Crossroads

Crossroads

Nikita Lynnette Nichols

www.urbanchristianonline.net

Urban Books, LLC
97 N18th Street
Wyandanch, NY 11798

ISBN 13: 978-1-60162-713-1
ISBN 10: 1-60162-713-0

First Mass Market Printing February 2014
First Printing February 2011
Printed in the United States of America

10 9 8 7 6 5 4 3 2 1

Distributed by Kensington Publishing Corp.
Submit Wholesale Orders to:
Kensington Publishing Corp.
C/O Penguin Group (USA) Inc.
Attention: Order Processing
405 Murray Hill Parkway
East Rutherford, NJ 07073-2316
Phone: 1-800-526-0275
Fax: 1-800-227-9604

Also by Nikita Lynnette Nichols

None But The Righteous

A Man's Worth

Amaryllis

A Woman's Worth

Lady Elect

You can reach the author

kitawrites@comcast.net
www.nikitalynnettenichols.com
http//:nikitalynnettenichols.blogspot.com
facebook.com

Dedication

*My wonderful parents, William and
Victoria Nichols, you are golden.*

Acknowledgments

When I look back over my literary career, I can't help but think about all of the love, dedication, and support that my loyal fans have given me. I'll be honest and admit that I didn't want to write this book. I knew it was going to be a headache and a migraine, and it truly was.

When I received the first revisions from my editor, I wanted to crawl beneath a rock and never come out. Every single page was marked with red ink. The second revision was marked with even more red ink. I really felt as though my character, Amaryllis Price, was trying to kill me. She haunted me in my sleep, taunted me during the day, and stomped on my brain constantly.

This is my fifth novel, and by far, the most difficult. I was informed that I was thousands of words short and didn't have enough pages to meet the requirement for publication. That's when I cried like a two-year-old that had her favorite candy taken away.

Pressure had gotten the best of me, and there were times when my mother would call to offer encouragement. She knew that I was discouraged and on the brink of throwing in the towel. I felt like putting the pen down, stepping away from the computer, and aborting this project. My mother reminded me of my fans that were waiting to read what Amaryllis was up to since my last book. She told me that I had no choice but to believe in myself and trust that God would get me through to the last page, and He did just that.

I'm truly thankful that my readers wouldn't leave me alone. They were contacting me on Facebook. Every day, when I opened my e-mails, I saw "When is *Crossroads* coming out?"

So, to all of my readers who just had to have your way, this one is for you!

Happy Reading, Kita

crossroad: (kros-ro¯d) a crucial point especially where a decision must be made

Merriam-Webster's Dictionary

crossroad: (kros-ro¯d) "When I'm trying to do right but come face to face with a situation that makes me wanna act like a straight-up ghetto fool."

Amaryllis Theresa Price

Prologue

"The doors of the church are open," Apostle Donald Lawrence Alford announced. He stood in the pulpit behind the podium and spoke to the congregation at Progressive Life-Giving Word Cathedral in Hillside, Illinois.

Amaryllis Price and her best friend, Bridgette Nelson, stood up from the pew and walked to the front of the church. They joined others at the altar who were eager to give their souls to the Lord or join the church.

It had been seven days since Amaryllis's return from visiting her sister, Michelle, in Las Vegas. And it had been seven days since Amaryllis had left the hospital, caught a taxi to Michelle's church, and threw herself at her sister's feet, begging for forgiveness.

Amaryllis was keeping her promise to Michelle, that she'd join a church when she returned home to Chicago. As the two friends stood to confess their love and devotion to God, Amaryllis reflected back to what had brought her to this point in her life.

She had been trained by her mother, Veronica, to be a product of her environment. During Amaryllis's teenage years, the back door to the home she had grown up in on the south side of Chicago was never locked. In fact, Amaryllis remembered it as a revolving door that constantly moved back and forth. As a drug addict left with his next fix he'd bought from Veronica, a pimp entered to collect what was due him: a peek at Amaryllis's body.

At the impressionable age of thirteen, Amaryllis had been sold into a life of drugs and sex. She had been taught how to walk into the back room off the kitchen and strip for various men. Veronica had convinced Amaryllis that she was safe because the men weren't allowed to touch her. She was only there for their viewing pleasure. All Amaryllis had to do was turn around, bend over, or spread her legs when the men told her to. She was forced to watch men satisfy themselves in her presence.

Because of Amaryllis's obedience, she had become the envy of every teenage girl in her school. Veronica had made sure to splurge where her daughter was concerned. A genuine Gucci bag, Fendi bag, Prada bag, or Louis Vuitton backpack was Amaryllis's reward for helping Veronica keep food on their table.

"See, baby, Momma didn't forget about you," is what Amaryllis remembered Veronica saying when she came home, often with gifts.

"My heart is beating overtime, Amaryllis," Bridgette said as she snapped Amaryllis out of her thoughts. "I mean, what do we say when Apostle Alford gets to us?"

As he got closer to where she and Bridgette stood, Amaryllis saw the apostle shaking the hands of everyone standing at the altar. "I don't know, but I remember Michelle mentioning something about receiving the right hand of fellowship."

Amaryllis looked to her left and saw the organist smiling at her. She returned the smile, but it was his wink that made her turn her head quickly. As soon as she did so, Apostle Alford was standing directly in front of her.

"Praise the Lord, daughter." Apostle Alford's smile was illuminating.

Amaryllis didn't know how to respond to his words. Had he given her an order?

Apostle Alford repeated himself. "Praise the Lord, daughter."

Amaryllis became nervous. Oh, God, what is this man talking about? She didn't want to appear to be ignorant or dumb, and she didn't want to be disobedient. She lifted her hands in the air, closed her eyes, and did what she thought she was supposed to do.

"Hallelujah. Thank you, Jesus. Glory to God."

When Amaryllis opened her eyes, she saw that Apostle Alford and everyone else was gaping at her. No one said a word. Uh-oh. What did I just do? Amaryllis became embarrassed. He'd told her to praise the Lord, hadn't he? Well, that's what she'd done, or so she thought.

"What's your name, daughter?" the apostle asked.

"Amaryllis Price."

"And what brings you to this altar today?"

"I need to change my way of living, and I need God to help me."

"Do you believe that Jesus is the Savior of the world?"

Amaryllis thought about the apostle's question. "Yes, I do. I believe that Jesus died for my sins. I also believe that He is risen."

Apostle Alford smiled again and extended his right hand to Amaryllis. "Welcome to Progressive Life-Giving Word Cathedral."

Amaryllis placed her right hand in the apostle's hand and smiled. She now had a pastor. Amaryllis Theresa Price, who was once a teenage visual prostitute and had grown into a devious, scandalous, vindictive woman, had a church home and pastor.

Chapter 1

How long will your car be in the shop this time, Amaryllis?" Bridgette asked one evening as she and Amaryllis jogged along a bike trail beneath the smoldering sun. The trail was located a half-mile east of Ashland Avenue, on the south side of Chicago.

"It'll be ready tomorrow. Tyrone said that he'd give me the money today to get my window fixed. This is the second time someone has smashed my rear window this month alone, and it's starting to scare me."

"I know what you mean, girl. A few weeks ago all four of your tires were slashed, and now someone keeps smashing your window. Are you sure you don't have any enemies lurking around?"

Amaryllis hesitated before she answered. "No. Not that I know of."

This time last year, Amaryllis Price had been a professional husband stealer. Her sister, Michelle, who lived in Las Vegas where Amaryllis was visiting, sounded convincing when she came to the airport to see Amaryllis before she boarded her plane back to Chicago. Michelle had told Amaryllis that she'd forgiven her for drugging James Bradley, Michelle's then fiancé, and taking nude photos of him and Amaryllis. Amaryllis turned one of the photos into a puzzle and basically stalked Michelle by sending her the puzzle piece by piece for eight weeks leading up to her wedding.

Michelle fought back tears. "Listen, in spite of what happened, we are still sisters, you hear me? I told you that we only got each other, so we gotta take care of one another."

Amaryllis's eyes also started to flood. "How can you still love me after what I've done?"

"Amaryllis, no one in this world is perfect. Now that you have a Bible, I want you to read Colossians, chapter three, verse thirteen. It tells us that if we don't forgive others, we won't be forgiven by God."

Just that morning, Amaryllis had told her father, Nicholas, that Michelle would get over the hurt she had caused her. Now she had a change of heart. "Yeah, but still, I've done some evil things to you. I can't imagine that I'd be as forgiving if I were in your shoes, Michelle."

"It comes with growth. In time you'll get there."

Amaryllis's flight number was called. "Well, I guess that's my cue."

Michelle helped her gather her bags. "Make sure you find a church home when you get back to Chicago."

Amaryllis placed her carry-on bag on her shoulder and stood, still looking at Michelle.

"Why are you looking at me like that?" Michelle asked.

"Because we look identical, but we're so different."

"You have the power to change that, Amaryllis."

"Michelle, you are a great example for me to follow in this walk with God, and I love you for who you are. If I can be half the woman you are, my life would be just about perfect."

That statement brought more tears to Michelle's eyes, and she hugged Amaryllis again. "That's the nicest thing you've ever said to me."

They held each other for a long thirty seconds, then Amaryllis's flight number was called again. Michelle broke the embrace and held Amaryllis's face in her hands. "I'm proud of you, little sister."

After that, Amaryllis recalled her ex-boyfriend, Randall Loomis, telling her that he'd forgiven her for various devious acts she had performed while living with him for two years.

Bridgette was driving them home from work one evening when they were just about to pass by Randall's church. Amaryllis asked Bridgette to pull over because she had some unfinished business with Randall and she needed to get some things off her chest.

Prior to Amaryllis arriving at Randall's church to speak with him, it had been exactly an entire year since the last time she had seen him. She stood across the street from Holy Deliverance Baptist Church, watching the festivities, the day that Randall and his best friend, Pastor Cordell Bryson, had gotten married to identical twin sisters. It had been a double ceremony. Eight months prior to his wedding day, Randall's last words to Amaryllis were to pack her things and get the heck out of his house.

She knew that all of the grief she'd caused Randall had left a bitter taste in his mouth but she had to face him. After getting out of Bridgette's car, Amaryllis walked up Holy Deliverance's steps and entered the vestibule. Immediately she saw Randall in the sanctuary speaking to a group of young men. It was a Monday evening. Amaryllis remembered that Randall spent "Men's Night" every Monday evening at church, mentoring young men. When Randall saw Amaryllis standing in the vestibule, he motioned for another man to take his place. He then excused himself, exited the sanctuary, and approached Amaryllis.

She had expected Randall to be angry. Amaryllis was prepared for him to show that he still held the grudge for all the trouble she had put him through. Had Randall thrown her out of the church without listening to a single word she said, Amaryllis was ready.

What she wasn't prepared for was the huge smile on Randall's face when he stood in front of her. Amaryllis was nervous and didn't know how she would get the words out, but his smile had soothed her.

After Randall greeted her, Amaryllis asked him listen to what she had to say and not interrupt her. He obeyed and kept quiet as she confessed to gambling his tithe money and not giving him messages when his mother had called their home wanting to speak to him.

Randall was calm, cool, and collected as Amaryllis poured her heart out and asked him to forgive her for going to church with him and acting out. She begged him to forgive her for coming out of their bedroom, naked, and walking into the kitchen when she knew that Pastor Bryson was visiting. Amaryllis had confessed to Randall that she asked Darryl and his goons to pour acid on Randall's car and put sugar in his gas tank. Then she confessed to powering off Randall's cell phone that night when Pastor Cordell tried to reach him for an emergency at the church. That was the fatal night when Brandon, a sixteen-year-old boy, came to the church, distraught, looking for Randall.

Randall had met Brandon one morning on a train that Randall was driving for the Chicago Transit Authority. Randall sensed that the young man was troubled. When he approached the young man, Randall had asked him his name. Brandon introduced himself to Randall but wondered what he wanted. Randall, the director of "Men's Night" at his church, had created a program where troubled youth could come and speak about their problems and get the proper help and guidance they needed. Just looking at Brandon's tattered clothes and shoes told Randall that the young man was trying to catch up to life.

Randall told Brandon about "Men's Night" and invited him to come that evening. Brandon had informed Randall that he couldn't make any promises because he was the primary caretaker for his younger siblings. His mother was a dope addict. After hearing the youth's story, Randall knew that he had to get him to his church that evening for mentorship.

Because Brandon was the sole provider for his family, he was forced to drop out of high school and work two part-time jobs. When he had finished his second shift, Brandon arrived home to find his next-door neighbor, Mrs. Beasley, banging on his front door, yelling for Brandon's mother to open the door. Mrs. Beasley told Brandon that The Department of Children and Family Services had come by earlier that day and taken his younger brother and two younger sisters away. When Brandon opened the lock and entered the run-down apartment he shared with his family, he found his mother lying on the floor, unresponsive. A needle was found near her arm. When the paramedics arrived, they tried to resuscitate her but failed.

That evening, Brandon found himself at Holy Deliverance Church looking for Randall.

It was Pastor Bryson that saw how troubled and out of sorts the youth was and invited him to his office. Randall had called Pastor Bryson that afternoon and informed him that instead of keeping his commitment to "Men's Night," he'd be spending time with Amaryllis. Randall had also told Pastor Bryson that he'd met Brandon on the train that morning and to look out for him and treat him well but Brandon would only speak to Randall. Pastor Bryson had called Randall's home and cell number but couldn't reach him.

Amaryllis was home when the call came in from the church. After Pastor Bryson had left his message for Randall to call him back as soon as possible, Amaryllis erased it. It was then when Randall's forgotten cell phone rang and again, Amaryllis listened to Pastor Bryson's message, then erased it before leaving the home she and Randall shared.

Randall was in his car waiting for Amaryllis. She had insisted that she be the one to go back inside and get his cell phone when he realized he'd left it behind. When she gave Randall the cell phone, he didn't look to see that the power was off.

The next morning, Randall read in the Chicago Sun-Times newspaper that Brandon had died. It was printed that the police had assumed he committed suicide.

As Amaryllis stood in Randall's presence and confessed that she was the reason that Pastor Bryson couldn't reach him to come to the church and counsel Brandon, she was sure that it would send Randall into a rage. Randall had done the exact opposite. He assured Amaryllis that she had already been forgiven for the things she'd done. Randall was more than happy to share with Amaryllis that he and his wife had adopted Brandon's brother and sisters and the family of five were living happily ever after.

Randall was more than pleased to learn that Amaryllis had gotten saved when she was in Las Vegas. He prayed with her, giving her advice on how to survive in the Christian world, and sent her on her way with a clean heart.

Amaryllis knew without a shadow of a doubt that Randall hadn't vandalized her car.

"What about Darryl?" Bridgette asked.

Darryl. That was a name that Amaryllis had hoped to go to her grave without ever hearing again. "I haven't seen or talked to him in a long time, Bridgette. Last I heard, he was doing time for rape."

Bridgette exhaled a sigh of relief. "Good for him. But had you pressed charges against that fool and his boys for raping you, he wouldn't have had the chance to rape another woman."

Chills ran down Amaryllis's back in the ninety-degree late August heat. She'd never forget the horrible pain that Darryl, a guy who had much more money than Randall, and three of his professional athletic friends, had inflicted on her. She had gone to Darryl's house for what she thought was one of their regular booty calls. It turned out that Darryl had another plan in mind when Amaryllis arrived at his mansion in Long Grove, Illinois.

What started out as a one-on-one fling went wrong when Amaryllis felt a hand—not belonging to Darryl—caress her back. That visit had ultimately landed Amaryllis in the hospital with a broken pelvic bone and plenty of bruises.

She remembered arriving at Darryl's mansion. When she walked in the unlocked front door, Darryl had yelled for her to come upstairs. In the master bedroom he was lying on the California king-size bed. Darryl was naked, and Amaryllis knew that foreplay wouldn't be necessary. He was ready for her.

She asked Darryl who the other three cars parked in his driveway belonged to, and he told her that friends of his had stayed over the night before.

Amaryllis undressed and got into bed with Darryl. He sat up and asked her how freaky she could be and how far between the sheets was she willing to go. Amaryllis told Darryl that for the right price she could be very freaky. In other words, as long as the money was right, there were no limits. He reached beneath his pillow, pulled out a money clip full of dollar bills, and gave it to Amaryllis. She removed the clip and counted ten thousand dollars. Amaryllis smiled at Darryl and said, "For this, I can be extremely freaky."

Soon after Amaryllis straddled Darryl, she felt a strange hand touch her right shoulder.

When she looked around, Amaryllis saw three naked men standing next to the bed. She recognized their faces from a time when she had danced at a bachelor party that Darryl had hosted at his home. The man who touched her shoulder was the groom. She saw the ring on his finger.

When she tried to hop off Darryl and cover herself with the sheets, Darryl yanked her arm and pulled her back on the bed. He reminded her that she had just been paid to allow the three men to have their way with her as well.

"You said that you could be very freaky," Darryl smirked.

"Yeah, as you wanted me to be, Darryl, not them." As she responded to Darryl, Amaryllis eyed the other men in disgust.

When Amaryllis told Darryl that his strong grip was hurting her arm, he gripped even tighter and held her down while the men raped her one by one. As much as Amaryllis fought back and screamed, they had overpowered her.

Later, Amaryllis left Darryl's house with a broken pelvis and was driving herself to Illinois Masonic Hospital when she passed out behind the wheel of her late model Nissan Maxima. She veered into a ditch on Interstate 294. It was only by the grace of God that she survived such an attack and car accident.

When Amaryllis woke up at the hospital, she couldn't remember how she got there, but she did recall Darryl telling her that if she mentioned his name in what had happened to her, he would kill her. So she lied and told the doctor that she had slipped and had fallen down the stairs at her house.

Amaryllis shook the shivers and all thoughts of Darryl from her mind. "Look, Bridge, Darryl basically told me that if I even thought of mentioning his name in what happened to me, he'd kill me. You know, as well as I do, that he's crazy enough to do it but I honestly don't believe that he's terrorizing my car."

The sun was beginning to set as their three-mile run was coming to an end.

"Well, if Darryl isn't your stalker, who could it be?"

Amaryllis stopped running and bent over to place her hands on her knees. She panted for air. "Your guess is as good as mine."

Bridgette mimicked Amaryllis and placed her hands on her knees, barely getting enough air into her lungs. "What . . . about . . . Randall?"

Amaryllis looked at her running buddy. "No way. Absolutely not. Black is happily married with three kids now. He's also an assistant pastor. He ain't thinking about me."

It hadn't gone over Bridgette's head that Amaryllis still referred to her ex-boyfriend, Randall, by the nickname she'd given him years ago. "You still call him that, huh? You still call him Black?"

"Yeah, I guess so." Amaryllis shrugged.

A very dark-skinned man with dreadlocks jogged passed them. "Good evening, ladies." His Jamaican accent was evident.

"Good evening," Amaryllis responded.

Bridgette took a good look at him when he ran by. His glistening muscles sparkled.

"It is now." Bridgette got a whiff of his cologne in the wind. "Ooh, he smells good. Did you hear his accent?"

"Yeah, it kinda makes you wanna go to Jamaica, doesn't it?"

Bridgette thought about that question. "Let's do it, Amaryllis. Let's go to Jamaica."

Amaryllis stopped panting and looked at her friend. "Are you serious? When?"

Bridgette raised the tone in her voice. "Yes, I'm serious. We both have a week off in November."

"Really? I mean, are you really serious, Bridgette? Don't play with me."

Bridgette raised the octave in her voice to prove her point. "Yes, I am."

The roommates started to walk toward their apartment building. "Okay, I'm game," Amaryllis agreed. "When we get home, we'll search the Internet for prices on all-inclusive packages. I can go for some fun in the sun."

Bridgette looked behind them and saw the man with the dreadlocks a quarter of a mile away and said with a Jamaican accent, "See ya' in Jamaica, mon."

When the two women turned the corner on Ada Street, Amaryllis noticed a light-skinned woman wearing dark sunglasses and a long black wig. She was sitting behind the wheel of a black Lexus SUV parked across the street. As they got closer to their high-rise building, Amaryllis was sure that the woman was watching them.

"Hey, Bridge, is that woman in the Lex watching us?" she discreetly nodded in the woman's direction.

Bridgette looked in the direction that Amaryllis had nodded. "Who is that?"

Amaryllis shook her head. "Heck if I know."

They stared at the woman as she stared back at them. They watched as the mysterious woman inhaled smoke from a cigarette and blew it in their direction. She then tossed the cigarette out of the driver's window, switched the gear from park to drive, pressed down on the gas pedal, and burned rubber away from the curb.

Bridgette got a glimpse of the license plate that read HOT ICEE "Who's Icee?" she asked.

Amaryllis didn't have a clue. "Icee? I don't know anyone named Icee, but I sure could use one in this hot weather."

They quickly dismissed all thoughts of whom Icee could be and entered their condominium building. Upstairs on the seventh floor, after entering their unit, Amaryllis pressed the play button on their answering machine that sat on an end table in their living room.

"Hey, baby, this is Ty. I'll be over there around eight o'clock tonight to bring the money for your window. Can you make some of that spaghetti? The kind you put your feet in."

Then she walked into the kitchen and saw Bridgette standing there laughing. She knew Bridgette's chuckles were a result of Tyrone's message.

"Amaryllis, you got that brotha hooked. I remember that time when you actually put your foot in a pot of spaghetti and stirred it. Tyrone licked it off your toes like he was eating peach cobbler."

Amaryllis laughed at the memory. "Yeah, Tyrone is a fool."

"I don't know who's the fool. You for sticking your bare foot in a pot of spaghetti, or Tyrone for sucking tomato sauce from beneath your toenails."

Amaryllis chuckled as she filled a pot with water to boil noodles and set it on top of the stove. "Apparently, Tyrone thought he was gonna get some nooky that night. I have to constantly remind him that I'm not knocking boots with him."

Bridgette gave her friend a high five. "All right, Amaryllis, go on with your bad self. You ain't done the nasty in how long?"

Amaryllis was proud of herself for keeping her legs closed. She had reached a milestone. She was saved, looking forward to becoming sanctified, and actually enjoying being celibate. Though it had been a struggle, she had managed to keep her promise to God. She vowed to remain celibate until marriage. There had been nights when Amaryllis slept with a pillow between her legs, crossed her ankles, and prayed to the Lord to keep her from giving in to her boyfriend's advances.

"It's been a few months. And if that's what Tyrone is hanging around for, then he can just press on, because my thighs are closed and under construction. God is repairing some thangs. Tyrone can't even sniff it."

Bridgette laughed and gave Amaryllis another high five. "I'm with you on that, girl. You sho' can't let him get close to it. 'Cause if you do, it'll be all over. Tyrone will be following you around like a puppy dog with its tongue wagging. I can just picture him out in the hallway, sniffing and scratching all around the door sayin', 'Open the door, Amaryllis, I know you're in there.'"

Amaryllis laughed. "That's true, Bridgette. These fools out here are crazy. Back in the day when I was in the world doing my thang, I dealt with this guy who wanted to have my scent in his mustache just so he could smell me all day."

Bridgette's mouth dropped wide open. "Ooh, Amaryllis, you ain't saved."

"I am saved. I said that happened back in the day."

Bridgette exited the kitchen and made her way toward the back of the apartment.

"I'm gonna hop in the shower. Before you stir the spaghetti with your foot, set aside a bowl for me."

At two minutes after eight o'clock, Bridgette answered a knock at the door. She looked through the peephole, then opened it. "Hey, Tyrone, come on in."

Amaryllis's boyfriend entered the condominium and closed the door behind him.

"What's up, Bridge? Where's my baby?" Tyrone greeted.

"She's in the shower. Have a seat in the living room. She'll be out soon."

"Maybe I should, uh, go and hurry her up," Tyrone said mischievously.

Bridgette gave him a stern glare. "Maybe you should sit your behind down in the living room like I said."

Amaryllis's celibacy was in full swing and going strong. Bridgette intended to keep her friend on the fast track. That was the deal they had made with one another when they had gotten saved a month ago. Bridgette would do all she could to help keep Amaryllis's panties on, and Amaryllis would return the favor and help Bridgette stop cursing.

Tyrone knew that Amaryllis and Bridgette were straight-up ghetto and didn't take any mess from no one. So he did exactly as he was told. In the living room he sat on the sofa, grabbed the remote control, and surfed through channels.

Bridgette filled a bowl with spaghetti from a green pot. While she was showering, Amaryllis had opened the bathroom door, poked her head outside, and told Bridgette not to eat from the black pot. Bridgette got a glass of grape Kool-Aid, then took it and her bowl of spaghetti to her bedroom, closing the door behind her.

Tyrone was into a wrestling match when Amaryllis came into the living room, dressed in a pair of jogging pants and a tank top.

"Hi, honey," she greeted him.

Tyrone admired her beauty as she came and sat next to him. When she plopped down on the sofa, he inhaled her aroma. "You smell yummy. What is that?"

"It's the new body wash by Issey Miyake. My sister, Michelle, sent it to me from Vegas."

Tyrone pulled Amaryllis into his arms then sniffed and kissed her neck. "Well, I'm gonna have to make sure you don't run out of that stuff, 'cause I likes me somma dat."

When he released Amaryllis, she saw a long scratch on his right arm. "What happened to your arm?"

"What do you mean?"

She ran her fingers over the scratch. "This scratch on your arm, it wasn't there yesterday."

Tyrone looked at his arm as if seeing the scratch for the first time. "I don't know. I guess it must've happened at work today."

"Ty, you teach the eighth-grade. How can you get a scratch like that while grading papers? This looks like a knife cut."

Tyrone snatched his arm from her grip, then stood up. It wasn't his intention for Amaryllis to see the wound. He reached in his pocket, pulled out three one hundred-dollar bills, and handed them to Amaryllis. "Here's the money to get your window fixed.

I can come by here tomorrow evening and take you to get your car from the shop."

Amaryllis took the money from him, folded the bills, and inserted them in her bra.

"Thanks for the offer, but Bridgette will take me to get my car after work tomorrow."

"Cool. Did you cook the spaghetti?"

Amaryllis wasn't done with her interrogation. "Is that a knife cut on your arm?"

The octave in Tyrone's voice changed. Clearly he was becoming irritated. "No. It's not a knife cut, Amaryllis. I don't know how the cut happened, okay?" He turned and walked toward the kitchen. "Can we please eat?" His words were quick and to the point, as though he really wanted to change the subject.

A warning siren went off in Amaryllis's head. She sat on the sofa wondering what the heck his problem was. She was only showing concern for Tyrone, but his strange behavior caused suspicion. Now, she became even more curious about the wound.

They had only been dating for three weeks. The wound on Tyrone's arm was fresh. Amaryllis didn't want to believe that he had gotten caught up in domestic violence with another female; however, Amaryllis was from the streets. She had seen it all, and she had done it all, and the only way to remind Tyrone that she wasn't to be played with or played on was to put fear in his heart.

She followed him into the kitchen and got a plate from the cupboard, then topped his plate with spaghetti as she spoke softly to him. "You know, Ty, where I come from, all I have to do is buy a crackhead a pack of cigarettes and a forty-ounce, and they'll do almost anything. For example, if I ever caught you cheating on me, I could have you kidnapped, then taken to a secluded area where you'd be tortured and buried alive." Her tone was calm and mellow. She spoke as if she were simply asking Tyrone what time of day it was.

Tyrone sat at the kitchen table looking at Amaryllis. She stood at the stove, in front of a black pot, preparing a plate of spaghetti with her back to him. He didn't say one word as she brought his plate to the table and set it in front of him. He watched as she filled another plate of spaghetti from a green pot and placed that plate on the table, then sat across from him, bowed her head, and closed her eyes.

"Father God, we thank You for this meal . . ." she began to pray.

Tyrone swallowed hard and didn't close his eyes. He kept them open throughout Amaryllis's entire prayer. Deep down inside, he knew she meant what she had just said.

Anybody who could make a statement like that and immediately pray to God was unstable and not to be played with. And they were eating spaghetti from two separate pots. Tyrone couldn't help but to wonder why.

". . . in Jesus' name, amen." After saying her prayer, Amaryllis opened her eyes, looked across the table at Tyrone, and blew him a kiss. She could tell by the expression on his face that she'd put something on his mind, and that was exactly what she had meant to do.

Amaryllis inserted a forkful of spaghetti into her mouth and noticed that Tyrone wasn't eating. "Go ahead and eat, honey. I put my foot in it, just like you requested," she teased.

Tyrone looked at the spaghetti and wondered what else Amaryllis was capable of putting in it. At that moment, he thought that maybe she really was unstable. She was Creole, after all. Tyrone had heard horror stories about Creole women and the lengths they'd go to get what they wanted. He could only imagine what was in his spaghetti.

The sauce wasn't orange, but a deep red. Maybe that was why Amaryllis was eating from a different pot. He took a bite and swallowed.

All of a sudden, Tyrone got sick to his stomach. He put his hand over his mouth and ran to the bathroom. He made it to the toilet just in time. Amaryllis heard him in the bathroom hacking and coughing and puking his guts out, but she remained at the kitchen table enjoying her dinner. There was a time when she could have taught a class on cheating. She was the champ at doing it. But cheaters don't like to be cheated on.

Bridgette was already dressed for work Friday morning when Amaryllis stepped out of the shower. As usual, Amaryllis was causing them to be late.

Bridgette was at the bathroom sink putting the finishing touches on her makeup.

"Amaryllis, would you please hurry up?"

Amaryllis quickly dried her body and hurried to her bedroom. "Okay, Bridge. I promise I'll be ready in ten minutes."

Bridgette followed her. "You should've been ready ten minutes ago. You know I'm trying to get this promotion, girl. I can't be late."

"Bridge, you ain't even gotta trip, because no one else applied for that job, which means it's automatically yours. Get somewhere and sat down before you bust a blood vessel."

Bridgette made fun of Amaryllis's newfound English. "Sat down?"

"You heard me." Then Amaryllis noticed the suit Bridgette was wearing. "And that's a bad St. John you got on. Where did you get it from?"

"Your closet."

Amaryllis stopped dressing and looked at Bridgette. "You got on my suit?"

"It's a shame to have so many clothes that you can't keep up with them."

Amaryllis couldn't believe the gall of her roommate. "Bridgette, is that really my suit?"

Bridgette opened the door to Amaryllis's walk-in closet. "Look at all of these tags still hanging on these sleeves. I figured that if you ain't gonna wear them, I might as well."

"That's what you figured, huh?" Amaryllis couldn't see herself just walking into Bridgette's closet and helping herself to whatever she wanted. Where was the respect?

Bridgette modeled the suit in Amaryllis's full-length mirror. "Yep."

"How about I figure out a way to snatch you bald for stealing my clothes?"

"Amaryllis, half of this stuff you don't even wear."

"Heck, I can't wear it if you got it on, and you look fat in my suit; take it off."

"Uh-uh. We are running late, and I already sprayed this jacket with Vera Wang cologne. I ain't taking nothing off. Let's go."

Time was of the essence. Amaryllis didn't have the time to bother with Bridgette right then. Truth be told, Bridgette really did look cute in the suit, and Amaryllis wasn't serious when she told her to take it off. She probably would've given Bridgette permission to wear the suit had she asked. Still, Bridgette needed to know and respect boundaries.

"That's all right, I'll fix you," Amaryllis threatened. "The very next time you touch my closet doorknob, there'll be a surprise waiting on you."

Bridgette wasn't the least bit fazed. She'd been borrowing Amaryllis's clothes, without permission, for years, and it was always the same threat. "Amaryllis, I couldn't care less about you putting a lock on this door."

"Oh, I ain't gonna put a lock on it. But the next time you touch my closet doorknob, your behind will fry like chicken wings in a deep fryer." Amaryllis walked to her closet and touched the doorknob, then started shaking as though she were having a seizure. After ten seconds of role playing, she looked at Bridgette. "That's gonna be you if you try to go into my closet again."

Bridgette chuckled at her roommate. She didn't take the threat serious. "Yeah, whatever. Let's go."

Amaryllis stepped into her Baby Phat stilettos, and Bridgette followed her out of the apartment.

When they stepped out of the elevator into the lobby, Amaryllis stopped at the security desk to talk to Marvin Johnson, the security guard on duty. Marvin was seventy-three years old and had been guarding the high-rise on the morning shift ever since Amaryllis and Bridgette moved in over a year ago.

Every morning at 6:15 a.m. sharp, Marvin made sure that he was alert and ready for Bridgette and Amaryllis to make their appearance. When the elevator doors opened and Amaryllis stepped off looking as fine as she wanted to look, Marvin's eyes would pop out of his head at the sight of her beauty.

Bridgette, on the other hand, was a different story. She and Marvin were like oil and water. The two of them just didn't mix. In an entire year, not one day had gone by that Bridgette and Marvin hadn't argued about something. Just as much as Marvin looked forward to flirting with Amaryllis, he also got a kick out of arguing with Bridgette.

As the two women approached Marvin's desk, he adjusted his eyeglasses and spoke first. "Good morning, Beauty and the Beast."

Bridgette rolled her eyes at him, and Amaryllis chuckled. Amaryllis knew Marvin had a crush on her, and she also knew he craved to meddle with Bridgette.

"Hi, Marvin, how are you this morning?" Amaryllis asked.

He showed Amaryllis the few teeth he had. "I'll be doing much better if you come around this desk and sit on my lap."

She laughed at him. "Marvin, you are a married man with grandbabies. You can't do anything for me."

Just talking to Amaryllis caused him to drool. He wiped his mouth with the back of his hand.

Bridgette looked at him in disgust, already upset that he referred to her as "the Beast."

"If she did sit on your old wrinkled lap, she'd slide right off because you got so much Ben-Gay on your legs."

Marvin looked at Bridgette. "You're just jealous because I ain't giving you no play."

Bridgette placed her hand on her hip and shifted all of her weight onto one leg. Every morning she made a vow to not let this man take her out of her anointing, but she lost the battle each time Marvin opened his mouth. "Jealous of what, Marvin? The only thing you can play is blind man. You're cockeyed in one eye and can't see out of the other. Each one of your eyeballs is rolling in different directions. Heck, I don't know if you're looking at me right now or someone across the lobby. And those aren't glasses on your face, those are telescopes. The lenses are so thick I bet you can see what the Martians on Mars are doing, can't you, Marvin?"

Amaryllis laughed. "Ooh, Bridgette, you promised God you'd tame your tongue."

Bridgette pulled on the coattail of her suit jacket, already angry that she had to repent so early in the morning. "Girl, he takes me there."

Marvin wasn't done with Bridgette. "You ain't saved. You ain't nothing but a witch sittin' up in church."

"At least I go to church. On Sundays, your antique-looking behind sits around the house all day waiting on somebody to come by and change your diaper. You know what, Marvin? You're gonna mess around and find out how much of a witch I can be. I can say two words that'll make all three of your teeth fall out. You look like a snaggletoothed pumpkin. You better be glad I don't celebrate Halloween, because I would stick a candle in your mouth and sit your old behind in my window."

Amaryllis hollered out and laughed so loud at Bridgette she got everyone's attention in the lobby.

Marvin was used to Bridgette's harsh words. He had become immune to her confrontational attitude. He loved to get her riled up in the morning. Bridgette didn't know it, but she was like a cup of strong black coffee for Marvin; she kept his adrenaline flowing.

It made Marvin's day when Bridgette argued with him. He didn't know if Bridgette was serious or not, but Marvin enjoyed every minute of it. "Who you callin' old? The cracks in your face is deeper than the crack in my—" Marvin started.

"Marvin, don't you dare!" Amaryllis scolded him before he could finish his phrase.

She looked at Bridgette and Marvin. "You two go through this every morning. You need to charge people to watch the show you put on."

At Marvin's last, unfinished statement, Bridgette was hot and ready to fight. "Uh-uh. It ain't about no money. I'm getting ready to jack him up for free." Bridgette stepped out of her heels and pulled off her earrings. "Now you see what you did, Marvin? You got me out of my anointing. I ain't had to act a fool all weekend. Now come from behind that desk so I can knock the dust off your old behind."

Marvin stood behind his desk going back and forth with Bridgette, but he never moved from his spot because he knew just how crazy she really was. He'd seen Bridgette come out of her anointing, as she called it, plenty of times. There was a time when Marvin witnessed Bridgette curse at a man for taking his time going through the revolving doors to exit the building.

"You slow *$%#. Would you hurry your *@# up? I got somewhere to be."

When the man didn't move through the revolving doors any faster after Bridgette's outburst, Marvin saw her step in the next opening of the doors and place both of her hands on the glass in front of her and push the doors to go around faster. The poor man didn't know what to think when the sliding glass door slammed into his back and forced him ahead. He lost his balance and fell forward on the ground just outside of the building. When Bridgette had made her way out of the building, Marvin saw her put her sunglasses on her face, step over the man, and proceed to walk down the street. It was a passersby that helped him stand. By the time he was on his feet, Bridgette was long gone.

Each time Bridgette challenged Marvin to come from around his desk to fight, he stood his ground where he was.

Amaryllis picked up Bridgette's shoes and gave them to her. "Girl, put your shoes and earrings back on."

Bridgette yelled over her shoulder as Amaryllis practically dragged her out of the building. "You better be glad I'm late for work."

Marvin stuttered when he got excited. "Nah, y-y-you b-b-b-better be g-g-g-glad you l-l-l-late for w-w-work."

Amaryllis almost had Bridgette out the door, but not out far enough. "You best not be here when I get home, Marvin," she continued yelling.

Of course she knew Marvin wouldn't be there. His morning shift ended at noon.

Finally, Amaryllis pulled Bridgette outside of the building. "Why do you let Marvin work your nerves and make you show your behind like that? Aren't you tired of repenting for the same thing every day?"

"Heck, he's lucky you were there to protect him. One of these days you ain't gonna be around, and I'm gonna whoop Marvin's old *#@."

Amaryllis shook her head at her roommate. "You can't stop cussing to save your life, can you?"

"I'm a work in progress. God ain't done with me yet."

They got into Bridgette's car and headed downtown. Had Bridgette looked in her rearview mirror while driving to work, she would've seen that HOT ICEE was hot on their trail.

Chapter 2

Saturday afternoon, Bridgette and Amaryllis were in the hosiery department of Macy's, in Chicago Ridge Mall, sorting through pantyhose.

Bridgette was frustrated and ready to go. They'd been in the hosiery department for half an hour. "Amaryllis, why do you just gotta have the Berkshire brand? Nylons are the same no matter what company makes them."

"It's that type of attitude, Bridge, that's got you looking jacked up when you think you're cute. The difference between you and me is the fact that you will wear tights in the summertime and I wouldn't. For your information, Berkshire is the best pantyhose that has ever been made. They have the perfect look and the perfect fit."

"Yeah, for fat folks."

Though she had managed to maintain her Coke-bottle frame that she worked hard to get in her early twenties, Amaryllis was now a size fourteen in her early thirties. But her curves were voluptuous. "I ain't fat, I'm thick, and don't you forget it." She pointed at Bridgette's belt buckle that was secured tightly around her waist. "And you're a Krispy Kreme doughnut away from shopping in the plus-size section yourself. All you gotta do is eat one more and kapow! All your buttons will be flying everywhere."

Bridgette dismissed the remark with a wave of the hand, but her belt was indeed tight. She was proud of her size twelve figure. She often teased Amaryllis that she could always put on Amaryllis's clothes and easily alter them to fit with a safety pin or belt, but Amaryllis couldn't squeeze into any of Bridgette's clothes. "Whatever, Amaryllis. I just don't see what all the fuss is about. The suit you bought today has a long skirt, and it drapes to your ankles. It's gonna be ninety degrees tomorrow, and you know the church will be packed. You need to put on a pair of flip-flops and call it a day."

Amaryllis stopped sorting through the hosiery and looked at her friend. "Flip-flops? With my Donna Karan suit? Girl, I should punch you in the face for even saying some crazy mess like that. I'm gonna teach you something about fashion, Bridge, so pay close attention. Don't even blink, because you'll miss it, I promise you. I paid three hundred dollars for this Donna Karan suit. It's elegant and semiformal. I wouldn't wear flip-flops because they'd cheapen the look of the suit. Instead, I'd wear pantyhose, preferably shimmers, and step into an elegant stiletto or a sling-back three-inch heel. I can also go without panty-hose altogether and step into a pair of open-toes since I got the French on my toenails, okay? Did you get that revelation?"

Bridgette didn't care for Amaryllis's so-called Bible lesson. "Whatever, Amaryllis. You think you're all that just because you're saved now. But trust me, honey, you're still just as ghetto as I am. So, come on down from that high horse."

"Oh, I never pretended not to be ghetto, Bridgette. I'll be the first to admit that I'm ghetto with a capital 'G,' because I'm real about who I am. But I'm high-class ghetto. Learn the difference and come on up a little higher. You're low-class ghetto. It's time for you to leave those corner-store stockings alone and graduate into some Berkshires."

"Girl, please. I'm not gonna pay twelve dollars for a pair of nylons."

"Uh-huh, and those stockings you wore to work yesterday with my St. John looked like the buck fifty you probably paid for them. Every time you got up from your desk, your knees were sagging. But that's on you. You can let the devil make a fool out of you if you want to. There's a difference between someone who thinks they look good and doesn't, than someone who wants to look good but does not care to."

Amaryllis found her size in the Berkshire brand, then found Bridgette's size. "You're graduating today, Bridgette. I'm buying these for you."

As they waited in line to purchase the pantyhose, Amaryllis and Bridgette heard a woman say, "No, Becky, I'm not buying the Barney pajamas. You have the exact pair at home."

Amaryllis and Bridgette looked over their shoulders and saw a woman trying to talk calmly to a little girl who appeared to be about seven or eight years old.

"But, Mommie, I want them," the girl whined.

"I said no, now put them back," the woman demanded.

"But why can't I have them, Mommie? Why?"

Bridgette couldn't believe the way the woman was handling that situation with her young daughter. "Umph, umph, umph. If that was my momma, I wouldn't have any teeth at this point. It only took Josephine one time to tell me no."

Bridgette and Amaryllis moved forward in line and continued to watch the drama unfold along with everyone within viewing.

"You can't have the pajamas, Becky. Put them back. I'm not gonna tell you again," the woman repeated to the child.

Everyone standing close by witnessed the young girl fall to the floor and throw a full-blown temper tantrum in the middle of Macy's. "But, Mommie, I want them. I want Barney."

"You stop that crying, young lady, or you'll find yourself in time-out. Get up from the floor right this minute. I mean it, Becky, get up right now."

"No, Mommie, no!"

To everyone's surprise, the frustrated mother relented and stood in line to pay for the pajamas.

Amaryllis was too outdone. "Bridgette, did you see that?"

Bridgette shook her head from side to side. "That's a shame. Josephine would've pulled down my pants right here in front of everybody and tore me up."

"Remind me to call my gynecologist when we get home," Amaryllis said.

"For what?"

"I just made up my mind not to have any kids. I'm gonna get on the pill."

"But you're not doing anything that requires the pill, Amaryllis."

"I don't care. After what I just witnessed, I refuse to get caught in that situation, because I will surely go to jail. Nowadays, you can't hit your kids."

"Amaryllis, you won't get caught up because you're not having sex, remember?"

"I wanna be ready just in case God decides He wants to do to me what He did to Mary."

Bridgette raised her eyebrows and the octave in her voice. "Mary who?"

"Jesus' mother. She wasn't having sex either, and you know what happened to her. She got caught up. So, in case God tries to do to me what He did to Mary, I'm gonna be ready for Him. I'm getting on the pill."

Bridgette let out a sarcastic chuckle. "Girl, please. First of all, Amaryllis, Mary was a virgin, and she gave birth to the Savior. You are a far cry from a virgin. And what's liable to come up out of you can hardly be called a savior. Trust me, honey, God ain't thinking about you."

Amaryllis looked at her friend and rotated her neck. "Excuse me, Miss Hoochiefied? You're not in a position to talk about anybody. Three of your ex-boyfriends paid you a visit in the bedroom and were never seen or heard from again. If you were to ask anyone about Robert, David, or Kevin, they'll say 'Last I heard, they were going over to Bridgette's house.'"

An elderly Caucasian lady standing in line ahead of them heard Amaryllis. She glanced over her shoulder to see the faces of the two women having such an inappropriate conversation.

As they were leaving Macy's, Amaryllis's cellular phone rang. She answered it just before the call was forwarded to her voice mail. "Amaryllis, speaking."

"Hey, baby, this is Charles."

At the sound of his voice, Amaryllis rolled her eyes at no one in particular. Charles Walker was from her past, and she wanted him to stay there. She knew that if she allowed him anywhere near her, she'd backslide for sure. He had always been her weakness. They dated for four years. She had met him at a club when she was hosting her twenty-first birthday party. They were introduced by a mutual friend that had brought Charles to the party.

After she and Charles shook hands, Amaryllis excused herself to mingle with all of her guests but there was something about Amaryllis that had mesmerized Charles. He didn't know if it was the color of her café-au-lait skin or the white halter top that cinched her tiny waist or the seductive perfume that she wore that night. Half an hour after they had met, Amaryllis's perfume still haunted Charles's nostrils. He didn't approach her again at the party, but Charles sat in a corner and watched every move she made that night. From the way she smiled to the way she sat and gracefully crossed one leg over the other, Charles was infatuated.

It was in the wee hours of the next morning when Amaryllis said good-bye to her last guest. The club owner walked her to her car, helped pack her gifts in the trunk, and wished her a good night. As soon as she sat behind the steering wheel and buckled her seat belt, someone knocked on her passenger-side window. She looked over and saw Charles hunched down with a smile that was to die for. She remembered his face from earlier that evening. She also remembered the feeling she got when she shook his hand.

It was electric, and Amaryllis knew, at that moment, that she was going home with Charles.

All throughout the party, Amaryllis felt Charles's gaze on her, so she had put on a show for him. As he sat in a corner and watched her every move, she made sure to sashay past him numerous times. She turned him on, and she knew it. Her promiscuity was evident when she allowed Charles into her passenger seat and also into her bed that night.

Their steamy relationship lasted for four years until Amaryllis got wind that she wasn't the only trick Charles was treating. But there was something about him that made her keep going back. It was the way he touched her that caused her knees to collapse.

Charles knew that Amaryllis was weak. Each time he called, she'd come a-runnin'.

The very last time Amaryllis left Charles's bed, she vowed to never return. She knew the quickest way to get over a man was to find herself another one. It wasn't long after when she was approached by her next ex-boyfriend, Randall Loomis. Just like most men, Randall had fallen for Amaryllis when he first saw her. She was trying on shoes in Evergreen Mall. He introduced himself and ended up buying her the shoes she was trying on. That day was the last day Amaryllis had any thoughts of Charles.

"What do you want, Charles? I thought I told you to never call me again," Amaryllis spat through the telephone receiver.

"Come on, Delicious. Don't be like that."

"My name is Amaryllis. Don't make me cut you."

"That's what I said, Delicious Amaryllis."

Charles was still no different from any other man who approached her. The conversations

would start out sounding promising. They seemed
to be interested in her as a person. They'd want to
know what she did for a living or pretended to be
hanging on to every word she said, but eventually,
the true bow-wow in them showed up.

Charles made her weak in the knees. His
smooth, milk chocolate skin with sultry eyes
and a mustache and goatee that were always
trimmed perfectly had kept Amaryllis running
back to his bed.

Just two days after Amaryllis had given her life
to the Lord, and only one day after she had gone
to Holy Deliverance Baptist Church to apologize
to Randall, Amaryllis ran into Charles while
on her lunch break in downtown Chicago. She
tried her best not to look into his eyes because
she knew the affect they had on her in the past.
She had revealed to Charles that she was a new
creature and her old ways were behind her. They
had been out of touch for a while and Charles
wanted nothing more than to have a taste of her
again. He played the understanding part and let
her know that he fully supported her new way of
living and had no intentions of pulling her back to
where she had come from. Still, he pressed her for
her telephone number. She relented and allowed
him back in her life.

That following Saturday, Charles took Amaryllis on a horse and carriage ride in the Loop, then treated her to a formal dinner cruise aboard the Odyssey yacht over Lake Michigan. He dined Amaryllis and presented himself as a brother who appreciated a good woman's wonderful company.

For most of the evening, Charles had been the perfect gentleman. Complimenting her hair, makeup and perfume, added with pulling her chair out for her and sliding her napkin across her lap told Amaryllis that Charles had indeed changed and was a keeper.

When the evening was over, Charles did the proper thing by walking Amaryllis to her door. Her intentions were to thank him for a lovely evening and call it a night.

However, Charles had another plan to bring the evening to a close. He wanted to go out with a bang, a big bang. Amaryllis turned the key in the lock, then turned around to face him.

"Charles, I really had a wonderful time tonight. Dinner was lovely, and the conversation was great. Maybe we can do it again, soon. Next time, it'll be my treat. Thank you and good night."

Charles towered over Amaryllis's five feet four inches, so she stood on her tippy toes and kissed his cheek. Then she walked into her apartment, gave him one last smile, and gently shut the door. Charles stood in the hallway stunned for about ten seconds before knocking.

Amaryllis opened the door and looked at him confused. She couldn't figure out what part of good night he hadn't understood. As she opened the door wider, Charles thought that was his invitation to come in.

Abruptly, however, Amaryllis placed the palm of her hand on his chest to stop him. "Where are you going?"

Now, Charles looked confused. Did Amaryllis really think he was going to settle for a light peck on the cheek? The dinner cruise had cost him one hundred eighty dollars. To valet-park his car had cost sixty-five dollars. The horse-and-carriage ride had cost one hundred dollars. In less than five hours, Amaryllis received almost three hundred forty-five of his hard earned dollars.

Charles looked at it as an investment . . . or a down payment. But not for a soft kiss on his jaw. He had other things in mind he wanted to cash in on. "Uh, I thought we could sit and talk for a while and really get to know each other again," he said.

Amaryllis heard the emphasis he put on the word "really" and knew right then that Charles was still a playa. But little did he know two could play that game. She knew what to do.

"I'd like that, Charles. Come on in and have a seat in the living room," she stated. Then she excused herself and went to her bedroom to relieve her aching feet from the four-inch stilettos she'd worn that evening.

While she was changing, Charles could hardly keep still on the sofa. He remembered that Amaryllis was easy and always willing. But she came with a high price. Charles figured that spending three hundred forty-five bucks on her should send him home with a satisfied smile on his face.

Five minutes later, Amaryllis came and sat next to him wearing a light blue FUBU jogging suit. "Oh, I feel so much better now that I'm outta those heels. My feet were killing me."

Charles looked at the jogging suit. In the past when he brought Amaryllis home from an expensive date, she'd always excuse herself and say that she was going to slip into something more comfortable. When she reappeared, she'd have on a short teddy. She would come and parade before him in some type of feminine material like lace, silk, or satin. The short teddies were easy to maneuver around and gave him quick access to her body, but this jogging suit she was wearing right then threw him off.

"I thought you were changing into something more comfortable," he complained.

"I did. I'm very comfortable." In her hands were two books. She placed one in Charles's lap.

He looked at the front cover. *HOLY BIBLE* stood out to him in gold lettering. He read the words, then looked at Amaryllis. "What's this?"

"It's a Bible."

Charles inhaled deeply, then exhaled slowly. Amaryllis was killing his romantic flow. "I know what it is, Amaryllis. Why did you give it to me?"

"Because, you said you wanted to sit and get to know me again. This is who I am now. Every night before I go to bed, I do a little Bible study."

She opened her Bible, the King James Version, to Jeremiah 29:11–14. "I wanna share something with you, Charles. It's my favorite scripture that I read every night before bed."

She crossed her legs in a pretzel on the sofa and read the Word of God to the devil seated next to her. "For I know the thoughts that I think toward you, says the Lord, thoughts of peace and not evil, to give you a future and a hope. Then you will call upon Me and go and pray to Me, and I will listen to you. And you will seek Me and find Me, when you search for Me with all your heart. I will be found by you, says the Lord, and I will bring you back from your captivity."

Amaryllis closed her Bible and looked at Charles. The expression on his face told it all.

He wasn't there for Bible study; he wanted to study Amaryllis.

"Charles, I got saved last week in Las Vegas. I love this scripture because it tells me that if I continue to seek God, I'll find Him. I have been held captive by sexual sin for most of my life. But I'm free now. The Bible tells me that God will keep me if I wanna be kept. And I'm just that crazy to believe that. As long as I stay prayed up and ask God to keep me, I know He'll do it. I don't care if you accept that or not, but you must respect it, because that's how I'm living now."

That conversation over three weeks ago had sent Charles home quickly. It was the next day in church when Amaryllis had met and began dating Tyrone Caridine. Now, Amaryllis found herself standing in Chicago Ridge Mall fighting the wiles of the devil again.

She knew that she needed to end the telephone call quickly. "Good-bye, Charles, and please lose my number."

"Wait a minute, baby. Why are you treating me so cold?"

"Look, Charles, I can remember a time I called when you didn't recognize my voice. You called me by six other women's names before you got to mine."

"Girl, I was just playing with you. You are the only woman for me."

"Well, you're not the man for me."

"That's cold, Amaryllis."

Amaryllis signaled Bridgette by pointing to her purse then pointing to her own phone in her hand. Bridgette understood exactly what she meant.

"Charles, I'm gonna ask you one more time, why are you calling me?"

"I want to see you tonight."

Amaryllis knew exactly what Charles wanted to see. He'd made too many compliments about her voluptuous breasts, long hair, and curvy hips. Suddenly, both Charles and Amaryllis heard a beep on the phone line. "Hold on a minute, Charles." Amaryllis clicked over. "Thanks, Bridge. This fool is on a roll. You should hear the crap he's talking."

She clicked over again. "Charles, I gotta go. It's an important call."

"Okay, but what about tonight? Can I meet you at your place, let's say around eight?"

"No. But you can meet me at church tomorrow morning, let's say around ten."

"Church?"

"Yep. If you wanna see me, that's where I'll be."

It wasn't that Amaryllis was being disrespectful

to her boyfriend, Tyrone, the head musician. She simply knew that Charles wouldn't show up.

After a long pause, Charles replied with, "Uh, I'll call you back and let you know."

Amaryllis heard the click in her ear and knew that she wouldn't hear from Charles any time soon. Playing the church card seemed to work. She and Bridgette started walking again.

"Charles again, huh?" Bridgette asked.

"Girl, yeah. He has yet to figure out that he's got a better chance of rolling between the sheets with his momma before he can touch me again."

"Amaryllis, I gotta tell you that I'm extremely amazed at how you've been able to abstain from sex. I mean, this time last year, you were addicted. You sure you ain't got something long and hard stashed in a box under your bed?"

Amaryllis chuckled. "Let me tell you something, Bridge. If I just gotta have it like that, both Charles and Tyrone are on my speed dial. And if I do mess around and get caught up and have to go to the altar, it won't be for a toy. If I'm gonna repent, it'll be for the real thing. You can believe that."

They strolled past a gourmet popcorn shop and Bridgette's mouth started to salivate. "I haven't had gourmet cheese and caramel popcorn in a long time. You want some, Amaryllis?"

"I can go for a minimix."

At the counter, Amaryllis told the cashier that she'd be paying for both her and Bridgette's order. Her selflessness pleased Bridgette. "Thanks, Amaryllis."

"I'm paying for everybody's popcorn today."

Bridgette looked around the popcorn shop and saw that the two of them were the only customers. "Everybody, like whom?"

Amaryllis bent over and placed her face directly at Bridgette's pelvic area and spoke loudly. "Hey, David, Robert, and Kevin, y'all want some popcorn?"

Amaryllis laughed at herself so hard she was in tears. Bridgette looked at the clerk.

"Pray for her, she ain't saved."

The cheese and caramel popcorn was warm, fresh, and finger-licking good. The two best friends snacked, walked, and talked as they did a lot of window-shopping.

"Amaryllis, you know we gotta study the Sunday School lesson for tomorrow," Bridgette reminded her.

"Yeah, that's first on my list when we get home."

"I hope I don't fall asleep in Sunday School," Bridgette complained. "It's boring as heck."

"What's boring about it?"

"Sunday School, plus morning service and evening service? Girl, that's way too much church for me. Besides, I ain't trying to learn anything about Fatback, Tupac, and the big negro in the diary burner."

Amaryllis almost choked on her popcorn as she laughed. "Bridgette, your behind is going straight to hell. It's Shadrach, Meshach, and Abednego in the fiery furnace, you fool. That just goes to show that Sunday School is exactly where you need to be."

Bridgette shrugged her shoulders. "Whatever. It's still way too much church."

They heard ringing coming from Amaryllis's purse again. She exhaled loudly. "If this is Charles, I'm gonna put some papers on him for harassment."

Amaryllis saw PRIVATE CALL on the caller ID before she answered.

"Amaryllis speaking."

"I guess you think you're cute with all that weave on your head. And that pink sundress is too tight." It was a female's voice. Amaryllis could hear hostility as she spoke.

She instantly stopped walking. Bridgette stopped walking also and looked at her. Amaryllis looked all around at the people walking past her and Bridgette. No one seemed to be paying them any attention.

Bridgette saw the shocked expression on her friend's face and mouthed, "Who is it?"

Amaryllis waved Bridgette's question away and spoke into the phone. "Excuse me? You must have the wrong number, and I'll tell you why. First, wherever you are, you're not close enough to see that my hair is all mine. Second, my dress fits me well."

"Oh, I got the right number, and you are not excused. And tell your girl in the white pants and yellow top that I've got her number too."

Suddenly, Amaryllis's phone line went dead. She looked at what Bridgette was wearing. "Girl, some heifer just called us out. She described what we had on and said she had both our numbers."

Bridgette glanced around the mall. A man was seated on a nearby bench with bags from various clothing stores on the bench next to him. He also held a female's purse. Surely, he was waiting patiently for a wife or girlfriend to return. People were riding up and down the escalator in the middle of the mall. A couple held hands as they walked and enjoyed ice-cream cones. Bridgette saw a woman approach a security guard to ask for directions. No one looked suspicious.

Amaryllis placed her phone in her purse. "Whoever it was blocked the call, so I wouldn't know who she was. What does that tell you, Bridge?"

"That she's a coward."

Bridgette dismissed all thoughts of the call and went back to eating her popcorn and window-shopping. But Amaryllis couldn't help but wonder who the caller was and the reason she had called.

She was walking the straight and narrow now, but she had once been a husband stealer and relationship destroyer. It was possible that the caller was an angry wife or bitter girlfriend of one of the men Amaryllis had bedded before she decided to give her life to Christ. First, Charles reemerged, then a threatening telephone call from an obviously unsettled female. If Amaryllis's past were indeed catching up to her, and if it were true what was said about karma, the anonymous phone call proved to be what Amaryllis knew was inevitable. What goes around comes around. It worried her that she didn't know exactly what was coming her way or who may be bringing it. The one thing she did know for sure was that she had a lot to reap.

Chapter 3

At seven o'clock Sunday morning, Amaryllis and Bridgette were up and listening to WGOD, the FM gospel radio station. Edward Primer & The Voices of Joy Community Choir was blasting the entire condominium singing, "It Won't Work."

Bridgette was in her bedroom putting together what she'd wear to church. Amaryllis was in the kitchen frying ham and eggs. Unexpectedly, there was a loud knock on the front door. Amaryllis peeked through the peephole. She saw who it was, frowned, then yanked the door open.

"It's seven o' clock in the morning, and it's Sunday. What are you doing here, Ty?" she spat.

Tyrone could hardly keep his balance as he leaned against the doorway. "Good morning to you too."

Amaryllis noticed his speech was slurred and his eyes were bloodshot. "Are you drunk? And what did I tell you about coming to my house without calling first?"

"Why I gotta call? You got another man up in here or somethin'?"

Amaryllis could smell the alcohol coming through his pores. "I'm sick and tired of you coming here unannounced."

Tyrone could barely stand. "Baby, can I come in?"

Amaryllis almost lost her religion. "Heck, no, you can't co—Look, Ty, why are you trying to make me do tha fool on a Sunday morning? I'm in here getting my praise on. I ain't got time for this."

"Amaryllis, please. Can I have an aspirin or something? My head is killing me."

She looked at him with disgust. *Lord, you know I wanna kick him in the groin, don't you?* "Tyrone, get your drunk behind out of my doorway. And if you ever come to my house drunk or unannounced again, there's gonna be consequences and repercussions."

She slammed the door in his face, went into the living room, and turned the volume on the stereo up to the maximum as she began singing with Ed Primer's group. "Gotta go, can't stay. Can't remain feeling this way. Lord, please. See about me."

The sanctuary choir at Progressive Life-Giving Word Cathedral sang a capella during Sunday morning service due to the fact that Tyrone Caridine, who was not only Amaryllis's on-again, off-again beau, but also the church's organist, was a no-show.

If one other person asked Amaryllis the whereabouts of Tyrone, she would let the entire church know what a drunken lush he was and that he was probably lying somewhere in a gutter. Mother Caridine, who was looking mighty siddity sitting on the Mother's Pew with a lilac hat and a matching lilac feather sticking out of it, believed her son's poop didn't stink. Tyrone could play the heavens out of an organ, but he had a problem.

It was offering time, and so far, Amaryllis had gotten away with a simple "I don't know," when she was asked about Tyrone. When the usher got to her row, he extended his hand forward, motioning for everyone seated on that pew to stand and walk to the front of the church to pay his or her tithes and offerings.

Amaryllis dropped her envelope in the basket and proceeded to walk back to her pew when Tyrone's mother reached out and grabbed her hand as she was passing by.

Amaryllis knelt next to her and kissed her cheek. "Praise the Lord, Mother Caridine. How are you this morning?"

As she always did, Mother Roberta Caridine admired Amaryllis's hair, makeup, suit, and stilettos. "Sweet darlin' baby, every time I see you, you are always so pretty and elegant. And you smell good too."

"Thank you. That's a bad hat you got on. I see I ain't the only one hanging in the malls."

Mother Caridine chuckled and patted Amaryllis's hand. "As you young folks say, 'You know how I do.'"

Amaryllis laughed. "Amen to that, Mother."

Then Mother Caridine leaned forward and whispered in Amaryllis's ear. "Do you know where my son is?"

Mother Caridine was a righteous woman of God. However, she had a flaw. When it came time to tell others how to raise their offspring, she was the first. But where her son, Tyrone, was concerned, he could do no wrong. If anyone tried to tell her something negative about Tyrone, she was quick to say, "Oh no, honey, Ty wouldn't do or say anything like that" or "The person may have looked like my son, but it wasn't him" or "Ty wasn't raised like that, so it couldn't have been him."

When Tyrone Caridine approached Amaryllis three weeks ago, he had welcomed her to the church. She and Bridgette were new members and hadn't made any friends.

Tyrone introduced himself as the church's musician. He told Amaryllis that she looked like she could sing. Amaryllis knew by the look in his eyes that he was flirting with her. He was handsome, so she played along.

"I do my best singing in the shower," she said. "I don't think my voice is good enough to be in the choir, though."

Tyrone believed Amaryllis to be the most beautiful creature God had ever created. He was drawn to the way her lips moved when she spoke.

"I could test your voice," he suggested.

"And how exactly would you do that?"

"You'd have to sing for me."

Amaryllis blushed. "No, I don't think so. I know my strong points, and singing is definitely not one of them."

"Are you a model?" he asked.

She blushed again. "No."

"What do you do?"

Amaryllis cocked her head to the side. "You certainly ask a lot of questions, you know that?"

Tyrone laughed out loud. "Yeah, I guess I do. That's because I wanna get to know you. Can I get your number and call you?"

It had been a year since Amaryllis's breakup with her last boyfriend, Randall. She was finally turning her life around and Charles's attitude the previous night was still fresh in her mind. The last thing she needed was to get involved in a new relationship. She wanted to devote her time to God and get to know Him.

"Not today, but it was nice to meet you, Tyrone."

As she turned away from him, he reached out and grabbed her by the elbow.

"Please don't walk away from me," he pleaded. "Do you want me to beg? I ain't too proud to beg."

Amaryllis found Tyrone to be charming. She smiled, then relented and gave him her telephone number. That Sunday night, Tyrone called her, and they talked for more than five hours. She invited him to her and Bridgette's condo the next evening, and she cooked for him. Later that evening, he came on to her. Amaryllis clearly stated to Tyrone that she was living a life of celibacy. What had impressed Amaryllis was the fact that he didn't get upset or even question her about the choice she had made. He told her that he respected her decision and wanted to continue a relationship with her.

During the three weeks they'd been dating, the two of them had become close. To Amaryllis, they had the ideal relationship. It was a relationship she was proud of. They went to the movies, to restaurants, and enjoyed each other's company. She thought that she had finally hit the jackpot with Tyrone. He was the first boyfriend she had that didn't pressure her for sex.

But Tyrone had a drinking problem. Amaryllis knew it when he had brought a case of beer to her house the first night she cooked for him but she overlooked his addiction.

She chose her battles. Amaryllis felt that she'd rather put up with his alcoholism than have to give him sex, but showing up drunk at her condo that morning wasn't cool. Tyrone loved to drink. It was a passion for him. However, now, Amaryllis figured that three weeks of dating an alcoholic was enough. Maybe it was time to call it quits.

Amaryllis saw Bridgette standing in the vestibule motioning for her to exit the sanctuary. "Mother Caridine, you may not want to hear this, but Tyrone was at my house early this morning, reeking of alcohol."

By the look on Mother Caridine's face, Amaryllis may as well have told her that there was no God.

"Alcohol?"

"Yes, ma'am."

"Ty doesn't drink."

"Mother Caridine, I know you love Tyrone but he was lit this morning. He may not have drank tea, coffee, or Kool-Aid this morning, but he was definitely sipping something."

"Uh-uh. That's not Ty's character. My baby knows better," she said while shaking her head in disbelief.

"Your baby is thirty-eight years old, Mother Caridine."

Before she could defend Tyrone again, Amaryllis kissed her cheek softly, stood, and walked down the center aisle. She unknowingly turned heads, men's and women's, as she sashayed out of the sanctuary.

Outside, Bridgette was waiting impatiently. "It's about time. What were you and Mother Caridine so engrossed in conversation about?"

"She asked if I knew where her son was. I told her he came by this morning and did a great impression of Woodrow from Sanford & Son, but her guess was just as good as mine where he is right now."

"Did she defend him?"

"You think she didn't?"

In the church parking lot, Amaryllis and Bridgette spied a black rose with a small white envelope attached to it. It was being held in place under the left wiper blade on Amaryllis's red, late model Ford Mustang.

Bridgette picked up the envelope, opened it, and read what was written on the card inside.

"I care enough to send the very least. From, Icee."

Amaryllis frowned. She had just gotten her window replaced two days ago. "Who is this Icee chick, and why is she stalking me?"

Bridgette opened the passenger door and got in. "We'll ask Deacon Brown on our way out of the parking lot. He's in charge of security. Maybe he saw the woman who put this on your window."

Amaryllis drove to the security booth. Bridgette rolled down the passenger window and yelled, "Deacon Brown."

He graciously walked over to their car all smiles, then knelt by Bridgette's window and poked his head inside the car. "Hey, there, Sister Bridgette. What can I do for you?"

Bridgette pressed the back of her head into the headrest to keep his lips from making contact with hers. "First, you can back up."

Deacon Brown eased out of the car a bit, but he was still too close for Bridgette's comfort. She looked over at Amaryllis who smirked and turned her head the other way.

Deacon Brown was smiling flirtatiously at Bridgette, and she saw that his teeth were beige. She could only hope that drinking too much coffee was to blame. It would be a shame to have a mouth full of rotten teeth. Then to her horror, she saw a putrid brownish liquid oozing from the corner of his mouth. She grimaced and squirmed in her seat. "Uh, Deacon, your lips are leaking."

He wiped his mouth with the back of his hand. "That's just a li'l snuff."

Bridgette and Amaryllis watched in disgust as Deacon Brown squirted a brown liquid clot between his two front top teeth beside Amaryllis's car. It took all that was in Bridgette to keep her breakfast down in her stomach. She placed her hand over her mouth and swallowed repeatedly to control the urge to vomit. Deacon

Brown leaned in a little closer to her. "What do you wanna ask me with your fine self?"

Now Bridgette inhaled a vile stench coming from his mouth. She pressed her head deeper into the headrest. Quickly, she held up the rose and card. "We were wondering if you saw who put this on Amaryllis's windshield."

To escape the stench while he spoke, Bridgette turned her head and pretended to reach behind Amaryllis's seat for something—anything.

"I sho' didn't," he replied.

Bridgette faced him again. "Okay, Deacon Brown, thanks."

"That's all you want? I thought you was gonna ask me to go on a date with you."

Bridgette snapped her head. Had she heard him right? "You can't be serious, Deacon."

"Oh, yeah, yeah, yeah. I'm serious," he panted.

Amaryllis chuckled at Bridgette's latest pursuer. Somehow, she always attracted men over the age of sixty.

Bridgette saw more brown saliva escaping the corners of his mouth. "Deacon, isn't your wife down in the fellowship hall, selling chicken dinners as we speak?"

"This ain't about my wife. Besides, she works nights; we can go on a date then."

It's not that Bridgette would entertain the thought of him escorting her anywhere, but she was curious about what Deacon Brown, whose entire wardrobe consisted of seersucker suits, white patent leather shoes, and short fat neckties, considered a date.

Today, he wore a red shirt, a white paisley printed tie, white pants, and a red belt with white shoes. It would be hard for a visitor to tell if Deacon Brown was the head of security or a member of a Baptist church men's choir.

Bridgette entertained him. "Where would we go, Deacon?"

As he answered her and his fetid breath escaped his lips, Bridgette kept telling herself, Don't throw up. Keep swallowing. Breathe only a little bit of air at a time.

"Well, if you like soul food, we could take a ride over to Betty's Soul Shack for fatback, pinto beans with gravy, and hoecakes." Deacon Brown licked his lips just thinking about the food he'd listed to Bridgette. "Mmm, that's some good eatin'."

Amaryllis leaned into Bridgette and asked, "What are hoecakes, Deacon?"

Bridgette answered for him. "Probably cakes that ho's eat."

Deacon Brown opened his mouth wide and released a foul smell and laughed.

"Bridgette, girl, you sho' 'nuff crazy. Hoecakes ain't nothin' but hot-water corn bread."

She had reached her limit. No longer could Bridgette sit and let what smelled like ten-day-old cabbage coming from Deacon Brown's mouth invade her nostrils. She looked at Amaryllis. "When I say 'drive,' floor it."

She glanced at Deacon Brown's chin. The brown saliva was on the verge of dripping onto her lap. "Uh, Deacon, back up, honey."

He brought his head out of Amaryllis's car just in time for the drool to hit the ground. Again, he wiped his mouth with the back of his hand. "So, uh, Sister Bridgette, you wanna go on a date with me or what?"

"You ready?" Bridgette asked Amaryllis.

Amaryllis pressed on the brake pedal and shifted the gear in the "D" position. "Just say the word."

Bridgette looked at Deacon Brown. "The only place we can go together is to Wal-Mart on Wednesday so I can use your senior citizen's discount. And you better pray real hard that Sister Brown doesn't receive a videotape of you out here willing to commit adultery." With her eyes still fixed on Deacon Brown, Bridgette yelled out to Amaryllis, "Drive!"

Chapter 4

At TGI Friday's restaurant, Amaryllis and Bridgette enjoyed Buffalo wings with blue cheese dressing as an appetizer. For their main course, Amaryllis ordered a grilled chicken Caesar salad while Bridgette opted for chicken teriyaki. After eating, Amaryllis leaned back in the booth to unbutton the back of her skirt. "Whew, that was good."

Bridgette withdrew a string of dental floss from her purse and put it to good use. She belched loudly before she spoke. "I know what you mean, girl."

Their waiter passed them by, and Amaryllis called out to him. "Excuse me, can you bring us two take-out containers, please?"

"Absolutely, ma'am. Would you ladies care for any dessert this afternoon? The vanilla cheesecake covered in hot chocolate sauce is magnificent," the waiter replied.

Amaryllis shook her head from side to side. Bridgette wasted no time in saying, "Yes, but make mine to go and feel free to get heavy on the chocolate sauce."

When they were alone, Amaryllis looked across the table at her friend. "Bridge, you know you don't need any cheesecake."

Bridgette was offended. "Excuse you? I'm not the one who had to unbutton her skirt just now."

"So?"

"So, who's the hippo—you or me? Until I have to do what you just did, shut the heck up. And if I catch you sneaking a piece of my cheesecake when we get home, I promise I'm going to jail."

Just then the waiter set two drinks on their table. "These are from a friend."

Bridgette and Amaryllis looked at each other and asked the waiter at the same time, "What friend?"

He looked over his shoulder and pointed to an empty booth. "She was sitting over there. She said to tell you the drinks are compliments of Icee."

Amaryllis's heart skipped two beats. Who the heck is Icee?

Bridgette told the waiter to take the drinks away and to please hurry and bring their containers. For the next five minutes, they sat waiting for their containers and contemplated who Icee could be.

Then Amaryllis looked at her wristwatch. "What is taking him so long to bring the containers? We're gonna be late for the four o'clock service. I still have to go home, track Tyrone's drunk behind down, and change outfits."

Bridgette glanced at her own wristwatch. "It's already three-fifteen. We're not gonna get any good seats if we don't leave now."

The afternoon service at Progressive Life-Giving Word Cathedral began on time at four o'clock and was always Holy Ghost-filled. Churchgoers from all across the city of Chicago made their way to the western suburb of Hillside in hopes of claiming a seat on one of the pews. People had learned that if they weren't seated at least fifteen minutes before praise and worship began, there would be standing room only.

Amaryllis exhaled frustratingly. "We can't wait any longer for the containers, Bridge. Let's just pay the bill and go."

"Are you cooking dinner tonight?"

"No."

"Then you're taking the rest of your salad, and I'm taking these Buffalo wings home."

Amaryllis looked at her wristwatch again. "Let's go. We'll stop after church and get something to eat if you're still hungry."

Abandoning her half-eaten dinner was not an option for Bridgette. "I am not leaving these wings. Get your purse and let's go."

Amaryllis watched as Bridgette placed her purse on her shoulder, stood, and picked up their plates. "Bridgette, you can't take those plates out of here."

She ignored Amaryllis and walked to the front of the restaurant and stood at the counter next to the cash register. There was no one standing behind the counter.

Bridgette looked around for a bell but didn't see one, so she yelled, "Ding, dong, ding, dong."

Immediately, a manager came from the kitchen. "Yes, ma'am. How may I help you?"

Bridgette dropped the plates on the counter. "Can we please have pieces of aluminum foil to wrap our plates so we can get out of here? We're trying to get to church on time."

The manager looked at the plates. "Who was your server, ma'am?"

"The heck if I know. We might as well have served ourselves." Bridgette was very loud. The customers seated close by gave her their undivided attention.

The manager saw that she was causing a scene. "Ma'am, please lower your voice. We are short-staffed today. I apologize for your inconvenience."

"Well, since you don't have anyone to serve me, I guess there's no one to take my money for the bill, right?"

The manager understood all too well where Bridgette was going with this. "Yes, ma'am. Your meals are on the house."

Without saying thanks, Bridgette turned to walk away, then stopped and turned around. "What about my dessert?"

The manager exhaled. Anxious to get the loud-mouthed woman out of his restaurant, he asked, "What would you like?"

"I want a slice of the vanilla cheesecake. And don't forget the chocolate sauce."

One minute later, the manager brought Bridgette a whole vanilla cheesecake, neatly wrapped, and a cup of chocolate sauce. "Is there anything else I can get you, ma'am?"

"A container for my chicken wings."

After the manager had wrapped Bridgette's chicken wings neatly in a container, they left the restaurant.

"Bridgette, you know you were wrong asking for dessert after the manager had said that our meals were on the house."

"Yeah, I should have left the restaurant without the cheesecake, but I wasn't gonna leave my wings, Amaryllis. Free or not, they were good."

Chapter 5

On the elevator going up to their condo, Bridgette looked at her wristwatch again.

"Amaryllis, it's almost twenty to four. Will you please hurry up and change? You know Progressive is always packed, and I don't wanna have to stand throughout the entire service."

"All I gotta do is slip on a pair of slacks and a blouse."

"Why do you always have to change outfits between services, anyway?"

"Because it's a sin to wear the same thing to two separate services, Bridge."

Bridgette frowned at Amaryllis's logic. "Says who?"

"Says Saint Amaryllis."

"Well, all I know is if I have to sit in the balcony, Saint Amaryllis is gonna suffer."

The elevator doors opened, and they stepped into the hallway. Tyrone was sitting on the floor with his back against the door to their unit. His legs were propped up, and he hung his head between them. Amaryllis stood in front of him and called his name. He made an attempt to lift his head but couldn't do it. She knew he was intoxicated and got angry. "Uh, Bridgette, you go ahead to church."

By the tone of Amaryllis's voice, Bridgette knew Tyrone was in deep trouble. "What are you gonna do to him, Amaryllis?"

"I warned this fool about coming over here drunk, but he doesn't think boo-boo stank. I'm gonna make sure that this is the last time Ty comes over here like this."

"Amaryllis, don't do anything crazy," Bridgette warned her friend.

Amaryllis looked at Bridgette. "You think I'm crazy?"

"Heck, yeah. With a capital K."

Amaryllis gave Bridgette a mischievous grin.

"Am I gonna have to bail you out of jail to-night, Amaryllis?"

Amaryllis ignored her question and took the cheesecake and chocolate sauce from her hands. "I'll put these in the refrigerator for you. You're hollering about being late for church, so you better go ahead."

Bridgette asked Amaryllis the same question again. "Am I gonna have to bail you out of jail?"

"No, I got a get-out-of-jail-free card."

Bridgette turned to get on the elevator, and Amaryllis waited for the doors to close before opening the door to their unit. She placed Bridgette's food in the refrigerator, then pulled Tyrone inside by dragging him by his arms. She left him lying unconscious on the living room floor and went into her bedroom to change into a pair of jeans, a T-shirt, and gym shoes. After changing clothes, she left the condo. She rode the elevator down, got into her car, and drove two miles to Home Depot. It was time for Tyrone Caridine to learn whom he was really dealing with.

About half an hour later, Amaryllis held a squirt bottle ten inches from Tyrone's face and sprayed water five times. He woke up coughing and gasping for air. He was lethargic and bewildered as he looked all around. His vision was obscured. He blinked four or five times and saw three Amaryllises. She sprayed water in his face again. This time, he coughed and almost choked. He tried to move but realized he couldn't. He lay in the middle of Amaryllis's bed wearing only his briefs. His arms were extended over his head. His wrists were tied tightly to the brass rails with white polyester rope. His legs were spread twenty inches apart, and his ankles were tied to the railings at the end of her bed. Although incoherent, Tyrone knew he was on lockdown. He blinked his eyes a few more times and finally, the three Amaryllises became one.

"Wha-what's going on?" he stammered.

Amaryllis stood next to the bed with a roll of duct tape in her hands. "Haven't I told you repeatedly to never come to my house drunk or without calling?"

Tyrone raised his head and saw that he was almost naked. "Huh?"

Amaryllis mocked him. "Huh?"

He saw the duct tape in her hand. "Wha-what you get-tin' ready to do with that?"

Amaryllis was angry. Angry that she was trying to live right but was constantly made to do wrong. It seemed like since she'd gotten saved, she was consistently walking into a crossroad. She was angry that this was another episode she was forced into that she'd have to repent for. What angered Amaryllis more than anything was that she was missing church. She was constantly on her knees asking God to deliver her from her wicked ways.

Looking at Tyrone lying in her bed completely helpless brought back memories of when she had attempted to steal her sister's fiancé. She recalled sneaking into James's apartment with a set of keys that she had made after stealing the original set from Michelle's purse. It was her plan to drug James by putting a large dose of Vicoden into a pitcher of Kool-Aid, wait until it made him unconscious, then take nude photos of James and herself. She reflected back on that day in Las Vegas.

After she spiked the Kool-Aid, Amaryllis loaded film into a tiny camera and hid it on a window ledge in between two large potted plants in James's living room. Then she went into his bedroom and undressed. After that, she crawled beneath his bed and waited for him to come home from a business trip. Her plan went perfectly when James got home and drank a glass of the spiked Kool-Aid. It took almost an hour for the Vicoden to take effect.

Amaryllis crawled out from under his bed and found him passed out on the sofa in the living room in front of his television.

She called his name three times to make sure he was asleep before she carefully removed his boxers and positioned him on the couch where the camera would catch his entire body. She set the camera for ten seconds and climbed her naked body on top of him with her back to the camera. Then she placed James's hands on her breasts. When she heard the camera snap, she climbed off him and set it for another ten seconds, then climbed on him again, this time bending forward, placing her lips on his. Her mission was accomplished.

Thinking back on that time caused Amaryllis's blood to run warm in her veins. Her plan to destroy her sister's relationship folded when Michelle found out what Amaryllis had done. She had written Amaryllis off until she received the news that Amaryllis had gotten robbed and beaten. When Michelle heard that her sister was left for dead and in a coma, she rushed to the hospital to be by Amaryllis's side and prayed her out of the coma.

Amaryllis was discharged from the hospital on a Sunday morning. She caught a cab to Michelle's church and threw herself at her sister's feet, begging for forgiveness. It was at that time when Amaryllis said to Michelle's bishop, "I need you to tell me what I gotta do to be saved."

Since then, Amaryllis had taken on her role as a new creature in Christ seriously. But, as she stood in her room holding Tyrone captive just as she did James, Amaryllis had yet to learn how to let the Lord fight her battles. She was hell-bent on teaching Tyrone a lesson, even if she had to repent for it later.

She tore eight inches of tape from the roll and spread it across Tyrone's hairy chest, then abruptly ripped it off. His eyes rolled to the back of his head in pain. Where thick, coarse hair once was, was now as smooth as a baby's bottom. He screamed out in pain. "Oww, oww."

Amaryllis walked around to the other side of the bed. "I told you there would be consequences and repercussions, didn't I? Why are you making me do this, Ty?"

Tyrone's chest was on fire. Tears came to his eyes as he watched in horror as Amaryllis tore another piece of the tape and spread it across his stomach, then viciously ripped it off. "Oww, oww, oww. Please stop, please!"

Amaryllis tore a third piece of tape and placed it beneath his navel this time. His eyes grew wide at the thought of what Amaryllis was about to do. He got delirious and yelled something he shouldn't have. "No, Icee, please stop!"

Amaryllis's fingers were on the beginning of the strip, ready to snatch it until Tyrone cried out the mysterious name. She paused and looked at him. "Who the heck is Icee?"

He didn't say a word. If he was in trouble a minute ago, he knew that he was really going to get it right then. Amaryllis saw tears streaming from the corners of his eyes down to his ears.

"Ty, I'm only gonna ask one more time." She spaced her words apart and spoke very slowly. "Who . . . is . . . Icee?"

If Tyrone told Amaryllis about Icee, she'd continue to torture him. If he didn't tell her, she'd still torture him, so he opted to change the subject. "Amaryllis, baby, you are sooo beautiful."

Amaryllis ripped the tape away. Tyrone screamed so loud, he almost shattered the bedroom window. She threw the roll of tape across the room and picked up a slab of wood she'd purchased from the store. She positioned it between Tyrone's ankles.

He got scared all over again and started to sweat. "Wha-what are you doing?"

From the floor by the bed, Amaryllis picked up a baseball bat, then looked at him.

"Have you seen the movie Misery, Ty?" she asked him calmly.

Tyrone began squirming on the bed, trying to escape the rope that tied his hands. "Oh, Lawd, Jesus. Help me, Lawd. Please help me."

Amaryllis positioned herself next to Tyrone's right ankle and raised the bat over her left shoulder. "Spare the rod, spoil the drunken boyfriend."

Tyrone lost his mind as he screamed, hollered, and cried. Amaryllis swung the bat but stopped short of his ankle and hit the mattress just two inches from his leg.

"Next time I won't miss. Who's Icee, and why is she stalking me?"

Tyrone was moaning and crying. "Please, Amaryllis, please."

She raised the bat over her left shoulder again. Tyrone screamed louder than any woman she knew. Again, she swung the bat and struck the side of the mattress, just inches away from his ankle. The shriek that came from his throat was piercing. He screamed and cried and cried and screamed as Amaryllis walked to the other side of the bed. Through his tears, he saw three Amaryllises raise three bats over three shoulders.

"Who is Icee?" Amaryllis demanded.

"Icee is crazy just like you."

Amaryllis was about to swing but paused. She gave Tyrone the widest grin and spoke like she was extremely happy all of a sudden. "You wanna see crazy?"

She dropped the bat and walked out of the bedroom. Because of the duct tape, Tyrone's chest, stomach, and the area beneath his navel were red and on fire. Crying, he tried to wiggle free of the rope that tied him to the bed but couldn't do it. Amaryllis came into the bedroom. In one hand was a bottle of isopropyl alcohol. In the other hand was a book of matches.

"What do you think Pastor Alford is preaching about this evening, Ty?" she asked.

Her voice had changed. Before Amaryllis left the bedroom, her tone was high. Now she was calm, cool, and collected.

At that exact moment, Tyrone knew that Amaryllis was as crazy as Jack Nicholson was when he was trying to kill his wife in the movie, The Shining.

"I don't wanna kill ya'. I just wanna bash your freakin' skull in."

Remembering those words sent chills down Tyrone's spine. He looked at Amaryllis, and for a split second, he could've sworn that he saw Jack Nicholson's head on her shoulders. When Amaryllis's face came back into focus, Tyrone wondered how she could be worried about what their pastor was preaching about while torturing him at the same time.

She stood over Tyrone and poured the entire bottle of alcohol beneath his navel. His eyes got wide, and he screamed so loud, his throat burned. "Oh, Lawd, Jesus, Jesus, Jesus. Help me, Lawd. Save me, Jesus, save me."

Amaryllis struck a match and held it six inches above Tyrone's private area. Snot ran from his nose down the sides of his face. He hollered out just as Amaryllis was releasing the match. "Okay,

okay. I'll tell you. Please don't burn me. I'll tell you."

Amaryllis calmly and slowly blew out the match. Of course, she wasn't really going to burn Tyrone. She only wanted to scare him. It had certainly worked. "I'm listening."

Tyrone was moaning and crying. How in the world did he end up with two crazy broads? In the two years he'd been with Icee, she'd stabbed him four times, pushed his car into Lake Michigan, and held him hostage in his own home for ten hours by pointing a gun at his head.

One night a year ago, she put a mayonnaise jar in a canvas bag and threw it on the floor. Then she stomped on the bag until the glass looked like little diamonds. In the midnight hour while Tyrone was asleep, Icee poured the glass across the bathroom floor. Lo and behold, like clockwork, Tyrone got up at two a.m. to use the bathroom. Three steps onto the floor, he screamed in pain. For the next three weeks, he went about his days wearing orthopedic shoes on heavily bandaged feet. Though it had been a year since that had happened, Tyrone sometimes still walked with a limp because a piece of glass couldn't be removed from his left heel.

Now he was tied to a bed with another psycho standing over him whom he'd only been dating for three weeks. She was threatening to set fire to what Tyrone considered his most prized possessions.

He confessed to Amaryllis that he'd been dating Icee for two years. When Amaryllis joined Progressive Ministries a month ago, it was love at first sight for Tyrone, but he didn't know how to break it off with Icee. He explained that Icee had followed him to her house one night. "That's how she found out where you lived."

"How did she get my cell number?"

"I guess she must've gotten it from my cell phone."

Amaryllis left the bedroom to retrieve Tyrone's phone from his jacket pocket. She brought the phone into the bedroom, stood by the bed, and began pressing buttons.

Tyrone prayed that she wasn't calling Icee; she would surely finish what Amaryllis had started to do to him.

"Amaryllis, please don't call her," Tyrone begged.

"I'm erasing all of my numbers from your phone. And if you ever call me again, for anything, I will personally see to it that all of your fingers are shot off your hand. I dare you to think that I'm playing with you."

After torturing Tyrone and making absolutely sure that he understood that she wanted nothing more to do with him, Amaryllis freed him and sent him on his way.

Then she changed the sheets on her bed and went into the living room. She sat down on the sofa with her cellular phone in her hand. She contemplated whether to make the telephone call she felt the urge to make. The more she thought about it, the more Amaryllis became convinced that she had to do it. She pressed the digits that she had retrieved from Tyrone's phone. Her call was answered on the third ring.

"Hello?"

It was her. Amaryllis recognized the voice as the same one that had called and threatened her when she and Bridgette were at the mall. "Is this Icee?"

There was a pregnant pause before a response came through on the other end of the line.

"Yes, this is Icee. Who is this?"

The same threatening tone that Amaryllis heard before came through the telephone line right then. She hoped that the conversation would go smoothly.

"My name is Amaryllis, and I'm calling to speak with you about Tyrone Caridine."

"What about Tyrone? What could you possibly have to talk to me about?" Icee spat the questions with fire. Amaryllis imagined her neck rotating with much attitude.

"Well, I wanted to inform you that as of today, I'm no longer seeing him. I had no idea that he was involved with someone else. Obviously you knew about me because I saw you outside of my building. I know that you put the black rose and card on my windshield. I know that you were the one who sent me and my friend drinks at the restaurant this afternoon. And I know you're responsible for smashing my car windows and slashing my tires."

Icee didn't respond.

Amaryllis could hear the television in the background but only silence from Icee. "Hello?"

"I'm here."

"Well, as I already stated, Tyrone and I are over. I apologize for upsetting you or hurting you, but I didn't know anything about you. He was playing both of us. But now that I'm done with him, I'm asking you to never call me again. Please do not place anything else on my windshield or slash my tires. There is no need for you to stalk me or sit in your vehicle outside of my building. I am no longer a threat to you."

Again, Icee didn't respond to Amaryllis at all. She simply disconnected the call.

Amaryllis sat on the sofa and thought about the love triangle she had unknowingly been a part of. "I thought I was done with this stuff, Lord. I'm trying to do right, trying to live right, but every time I turn around, something happens that makes me do things that I know I shouldn't do."

At that point, all Amaryllis could do was hope that Icee was mature enough to place fault where it belonged; on Tyrone. For once in Amaryllis's life, she realized that she wasn't the cheater in the relationship. She, indeed, had come a long way.

Amaryllis began to think about what her ex-boyfriend, Randall, said to her when she went to his church for forgiveness. His words of wisdom had comforted her. Randall had told Amaryllis to not be afraid of trials but learn to expect them. He reminded her that she had the power of the Holy Ghost to help her through anything.

Randall encouraged Amaryllis to stay in the Word of God because it was her weapon. He advised her to read her Bible daily and to never, under any circumstances, underestimate how low the enemy will go to destroy her. He also advised Amaryllis to keep her friends close and her enemies even closer. He assured her that God would protect her from all hurt, harm, and danger.

Amaryllis thought Randall's words were a personal short sermon written just for her. She got up and went into her bedroom and grabbed her Bible from the dresser. She realized that she had failed God today. Amaryllis knew that torturing Tyrone was the wrong way to end the relationship. She also knew that tomorrow was a new day. She could repent now and start fresh in the morning.

"Lord, if You give me another chance, I promise to do right by You."

Amaryllis prayed that God would give her another chance to make it right. She lay across the bed, opened her Bible, and read scriptures while she waited for Bridgette to return home from church.

Chapter 6

At six-fifteen Monday morning, Amaryllis and Bridgette stepped off the elevator. Marvin was anxiously waiting at his post for the roommates pass to him by. Amaryllis reached his desk first. "Good morning, Marvin."

If it wasn't a good morning five minutes ago, it was certainly a good morning now that Amaryllis was present. Marvin presented her with a dozen red roses. "Beautiful flowers for a beautiful lady."

Amaryllis took the roses from him and sniffed them. "Thank you, Marvin. These are beautiful. I'll place them in water and set them on my desk when I get to work."

Bridgette walked up. "Today is my birthday, not hers. Where are my darn flowers?"

Marvin looked at her. "I was running late for work this morning. I didn't have time to stop by the cemetery and pick 'em."

Bridgette moved closer to him. "Didn't I tell you that I could say two words that'll make all three of your teeth fall out?"

"See, you can't even count." Marvin held up two fingers. "I got fo' teef."

Bridgette looked at the two fingers he held up. "And you say I can't count? How many teeth do you have, Marvin?"

He held up two fingers again. "I got fo' teef."

Bridgette laughed, and so did Amaryllis.

"Bridgette, will you leave Marvin alone?" Amaryllis asked.

"He started with me about the flowers. Why do you always take his side?"

"Because Marvin is an old man." Amaryllis wanted to separate them before an argument erupted. "It's your turn to drive. Go get the car and drive around to the front of the building."

Bridgette looked at Marvin. "You better be glad I gotta go to work."

"Nah, y-y-you b-better be g-glad y-y-you g-gotta go to w-work."

Bridgette walked to the door that led to the garage then turned around. "Hey, Marvin, how m-m-many t-t-teefs y-you g-got?"

Marvin patiently waited for Bridgette to finish mocking him and held up two fingers.

"I got fo' teef."

Bridgette laughed and walked out the door. Amaryllis thanked him for her roses again. "I really appreciate my flowers, Marvin."

"You wanna come around my desk and sit on my lap?"

"You know what, Marvin? This time last year, I would've gladly sat on your lap and charged you fifty bucks. But I don't live like that anymore, sweetie."

"Is you a virgin?"

Amaryllis thought about his question. "I'm trying real hard to be."

She bid him farewell, then walked out of the building with her roses.

When she fastened her seat belt after getting into the car, Bridgette pulled away from the curb. Near the end of the block, before Bridgette reached the stoplight, a woman made a sharp right turn. She cut in front of Bridgette's car, nearly causing a collision.

Bridgette went into a rage. She honked her horn profusely and yelled obscenities at the driver. "You stupid . . . Can't you see my car?"

Her outburst startled Amaryllis. "Bridgette, would you please calm down?"

Bridgette unfastened her seat belt and exited the car on her way to confront the woman. "No, uh-uh. I'm gonna tell this trick a thing or two."

"Bridgette, get your behind back in this car!" Amaryllis demanded as she started praying. Just when Bridgette got to the rear of the woman's car in front of her, the light changed to green, and the woman sped off.

Bridgette was hot under the collar that she didn't get a chance to give the woman a piece of her mind. As she walked back to her own car, a man who sat in his vehicle behind hers blew his horn to get her moving. Bridgette looked at him and yelled, "Don't you see me getting in the car, you idiot? Huh? You wanna die this morning? Press that horn again and see what happens."

Amaryllis was in the passenger seat with her eyes closed. She was still praying.

Bridgette got back in the car and sped all the way downtown to the law office where the two of them worked. Amaryllis didn't say a word . . . she just prayed silently.

No sooner than Amaryllis sat at her desk, she heard Bridgette yell from across the office, "Who put these folders on my desk?"

She was yelling at no one in particular, but the entire office staff stopped what they were doing and looked at her. Bridgette had been employed at Parker & Parker Law Office as a paralegal for the past six years. For the entire six years, she'd started every morning off with a loud complaint. It was always loud enough to get everyone's attention.

On Mondays, it was, "Who put this on my desk?"

On Tuesdays, it was, "Who's been using my darn computer?"

On Wednesdays, it was, "Where is my darn coffee mug? I left it right here on my desk."

On Thursdays, it was, "Whoever stole my Winnie The Pooh ink pen better return it in the next five minutes, or else I'm gonna set it off up in this mutha."

Fridays' outburst were everybody's favorite. "It's eight o'clock. Where's my darn check?"

At around ten minutes before noon, Bridgette's intercom buzzed. "Yes, Mr. Parker?"

"Bridgette, can you come into my office, please?"

"Sure, Mr. Parker. I'll be right in."

She dialed Amaryllis's extension. "Girl, this is it. The boss wants to see me. It's promotion time," she sang.

"All right, girlfriend. I guess lunch is on you today, huh?"

"Lunch and dinner."

Bridgette hung up from Amaryllis and grabbed a notepad and pen then went and knocked on Mr. Parker's door before gently opening it. He was sitting behind his desk speaking into a Dictaphone. He motioned with his hand for her to come in and have a seat. Bridgette sat in a chair across from him and patiently waited for him to finish his thought. In a moment, Mr. Parker set the Dictaphone on his desk and looked at her.

"Bridgette, how are you feeling today?"

She smiled. "Fine, thank you."

"Tell me what happened in the break room earlier today."

Her smile faded. Mr. Parker was referring to the argument she had had with David, another paralegal that happened to be Mr. Parker's nephew.

"I don't know what you mean," she answered nervously.

"Did you and David argue?"

"We exchanged a few words, but it's all good now."

"What do you mean, 'it's all good'?"

"It's squashed."

Mr. Parker gave Bridgette a look that told her he didn't understand her language.

"We've settled the disagreement, Mr. Parker."

The boss folded his hands on the desk. "David said you threatened him when he changed the channel on the television in the break room."

"I was watching the The Young And The Restless, right? The idiot came in the break room and changed the channel like I was invisible."

It completely went over Bridgette's head that she had just called the CEO's nephew an idiot.

Mr. Parker picked up a sheet of paper from his desk. "Bridgette, I have a written statement from David that reads, 'I thought Ms. Nelson was asleep, so I changed the channel on the television. That's when she jumped up from the sofa and said that she would throw me out of the *$@&^ window if I touched the television again.'"

He laid the sheet of paper back on the desk and looked at Bridgette. "Is that a true statement, Bridgette?"

"Nope. I told that idiot I would throw his punk behind out of the *$@&^ window if he touched the television again. You tell that nerd that I said if he's gonna quote me, quote me right."

Ten minutes later, Bridgette left Mr. Parker's office and walked straight to Amaryllis's desk. "Girl, you ain't gonna believe this sh . . . uh, stuff." She had almost cursed but caught herself.

Amaryllis kept typing. "What?"

"He didn't give me the promotion."

Amaryllis looked up at her with a surprised expression on her face. "Why?"

"Because I cussed David out this morning and threatened to kill him. Can you believe something that minor stopped me from getting my promotion? Mr. Parker said he'll consider my application for the promotion if I take an anger management class. Girl, when he suggested that, I almost went to jail. I looked into the future and saw myself leaping across his desk and choking the sh . . . uh, mess out of him. Then I heard God say 'Peace, be still.' " Bridgette held up her right hand. "But I promise, I was ready to go to jail."

"So, what are you gonna do, Bridge?"

"I'll tell you what I'm not gonna do. I'm not taking an anger management class. Can you imagine me sitting in a circle with a bunch of crazy folks? What am I gonna say, 'Hello, my name is Bridgette Nelson, and I'm a mad $#@&%'?"

There was a time when Amaryllis would laugh whenever she witnessed Bridgette let loose her tongue. But witnessing her best friend lose a promotion because she couldn't control her mouth wasn't a funny matter to her. Bridgette had made a promise to stop using so much profanity, and Amaryllis wondered when she would start to make good on that promise.

"Do you remember the promise you made to God to stop cursing, Bridgette?" Amaryllis reminded her best friend.

Bridgette leaned against Amaryllis's desk and picked lint from her sleeve. "Uh-huh."

"Well, it's about time you made good on your word, don't you think?"

"I'm trying to."

"How? How are you trying? Were you trying this morning when you cussed out that lady who cut you off? Were you trying when you cussed out the man when he blew his horn at you? How about cursing out Mr. Parker's nephew? Were you trying then too?"

Bridgette became defensive. "Don't preach to me like you've been saved your whole life, Amaryllis. You ain't nowhere near perfect. Hmph, I know what you used to do."

"You said the magic word. Yeah, I used to do some wild stuff, but I don't anymore. You and I made promises to God together, and we swore to keep each other on the right path. I kept my promise. I haven't rubbed up against a man in a long time. And trust me on this—staying away from a man's bed is just as difficult for me as controlling your mouth is for you. But this conversation isn't about me, Bridgette. I'm not the one who just lost a promotion—you are."

With that being said, Amaryllis turned her attention back to her computer. Bridgette stormed across the office to her desk and plopped down in her chair. Five seconds later, the entire office staff, including Mr. Parker, heard Bridgette yell, "Who turned the volume down on my radio? I was listening to Bishop T. D. Jakes preach."

Amaryllis looked at her best friend and shook her head, then mumbled, "What for? It ain't doing you no good."

Chapter 7

After their evening run on Tuesday, Amaryllis and Bridgette walked two blocks from their condominium to Estella's Shrimp Basket. They left the restaurant with three pounds of jumbo shrimp and a large container of fried okra. Back in their building, they passed the security desk on their way to the elevator when the guard who worked the evening shift spoke to them. "Hey, you ladies hear about Marvin?"

Bridgette set their food on the security desk. "What about him?"

"He had a heart attack this afternoon. From what I hear, he was in bad shape."

Amaryllis placed her hand over her heart. "Oh, my goodness. What hospital is he in?"

"The paramedics took him to Loyola University."

The two women went to their unit and put their dinner on top of the stove.

They both showered and dressed in nylon jogging suits, then headed to the west side of Chicago to Loyola University Medical Center.

At the receptionist's desk, they were told that Marvin was in the Intensive Care Unit and visiting hours would be over in twenty minutes.

Amaryllis and Bridgette expected to see Marvin attached to many machines and barely conscious. They stopped in the gift shop where Bridgette bought get-well balloons. When the ladies walked into Marvin's room, he was sitting up in bed, watching Sanford & Son and eating ice-cream sherbet.

Bridgette heard Fred Sanford when he insulted his sister-in-law, Esther.

"I could stick your face in some dough and make gorilla cookies," Fred Sanford teased.

Marvin laughed at the television, and Bridgette went and stood next to his bed. "Get the heck up out of this bed. Ain't nothin' wrong with you. Here I am driving like a maniac across the city, rushing to get here because I thought you were knocking on death's door. Yet, you're in here having a miniparty."

Amaryllis looked at her. "What do you mean 'like a maniac'? Shouldn't you have said, 'Being the maniac that I am, I drove like a fool'?"

Bridgette ignored her and spoke to Marvin. "If you had a heart attack, why are you laughing at the television and eating ice cream?"

Marvin raised his eyebrows. "Who told you I had a heart attack?"

"The guard who works the evening shift."

"Well, he lied. I was having chest pains and a hard time breathing, but the doctor's ruled out a heart attack."

Amaryllis patted Marvin's foot. "I'm glad you're okay, Marvin."

Bridgette tied the balloons to the railings on his bed, and Marvin smiled at Amaryllis.

"Thank you, sugar."

Bridgette was offended. "What the heck are you thanking her for? I was the one doing eighty all the way over here. And it was my twenty dollars that bought three darn balloons. I bet the next time I hear about you riding in an ambulance, I'll wait until I get an invitation to the funeral before I buy anything else."

Marvin grabbed Bridgette's hand and kissed the back of it repeatedly. "I'm sorry, sugarplum. Thanks for my balloons. I knew you loved me."

Bridgette snatched her hand from his grip. "Uh-uh. Don't be trying to make up for it now. And I don't love you. I just wanted to see for myself that you were dead." The mushy card Marvin was playing wasn't working for Bridgette. She preferred to be at war with him.

Marvin teased her and sang, "Bridgette and Marvin, sittin' in a tree. K-i-s-s-i-n-g."

Bridgette looked at his wrist. "Sing it again and I'll snatch that IV right out of your arm, I promise. And if you're sick, you don't need to be eating ice cream. It could freeze your heart." She sat down in a chair next to his bed and grabbed the cup of sherbet off his tray. She made herself comfortable and ate what was left of it.

Amaryllis scolded her. "Bridgette, you can't take his ice cream."

Bridgette looked at her. "Look, Amaryllis, we didn't get a chance to eat our shrimp, which means I'm hungry."

"But the sherbet is for Marvin."

Bridgette pressed the nurse button on the remote control, then looked at Marvin.

"When she answers, tell her to bring you another cup of ice cream because I'm eating this one."

On the way home from the hospital, Amaryllis asked Bridgette to stop at Wal-Mart. There were only a handful of customers in the store. In the feminine hygiene aisle, they were comparing prices of maxipads when Amaryllis noticed a young Caucasian store clerk watching every move she and Bridgette made. He pretended to arrange items on a nearby shelf while at the same time keeping one of his eyes on them.

Amaryllis whispered to Bridgette. "Bridge, that guy thinks we're shoplifters."

What Amaryllis had said was all the fuel Bridgette needed to start a fire. She looked at the young clerk. "What the heck are you watching us for? How come you ain't watching the white folks? We ain't gotta steal a darn thang."

Though the clerk would never admit it, Bridgette's outburst and forwardness caught him off guard. "I wasn't watching you, ma'am. I was just stacking these products."

Bridgette looked at what he was supposedly stacking. "Well, how long does it take you to stack douche bottles that were already on the shelf?"

He quickly removed his hand away from the shelf. "I'm just doing my job, ma'am."

"Is it your job to watch me like a hawk?" Amaryllis asked.

"It's my job to assist you."

Amaryllis held up the boxes of maxipads she was holding. "Okay, well, sometimes, when I bleed, it comes out clotty and real heavy. Which of these brands do you recommend I use to keep from having to soak my panties in the bathroom sink every month?"

Bridgette couldn't help herself. She held up the box of tampons. "And can you demonstrate how to properly insert these?"

The young clerk's face turned completely red. "Uh, I'll get someone else to help you."

He practically ran away from them. Amaryllis looked at Bridgette. "Bridge, we're ignorant."

Chapter 8

On Wednesday morning, Amaryllis was typing at her computer when her extension rang. She wasn't in a talkative mood and decided to let the caller talk to her voice mail instead. After a few minutes, she called her mailbox and heard, "Hey, sis, just callin' to—"

Amaryllis quickly disconnected the call and dialed Michelle's number in Las Vegas. "Hi, Michelle."

"That was fast. What are you doing, screening calls?"

"Girl, I have to. I'm running from men these days. And I definitely don't wanna talk to Tyrone."

"What's this I hear? Is there trouble in paradise?" Michelle asked.

"Honey, please. What we had can hardly be considered paradise. So, let's change the subject. How's James?"

Michelle smiled at James's photograph sitting on her desk. "James. Now, he's Mr. Paradise. He's wonderful."

"I gotta give it to you, Michelle. If there was ever a near perfect man in this world, James is the one."

"I am blessed to have him."

"He's blessed to have you too. Don't ever forget that, Michelle."

"Thanks, sis. That was a nice thing to say."

"It's the truth. So, what's up?"

"Well, James's mother is flying in from Houston this evening. I'm hoping to be out of court in time to go with him to the airport to get her. James has been running around frantically, trying to make sure everything is perfect for his mommie."

"Aha, so James is a momma's boy, huh?"

"To say the least. Her bedroom at her house is decorated in pink and yellow. So, James decided he wanted to change one of our guest bedrooms to suit her taste. He redid the entire bedroom in pink and yellow. The neutral color carpet has been pulled up. He wanted her to walk on pink carpet. The bedroom you used when you were here is now fit for a queen."

If Michelle was upset, she didn't sound like it.

"Doesn't that bother you, Michelle?"

"Does what bother me?"

"All the trouble James is going through for his mother. I mean, I don't think I would tolerate my husband remodeling my house just to pacify his mother."

"Amaryllis, James is a good husband and a good son. Mother Bradley has no idea what James is doing for her. No, it doesn't bother me at all that he appreciates his mother and does all he can to make her comfortable in his home."

"Wait a minute, Michelle. That was your home first."

"But when James moved in, it became his home too. He's the head of this household. The name on the mailbox has been changed from Price to Bradley. I no longer have to pay folks to mow my lawn because that's my husband's job. Both of our names are on the title to this house, but his name is first."

Amaryllis couldn't understand Michelle. "Why did you add his name to your mortgage?"

Michelle let out a loud sigh. "Do I gotta go to church on you again?"

"Yeah, because I wanna know what you're gonna do if James decides he wants out and half of your house."

"First of all, James's name was added to the mortgage because it's his responsibility to pay it, not mine. I gave that up when I said 'I do.' We didn't go into this marriage thinking that in eight or ten years, we might be divorced so we better not get joint bank accounts, or we better not add his name to the mortgage, or we better sign prenuptials."

Amaryllis almost dropped the telephone. "Hold up, Michelle. Let's stop this conversation and rewind it for a minute. Did I hear you right? You didn't make James sign a prenup?"

"Why do you think that I should have?"

Amaryllis pressed her ear tighter against the telephone. "You own a law firm, Michelle. Hello?"

"Yeah, and . . . ?"

"You're worth millions."

Michelle didn't understand what Amaryllis was getting at. "How do you know, and what's your point?"

"I use to do the books there, sweetie. I replaced your secretary, Chantal, when she went on maternity leave, remember? I know what you're banking. My point is, if James decides to walk, he can easily take half of what you've built. Why give a man that much power over you?"

"Amaryllis, the only one that has power over me is God.

Let me explain something to you. I didn't go looking for James; God sent him to me. The man courted me right, and he loves me right. I believe with my whole heart that God has joined us together. Therefore, what's mine is his, and what's his is mine. In other words, we share everything, and everything we have is ours—except my chocolate. James knows that's the one thing he can't touch.

"God and I have an understanding. When He brought James to me for the very first time, I knew I had to have him. James is righteous, he's holy, and he worships the husk on my feet, as my friend, Jodie, would say. What more can a girl ask for? I told God that if He allowed me to have James, I would do everything that was within me to make him happy.

"And trust me, honey, my husband grins twenty-four seven. Even in his sleep he's smiling. His love for me is overwhelming. Everything I ask him for, he gives. I have more diamonds than I know what to do with."

"That's because he's buying them with your money," Amaryllis commented.

"It's our money, Amaryllis. And as long as I get the gold, I couldn't care less where the money came from. And James is not hurting; he's a homicide detective."

"That can't compare with owning a law firm, Michelle."

"Amaryllis, James is my angel. He's my soul mate. He comforts me, he covers me, he appreciates me, he adores me, and he loves me. We've been married for nine months, and he still carries me over the threshold whenever we walk in the front door. I haven't put gas in my car or truck, nor have I had to wash them since I met

James. I don't have to worry about mortgage or car payments. I haven't seen a light, telephone or gas bill in nine months. And whenever I shop, James sits and reads a magazine. But when I get to the cash register, he steps right up and asks for the total. He writes the check, not me. My welfare is his business. He's my pastor's armor bearer, and mine too."

"That might be all good, Michelle. Like I said, if there was ever a near perfect man, you got him. What I don't understand is why James feels the need to remodel your home to suit his mother," Amaryllis stated.

"Because she'll be here for a month, Amaryllis. He wants to make her comfortable, as he should. She's his mother, and I encourage him to do whatever he wants for her. James is just being James. The way a man treats his mother is the way he'll treat his woman. A man's mother will always be the queen in his life. And his woman can't do anything about that. If a woman tries to come between a man and his mother, she'll be the one getting left in the cold, not Momma.

"When Mother Bradley gets here, she'll be the queen of this house. I don't have a problem with respect. I give it where it's due."

"You only met her a few times, Michelle. It's not like y'all are buddy, buddy."

"Mother Bradley and I are very close. We talk on the telephone every week. Amaryllis, don't you know that if you get a man's mother to fall in love with you, you'll have no worries about getting the man or keeping him because she'll have your back? Mother Bradley raised James to be the man he is today. Now that I think about it, she raised him for me. So, when James gives me my nightly foot massage, I'll make sure that Mother Bradley has a Chunky in her hand and her feet on James's lap too."

"Oh, ain't that about nothing. You'll have three cows, two elephants, and a hippo if anyone touches your chocolate, yet you'll share it with a woman who's getting ready to take over your house."

"Listen, honey, the woman who gave birth to my destiny can have my chocolate and anything else she wants."

Just as Michelle was speaking to Amaryllis, James appeared in her office doorway with a dozen roses in one hand and a small white paper bag in the other. Michelle smiled at her husband. "Speaking of the angel, my armor bearer is here with chocolate and roses."

"Okay, I guess that's my cue. I'll talk to you later. Tell James I said hey."

"I will, sweetie. Look for something in the mail real soon."

"Like what? Some money?" Amaryllis was hopeful.

"No. Something else."

"Okay."

Michelle became concerned. "Hey, sis?"

"Yeah?"

"Do you need any money?"

"I always need money, Michelle."

"Which Western Union do you want me to send it to?"

After confirming with Amaryllis where to send money, Michelle placed the telephone on its receiver and looked at her husband. "Hello, gorgeous."

James presented his prize-winning smile that always melted Michelle. "I'm not the gorgeous one, Mickey, you are." Mickey was the nickname James had given her shortly after they had started dating.

"Not me, you are."

"No. You are, Mickey."

James came into her office, shut the door softly behind him, then locked it. He placed the roses and candy on a table by the door. He then walked to Michelle, picked her up from her chair, and sat her on top of the desk. He reached behind her and pressed the intercom button to speak with Michelle's secretary. "Chantal?"

"Yes, James?"

"Hold all of Michelle's calls, please."

Chantal chuckled. "Ten-four, Detective."

Chapter 9

At lunchtime, Bridgette stood next to Amaryllis at the counter in Western Union and watched as Amaryllis counted $2,000 in one hundred-dollar bills. "Dang, Amaryllis, how can a sister be down wit somma dat?"

Amaryllis kept counting as she answered Bridgette. "She can't."

"Come on, Amaryllis. I gotta get my manicure and pedicure. They are a week overdue."

Amaryllis stopped counting her cash and looked at her friend. "Bridge, I ain't your pimp. You better call Deacon Brown and tell him to get your nails done."

Bridgette's stomach turned, and her hand flew over her mouth. "Girl, you're gonna make me throw up."

Amaryllis looked down at Bridgette's high-heeled sandals. She saw the polish on her toes chipping and promptly gave her $100. "Here, I can't have you going anywhere with me looking like you got liquid paper on your toes. And why would you wear sandals if your toes ain't looking right?"

"Because these sandals match my outfit. You know I gotta be cute." Bridgette ran her hands down her sides and traced her silhouette.

"Bridge, ain't nothing cute about an outfit and matching sandals with jacked-up toes. You could have easily worn slip-on mules or pumps. Now, that would've been cute. But your toes cheapen the look of your sandals. I know how much you paid for them because I was with you when you bought them. If you're gonna wear expensive shoes, wear them right. And you have on Capri pants today. Why didn't you wear your silver anklet for daintiness?"

"I didn't think about it."

Amaryllis looked up toward the ceiling. "Lord Jesus, help your saint."

"What about you, Amaryllis? You're always in my Kool-Aid, even though you do know the flavor, but what about you?"

Amaryllis stepped away from the counter and spread her arms wide and looked at Bridgette. "What's up? What about me?"

Amaryllis was sporting a lavender silk pant-suit. The blouse was long sleeved and it wrapped around to tie on the left side. A silver rhinestone choker circled her neck and matching rhinestone studs decorated her ears. The lavender silk pants hugged her hips perfectly and draped to her ankles. On her feet she wore lavender patent leather, three-inch sandals that were crisscrossed on the top. Her second toe on her left foot sparkled with a rhinestone ring. And, of course, Amaryllis's toenails were freshly done.

She raised her right pant leg up a few inches to display a rhinestone anklet. Bridgette couldn't say anything. From head to toe, Amaryllis always had her stuff together.

"Yeah, okay, Amaryllis. I'll give you your props today," Bridgette complimented.

"Today? Is there ever any day I step out of our front door and I'm not flawless?"

Bridgette thought hard.

Amaryllis gave her ten seconds. "Don't work your brain, Bridge. You can't think of a time."

"Yeah, you're right. I forgot to whom I was talking. You put on eyeliner and lipstick just to take the garbage down to the dumpster or get the mail from the mailbox in the lobby."

Amaryllis placed her purse on her shoulder and headed for the door. "Because that's what true divas do. Graduate."

Amaryllis went back to the office while Bridgette opted to pay a visit to Kwong Dhan's

Nail Salon two blocks away from the law firm. Forty-five minutes later, Bridgette walked to Amaryllis's desk and lifted her left sandal up to the brief Amaryllis was typing from to show off her newly painted toes. "Check 'em out."

Amaryllis was impressed. "Very nice. Who hooked you up, Don Chyung?"

"Nah, he wasn't in the shop today. Sue Hang did my toes today."

Amaryllis took her anklet from her ankle and wrapped it around Bridgette's ankle.

"Now, you look cute."

"Thanks, girlfriend. I look and feel so good now nothing can upset me." Bridgette sashayed across the office to her desk and sat down. Two seconds later everyone heard, "Who put these darn sunflower seed shells over here by my chair?"

On Friday morning, Amaryllis was greeted with two red roses, two yellow roses, and two orange roses on her desk. They were in a glass vase filled with water. Baby's Breath surrounded each rose. Next to the vase was a pink envelope. She sat down, turned on her computer, then opened the envelope and read the card inside.

An orange rose represents friendship A yellow rose represents prosperity A red rose represents love I'm thinking of you, Charles

Yeah, right. No sooner had Amaryllis placed the card back into the envelope, her extension rang.

"Good morning. Parker & Parker Law Offices, Amaryllis speaking."

"Good morning, beautiful."

At the sound of his voice, Amaryllis rolled her eyes and exhaled loudly. "Whatever, Charles. What's up with these dry flowers and this bogus card you sent me?"

"Why you gotta be like that, Amaryllis?"

"Charles, I'm looking at these imitation roses. All six of them are dry and crusty around the edges. And this card is bogus, because we ain't friends, nothing between us is gonna prosper, and I sure as heck don't love you."

"Dang, Amaryllis. Did you wake up on the wrong side of the bed or something?"

"These flowers don't impress me, Charles. Because I know for a fact this is another one of your playa-playa moves to try and get some booty."

"Nah, baby, you got it wrong. This ain't about that. I'm really diggin' you, girl."

Amaryllis didn't believe Charles. It was always the same conversation with him.

He'd ask her for sex, and she'd turn him down. A few weeks would pass, and then he'd call again, always for the same thing.

"Whatever, Charles. Let me ask you a question. Why didn't you bring these flowers to my job yourself?"

"Because I knew you'd throw them in my face."

"True that. I gotta go. It's Friday, and Fridays are always hectic days."

"Can I take you to dinner tonight?"

"Nope. I'm going to the movies with Bridgette."

"Well, how about I take you to breakfast in the morning?"

"No can do, Charles. I got beauty duty in the morning."

"Beauty duty? How can you top perfection? There's absolutely nothing more that you can do to yourself that'll make you more beautiful than you already are."

She was not impressed with his words. "Whatever, Charles."

"Amaryllis, please. Give a brotha a second chance. I know I messed up the first time around, but you're all I think about. Can I at least buy you dinner tomorrow? I know you like to dress. I'll even take you shopping after dinner."

"Charles, you can't afford me. I'm high maintenance, honey."

"Try me, Amaryllis. Tomorrow night is on me. Whatever you wanna eat and wherever you wanna shop. The sky's your limit. And I promise you that I'm not trying to get in your panties. I just wanna spend some time and get to know the new you."

"Unadulterated time?"

"Absolutely."

Amaryllis paused, and Charles thought she'd hung up on him. "Hello?"

"I'm thinking, Charles. Do you remember the conversation we had at my house after the last time we went out?"

"Yeah."

"What did you get out of it?"

"I understood that under no circumstances were you having sex. I know and respect the fact that you are saved now. I remember you saying that you've changed and you're trying to live right."

"So, you feel me on the sex issue?"

"Yeah, I feel you."

Amaryllis wasn't sure if allowing Charles back in her life was a good move. He was sounding good, but she needed to know if he knew God. "Are you in church, Charles?"

"Believe it or not, Amaryllis, I went to church with my mother last Sunday, and I promised her that I'd go with her again this Sunday. I'm trying to turn my life around."

Amaryllis had a hard time digesting Charles's last sentence. But who was she of all people to judge? If God could give her a clean heart, maybe He could work with Charles too. Besides, Amaryllis knew all too well what it felt like to be constantly written off because of things done in the past.

"Okay, Charles. We can do this tomorrow night."

Charles was excited. "You plan the evening. Whatever you wanna do, I'll flow with it."

Amaryllis disconnected the call with Charles. Could this be another setup for her to fail? The two of them had great chemistry. Was it possible that they could actually spend time together and not end up in bed? It had never been done before. Amaryllis knew she was weak. Charles made her weak. But he said that he was attending church.

She sat at her desk and silently prayed. "Father, please help me. Keep me strong. Father, please don't let this be a setup. I don't want to have sex again until I'm married. Keep me, Jesus. Please keep me."

Chapter 10

On Saturday evening, Bridgette sat in the middle of Amaryllis's bed and watched her try on and model at least thirty to forty different outfits. "It really doesn't matter what you choose to wear, Amaryllis. Charles's mouth is gonna drop open because you're naturally beautiful."

She and Bridgette put together a look that would definitely knock Charles off of his feet. Amaryllis modeled tight-fitting Apple Bottom black denim jeans with black three-inch stilettos. A sheer blouse over a black bustier surrounded her torso, and it pushed her double Ds up and out. With every move she made, her cleavage gave Jell-O gelatin a run for its money. She decorated her neck and ears with a silver rhinestone choker and studs.

Being a babe in Christ, Amaryllis lacked in areas of her life where certain things should be changed. Though she had plenty of suits and dresses for church, and office attire for work, her wardrobe for the weekends had yet to receive a major overhaul. She had a killer body, and she knew it. Before she gave her life to Christ, Amaryllis used her seductive wardrobe to attract men to her. She didn't understand that even though her life had changed, her wardrobe needed to be changed as well.

Charles rang their doorbell at exactly five p.m. When Amaryllis opened the door, Charles couldn't utter a word. He made an attempt to speak but couldn't. Amaryllis was flawless, and she'd always been able to render a man speechless at the sight of her beauty. She watched as his eyes scanned her from head to toe, slightly pausing on her cleavage.

It was at that moment that Amaryllis realized that she had made a poor choice in what to wear that evening. The way Charles gazed at her breasts made her extremely uncomfortable. She knew that look. It was the same look that he gave her when they were fornicating awhile back.

"Wow, you look amazing," he said.

"Um, Charles, can you give me about five minutes? I need to change."

"Why?"

"Because I don't want to give you any mixed signals."

Amaryllis disappeared inside her unit without inviting Charles inside. She made him wait in the hallway while she rushed to her closet to find a more suitable blouse.

Bridgette came into Amaryllis's bedroom and saw her throwing different blouses and tops on the floor. "Is the date over already? What are you doing?"

Amaryllis grabbed a white loose-fitting top off the rack and studied it. It was long enough to cover her butt. "This ought to do."

Bridgette didn't understand. "Your outfit is cute. Why are you changing?"

Amaryllis quickly took off the bustier and put on a more comfortable bra. "How can I expect Charles to treat me with respect if my clothes tell him that I don't really want respect?" She slipped the white blouse over her head and looked at her reflection in the mirror. She was pleased. "That's perfect."

Amaryllis returned to her date in the hallway and found him leaning against the wall.

"I'm sorry to have kept you waiting, Charles. I'm ready to go now."

Charles glanced at her white blouse. "Why did you change?"

Amaryllis started to walk toward the elevator. "Because I needed to."

As he walked behind her, Charles saw that her long blouse hid her voluptuous behind from his view.

Amaryllis pressed the button for the elevator.

"I don't think I've ever seen you wear anything like that before," he said. "It's conservative, and I like it."

"Charles, you talk a good game, but I still ain't giving you any booty. So, you can just chill with the phony flattery, okay?"

That wasn't the response Charles was expecting. She had offended him. He grabbed both of her hands and turned her toward him, then looked into her eyes. "Why did you have to take it there? Can't you just relax and allow me to be a gentleman? I don't want any booty."

"Oh, really? Well, I couldn't tell by the way you were sopping me up with your eyes when I first walked out the door."

"You had on a sheer blouse. Did you really expect me to act like I couldn't see through it?"

The elevator doors opened, and they stepped inside.

"You know, Amaryllis, it really doesn't matter what you wear because you're naturally beautiful."

She smiled.

"I really wish you would allow me to treat you like the queen you are. Can you do that for me?"

Amaryllis looked deep into his eyes. He was so unlike the Charles she was used to. Back in the day every time they got together, they ended up in a bed somewhere. She wondered if it was possible that Charles was sincere. She had to constantly remind herself that she too had turned her life around.

"Okay, Charles. I gave Bridgette my itinerary, and I gave myself a curfew. I want to be back here no later than ten o'clock. If I'm not here by ten zero, zero, Bridgette is gonna come looking for me. And when she finds us, all heck is gonna break loose. I'm sure that I don't have to tell you that she's crazy. Trust me when I tell you that you don't wanna make me miss my curfew."

Amaryllis was impressed at the white stretch limousine waiting for them outside. "My, my, my. Charles, this evening is looking promising so far."

"Well, you kinda hurt a brotha's pride on the telephone yesterday when you said that I couldn't afford you. So I had to come correct and show you what Sir Charles was working with."

The driver opened the door for them. Once they were seated, Amaryllis looked at Charles. "Honey, you can't afford me. I could've hired a limo just like you did."

Charles reached under the seat and presented Amaryllis with a dozen red roses.

"I personally went to the flower shop and handpicked these one by one. They're fresh."

Amaryllis smiled and took the bouquet from his hand and sniffed the roses. "They're lovely, Charles. Thank you."

The driver got behind the wheel and asked Charles for their destination.

"Ruben, my man, wherever the little lady's heart desires."

Ruben positioned his rearview mirror so that he could see Amaryllis's face. "Where to, beautiful?"

Amaryllis sniffed the roses again and looked at Charles. "You can't afford me."

"Answer the man's question, Amaryllis."

She smiled, still sniffing her roses. Her eyes never left Charles's eyes as she answered Ruben. "Take us to Rush Street."

Every citizen of Chicago knew that one of the most expensive steak houses in the city was on Rush Street. It was now time for Charles to put his money where his mouth was.

Chapter 11

Charles wined Amaryllis at Gibson's Steak House with a bottle of Cristal that came with a price tag of $250. He also dined her with steak, lobster, and crab. Amaryllis got a big kick out of Charles feeding her from across the table where he sat. Not only did she enjoy dinner, but the conversation was equally enjoyable, if not more enjoyable.

From the moment Charles pulled out her chair and sat her down, he made her laugh. Not once had he directed their conversation to a sexual topic. When Amaryllis excused herself to go to the ladies' room, Charles stood with her. He couldn't help but notice men's heads turn in her direction as she passed their table. Amaryllis walked by a booth in which two women were sitting. Charles saw that they too admired Amaryllis as she sashayed by their table. Amaryllis didn't know that even in her loose-fitting blouse that hid her voluptuous butt, she was stunning.

When she returned to the table, Charles stood and pulled out her chair again.

"Aren't you the perfect gentleman," she complimented him as she sat.

Charles sat in his chair. "I'm just doing what a man should do."

Amaryllis paused before she spoke, but she needed to get something off her chest. "Charles, I owe you an apology."

"For what?"

"I came hard at you earlier this evening. You complimented me on my blouse, and I fired back that you weren't getting any booty. I'm sorry for that. That was out of line."

"Well, you know what? I get it. I get that you're trying to do the right thing. I get that your guard is up, and it should be. You are beautiful, Amaryllis. I mean beautiful. You should've seen the heads that turned to watch you walk when you went to the bathroom. And I think it's great that you've turned your life around. You inspire me to turn my life around too."

Amaryllis's smile lit up the dining room. The thought of her being an inspiration to anyone was mind-blowing. "Aw, that was a sweet thing to say, Charles."

"I mean it, Amaryllis. Being with you, like this, is good for me."

"What do you mean 'like this'?"

He leaned his upper torso over the table so that Amaryllis could hear every word that was about to come out of his mouth. "What I mean is that I dig the new Amaryllis. Your past is my past; we used to fornicate like forty going north. We had some good times, and I enjoyed every minute of it. And I'll even be honest and say that I don't apologize for what we did because I loved it. It felt good. But being with you tonight shows me that you and I can enjoy one another's company without taking it to the sheets. And I know that if I want a relationship with you, I have to be on the same level of understanding and spirituality as you.

"And I'm getting there. I'm getting there, Amaryllis. Do I want to rip your clothes off right now? Yeah, I do. It's a struggle for me to contain myself. But I want to have a relationship with you. And you've made it clear that in order for me to do that, I gotta change my life too. So, let's do it. Let's do it together. Let's talk this talk and walk this walk."

Amaryllis didn't know what to say, but she loved the words that were coming out of Charles's mouth. To hear him say that she inspired him to become celibate felt good.

Charles admitted that he was digging the new her, and truth be told, Amaryllis was beginning to dig the new Charles too.

"Okay," she said, "let's do it."

Charles smiled and picked up his glass of champagne. He held it across the table. "Here's to new beginnings."

Amaryllis met his glass halfway with her own. "To new beginnings," she smiled back.

The waiter placed the bill on their table, and Charles quickly snatched it up. Amaryllis was no stranger at Gibson's; she knew what the bill was going to look like. She watched as he took five one hundred-dollar bills from his wallet and lay them on top of the bill for the waiter to pick up. She examined his face, but Charles was calm, cool, and collected. Her eyebrows rose when she witnessed him place a fifty-dollar bill in the waiter's hand as they were leaving the restaurant.

In the limousine, Charles complimented Amaryllis on her beauty again. "I just can't get over how beautiful you look tonight. How much did it cost you to get your hair and nails done?"

"About ninety bucks."

He took his wallet from his pocket, pulled out a one hundred-dollar bill, and held it in his hand for Amaryllis to take. "For your trouble."

She looked at the money, then into Charles's eyes. "Is this where I'm supposed to say, 'Thanks but no thanks'? You know I don't turn money away."

"Absolutely not. I'm offering to reimburse you for the cost of your hair and nails."

Amaryllis took the money and put it in her purse. "Thank you."

Ruben adjusted the rearview mirror and looked at Charles. "Where to?"

"What's your pleasure?" Charles asked Amaryllis.

"You can't afford me."

Charles exhaled. "Here we go with that again. Amaryllis, are you enjoying the limo ride?"

"Yes."

"Did you eat well?"

She smiled. "Yes."

"Was the conversation great?"

She thought about Charles's lovely words. "I'll admit that you held my interest."

"Are your roses fresh enough to your satisfaction?"

Amaryllis picked up her bouquet from the seat and admired them. "Uh-huh."

Ruben sat in the front seat rotating his eyeballs from side to side, watching them in the mirror.

"I promised you yesterday that I was gonna take you shopping. And I meant it."

"Charles, I have expensive taste. You better quit while you're ahead."

She lowered her head into the bouquet and allowed the scent to tickle her nose. Charles placed two fingers underneath her chin and turned her face toward his own. "What's your pleasure, Amaryllis?"

She swallowed hard. Again, as she spoke to Ruben, she kept her eyes locked on Charles's eyes. "Ruben, I have to be home in two hours. Get me to Oakbrook as fast as you can."

The limousine pulled away from the curb. Charles grabbed Amaryllis's hand and held it all the way to their next destination. Amaryllis felt like Cinderella, happy and excited to be in the company of a man who was pulling out all the stops for her happiness. But unlike Cinderella, Amaryllis knew the limousine she was riding in wouldn't turn into a pumpkin at midnight.

Amaryllis saw it hanging the moment she and Charles walked through the revolving doors.

"Good evening. Welcome to Zola's Furs," they were greeted by a saleswoman.

Mesmerized, Amaryllis ignored her and walked to the back wall. She stood underneath a grey Chinchilla poncho and looked up at it in awe. She was so engrossed in the beauty of the coat she didn't hear the saleswoman approach her from behind.

"It's beautiful, isn't it?"

Amaryllis didn't turn around. "Yes, it is."

"Would you like to try it on?"

"Yes."

Amaryllis moved aside as the saleswoman lowered the coat. She helped Amaryllis into it, then stood back and admired her. "A beautiful woman deserves a beautiful coat," the saleslady said.

"I agree," Charles responded.

Amaryllis twisted and turned in the coat for five full minutes. Charles came and stood next to her. "By the way you're posing, I take it that you like it."

"How much is it?" Amaryllis asked the saleswoman.

"The price is inside the coat."

Amaryllis removed the coat and looked at the price tag. Her eyes grew wide, and she almost stumbled into Charles. He peeked at the price tag. Amaryllis searched his eyes for a reaction, but Charles didn't give her one.

The saleswoman looked at her wristwatch. "The store is closing in ten minutes. Perhaps you can come back tomorrow?"

Charles looked at her. "We'll take it."

Amaryllis's mouth went dry. "Charles, I don't really expect you to buy this coat for me. It's way too expensive."

"Why did you bring me here then, Amaryllis?"

"To prove to you that you couldn't afford me."

Charles opened his wallet and gave the saleswoman his Visa gold card. "Wrap it up with a big bow."

Amaryllis stood still while the saleswoman took the coat and walked away. "Charles, you're crazy."

"Yes, I am. But for you."

At the counter, the saleswoman gave Charles the receipt to sign. Amaryllis looked at him and smiled. "You still ain't getting any booty, Charles. I don't care how much money you spend."

Her smile confirmed to Charles what he already knew. Amaryllis was joking with him. They had already crossed that booty bridge.

"What can I get for a forty-dollar bouquet of roses, a three hundred fifty-dollar limousine ride, a one hundred-dollar cash gift, a five hundred-dollar dinner, and this coat?"

Amaryllis looked into his eyes. "A hug, a thank you, and a kiss on the cheek."

"I'll take it."

Amaryllis thought about something. "You know, Charles, if you ever got angry with me, you can easily take this coat back because you have proof that you bought it. So, legally, it's yours."

"That ain't never gonna happen, but what's your point?"

"How much does it cost to have my name embroidered inside the coat?" Amaryllis asked the saleswoman.

"Thirty dollars a letter."

Amaryllis did the math. "So, to get 'Amaryllis Theresa' embroidered costs about five hundred bucks?"

"Yes, ma'am."

Amaryllis looked at Charles. "I want my name in this coat just in case you decide to do tha fool and try to take it back. I want the heifer to know that it belonged to me first."

Charles frowned at her. "What heifer, Amaryllis?"

"Any heifer."

For the second time in one night, Charles withdrew five one hundred-dollar bills from his wallet and placed them on the counter.

The saleswoman gave him his receipt. "Thank you, Mr. Walker. The coat will be shipped to Ms. Price's address within two weeks."

Amaryllis and Charles exited the store and headed back to the limousine. Her thoughts took her back to the days when she and Charles were hot and heavy. Just like tonight, Charles had always spent money on her. But Amaryllis would always thank him with sex. As the limousine drove them back to her condominium, she silently prayed that everything Charles had said to her earlier that evening was true. She prayed that he wouldn't go back on his word.

The enemy spoke to Amaryllis. "You know good and well that you can't keep your legs closed where Charles is concerned. He spent a lot of money tonight. Nothing has changed. You're a fool if you think he won't expect you to repay him."

"Shut up, devil." Without realizing it, Amaryllis had spoken out loud.

Charles looked at her. "Huh?"

"Nothing. I was just mumbling." She knew better than to allow the enemy to take her thoughts there. That was exactly what her ex-boyfriend Randall told her to watch out for.

"Beware of destiny preventers and dream killers. Folks are going to come at you and remind you of the things you used to do." That was another bit of advice Randall had given to her when she stopped by his church after her trip to Las Vegas.

Thinking back on Randall's words, Amaryllis had made a decision. She decided that she was going to believe in Charles just as she expected him to believe in her. Surely the two of them had come full circle. Old things were passed away, and Amaryllis was looking forward to the new things ahead.

They arrived at her building, and Charles escorted her to her door. Just as Amaryllis slid her key into the lock, Bridgette yanked the door open. "It's two minutes after ten. You couldn't call?"

Charles spoke first. "I'm sorry, Bridgette, it's not Amaryllis's fault. I tried my best to get her here before ten o'clock."

Bridgette looked at her friend. "Are you all right? You want me to cut him?"

Amaryllis laughed, and so did Charles. "No, Bridge. Take the butcher knife out of your pocket and put it back in the kitchen drawer. I'm all right, and thank you for having my back."

"Are you sure?" she asked Amaryllis while glaring straight into Charles's eyes.

"Yes, sweetie, I'm sure."

Bridgette's eyeballs scanned Charles from his head to his feet before she walked away.

Amaryllis turned toward him. "Thank you so much, Charles. Maybe one day I'll be able to do for you what you did for me tonight."

Frustrated, Charles sighed and leaned against the wall. Amaryllis saw the disappointed look on his face. "What? Did I say something wrong?" she asked.

"You just don't get it, do you? I don't want you to do for me what I did for you. That's not what I'm about, Amaryllis. I showered you with gifts tonight because I wanted to. I enjoy being with you. I like it when you smile because that makes me smile. I promise you that I don't want anything from you."

Amaryllis was on the verge of tears. Charles didn't say anything else. He gently kissed her cheek and walked away.

After Amaryllis had showered and dressed for bed, she got on her knees to pray. "Father, thank You. Thank You so much." She didn't ask God for anything, nor did she complain about anything. She simply thanked Him over and over again for His grace and especially for showing her mercy.

Chapter 12

During morning service, Amaryllis was standing, clapping, and singing praises to God when an usher came to her pew and extended his hand. Suddenly, Charles appeared looking as fine as he wanted to look. Amaryllis noticed the Hugo Boss tailor-made suit the moment she saw him. Charles excused himself past six people, including Bridgette. He made his way to the middle of the pew and stood next to Amaryllis. He left a whiff of Pleasures by Estee Lauder behind him.

Bridgette looked at her best friend and couldn't remember the last time she'd seen Amaryllis smile at a man the way she was smiling at Charles. Silently, she said a little prayer for her friend. Please, Lord, work this out for her. At the smile on Amaryllis's face, Bridgette couldn't help but smile herself.

Throughout the service, Amaryllis was so proud to have her man at her side. There was a time when no one could've paid Amaryllis to step one foot inside church doors. The few times that she had allowed her exboyfriend, Randall, to talk to her into going to church with him, she had embarrassed him by picking at her fingernails when the pastor was preaching or simply yelling obscenities when she thought the sermon was written specifically for Randall to break up with her.

But Amaryllis's life had changed for the better. Now she was up on Sunday mornings before daybreak, excited about going to church. She looked forward to it. It was a thrill for her to sit in the presence of other saints and listen to what would be fed into her soul.

As the choir rendered in song, she noticed that Tyrone was absent. A guest musician, instead, was seated behind the organ. She shook her head thinking that it was just another Sunday morning that Tyrone was probably lying somewhere in a gutter, highly intoxicated. She looked at Charles who was standing, clapping, and singing along with the choir. Amaryllis was pleased with the decision she had made to get Tyrone out of her life and allow Charles back into it. She hadn't heard a peep from Tyrone since that day of torture at her place, and she hadn't seen Icee since she called to tell her that she was done with Tyrone. She'd killed two birds with one stone.

Standing next to Charles, Amaryllis heard him singing. "Please make me better. Better, Lord, better, Lord."

Amaryllis began singing along with him. "Even if it means that I have a lot to sacrifice, make me better, Lord." If someone had told her years ago that she'd come to love God the way she did, Amaryllis would've told that person that they were insane. But as she stood in church and praised God with her man at her side, Amaryllis sang until her heart was content.

During offering time, as Bridgette, Amaryllis, and Charles dropped their envelopes in the basket at the altar, Mother Caridine grabbed a hold of Amaryllis's hand. Bridgette proceeded to her seat, but when Amaryllis stopped walking, so did Charles.

Mother Caridine looked at the man standing so closely to Amaryllis before she spoke. "Hi, sugar."

Amaryllis kissed Mother Caridine's cheek. "Hi, Mother. How are you?"

Again, Mother Caridine looked at Charles. "Hello."

Amaryllis felt she had no other choice but to introduce them. "Uh, Mother Caridine, this is Charles."

Charles extended his hand to her. "It's a pleasure to meet you."

Mother Caridine didn't shake his hand. She ignored his remark as she spoke to Amaryllis. "I was wondering if you're going to stop by and see Tyrone today. You do know that he's in the hospital, don't you?"

Amaryllis's eyebrows shot up. "Uh, no, I didn't know that. Is he all right?"

"No, he's not all right. Haven't you spoken with him?"

"No, ma'am. Ty and I are no longer seeing each other. I thought he would've told you."

A shocked expression came across Mother Caridine's face. "Oh. Uh, no, Tyrone didn't inform me." She looked at Charles again. "This is news to me."

Charles sensed that it was an uncomfortable moment for Mother Caridine. He leaned close to Amaryllis. "Hey, uh, service is just about over. I'll just wait for you outside."

Amaryllis grabbed his hand to keep him right where he was. "You don't have to leave." She looked at Mother Caridine. "What happened to Ty?"

Even though Amaryllis hadn't introduced Charles as her boyfriend, Mother Caridine knew he was more than a mere friend when Amaryllis wouldn't let him walk away.

"He was in a car accident yesterday," she stated.

Amaryllis placed her free hand on her chest. "Oh, my goodness. Was he badly hurt?"

"He was banged up pretty badly. A few broken ribs and a fractured collar bone, but he'll pull through just fine."

"What caused the accident?" Amaryllis asked.

Mother Caridine pinched her lips together. Amaryllis knew right then that alcohol was what caused Tyrone's accident.

"Was he driving under the influence, Mother?"

Mother Caridine looked at Charles, then at Amaryllis. "Tyrone's blood alcohol level was a bit high over the legal limit, but not much. I really believe the police officer exaggerated the results. Tyrone said he only had one beer."

It never failed. Mother Caridine still defended her son, even when she knew it was against the law to drink and drive. Tyrone's accident was more confirmation that Amaryllis had done the right thing by ending her brief relationship with him.

"Mother, please give Ty my best and let him know that I'll keep him in my prayers."

They then went back to their seats and waited for the benediction. When the minister dismissed the congregation, Charles spoke to Amaryllis. "You know I don't mind if you want to go and check on your ex. Broken ribs and collar bone are serious business. It sounds like he's in bad shape."

It wasn't that Amaryllis was insensitive to Tyrone and what had happened to him. She was relieved to know that he had survived the car accident. But she hadn't vested any real time with him. Three weeks wasn't long enough to have fallen in love. Amaryllis hadn't slept with him, therefore, a stronghold, or soul tie, hadn't yet formed. "I really don't have the desire to see him. He has my prayers. That's enough."

Chapter 13

On Thursday morning, Amaryllis opened a letter addressed to her sent from Mrs. Michelle Denise Price-Bradley and showed it to Bridgette. "Look, Bridge, my sister's still attached to Daddy. She refuses to drop his name."

"Well, you said he raised her by himself. For her entire life it's been him and her. And for her to have remained a virgin until marriage lets me know that he's done a darn good job, if you ask me."

Amaryllis looked at Bridgette as she opened Michelle's letter. "Well, I didn't ask you. Michelle is snooty, and so is Daddy."

"If raising her to be snooty is what kept her legs closed, then I say 'hats off' to Mr. Nicholas Price. There ought to be more fathers like him. We got way too many baby daddies out there and too few fathers; there is a difference, you know."

"Yeah, I know all too well. He's my daddy and Michelle's father."

From the envelope, Amaryllis pulled out a flyer and read it silently.

Praise Temple Church Of God's
Women of Warfare
Present a one-night crusade
"God's Wailing Lady"
Prophetess Dr. Michellene Anderson of
Chicago, Illinois Guest Speaker
6:00 p.m. Saturday, September 15th, 2011
Praise Temple Church Of God 1751 Grace
Parkway Las Vegas, Nevada Ulysses R.
Graham, Senior Pastor First Lady Cookie B.
Graham, Sponsor & Coordinator

Bridgette saw a weird expression on Amaryllis's face as she read the flyer.

"Everything okay with your sister?"

"Yeah, it's just an invitation to Michelle's church's crusade in three weeks."

"So, why are you frowning?"

"Because, I have absolutely no clue what a crusade is."

In Las Vegas, Nevada, James Bradley, Amaryllis's brother-in-law, was walking out the front door on his way to work when the telephone rang. "Bradley residence."

"Hello, Mr. Bradley. What are you up to?"

"Hey, Mickey. I'm up to missing you."

Things hadn't changed. James still couldn't tell the difference between Michelle and Amaryllis when they were on the telephone.

"I'm up to calling from Chi-town," Amaryllis said.

James looked puzzled as he glanced at the caller identification box. Then he saw his sister-in-law's name. "Amaryllis?"

"The one and only. What's up, brother-in-law?"

"Thank the Lord for technology, because you almost had me. You and Mickey are so much alike that even your voices are identical."

"Everyone says that. So, how does it feel to be an old married man?"

"Well, I can't tell you how it feels to be old because I wouldn't know. But I can say that being married feels great. Michelle is a wonderful wife."

"Spoken like a man in love."

"True that."

"Can I speak to my sister?"

"You can if you call the firm."

Amaryllis glanced at her wristwatch. "James, it's eight a.m. my time and six a.m. your time. Michelle is at work already?"

He chuckled. "You know your sister, Amaryllis. Mickey's a workaholic, plus we're going on vacation soon so she's cramming right now."

"Well, good for her, because I ain't the one. How's work going for you?"

He let out a loud sigh. "Same old, same old. My partner, Alex, just called and said that a body was found in a trunk. I was on my way to the crime scene when you called."

Amaryllis remembered the time when she lived with Michelle how much James talked about despising his job as a homicide detective. "Well, don't let me keep you from death," she joked.

"That's not funny."

"Where's your sense of humor?"

"In this business we're not allowed to have one."

"Michelle mentioned that your mother was in town. How is she?"

"Mom is good. Thanks for asking."

"I'll let you get to work, James. It was nice talking with you."

James didn't seem the least bit bothered by Amaryllis's phone call. He'd spoken to her as though she had never set him up to make it seem like he was cheating on Michelle.

At Price & Associates Law Office, Michelle stood at Chantal's desk discussing an upcoming trial when the telephone rang. "Price and Associates, Chantal speaking."

"Good morning, Chantal. It's Amaryllis."

"Hi, Amaryllis, how are you?"

Michelle's face lit up at the sound of her sister's name.

"I'm fine, but the question is, 'How's that beautiful baby boy of yours?'"

"He's adorable and getting bigger by the minute, Amaryllis, thanks for asking."

"I saw the lovely pictures that Michelle sent me. She and James look so happy to be holding their godson. Is Michelle around?"

"Yes, hang on a second."

Michelle was already sitting at her desk waiting for Chantal to finish her conversation. As soon as she pressed the hold button, Michelle picked up the telephone. "Hey, sis."

"Hey, sis. Why are you and Chantal at the firm at six a.m.?"

"Because James and I are going on a lengthy vacation soon, and I need to get a few cases in order."

"What about your mother-in-law?"

"Mother Bradley is coming with us."

Amaryllis didn't understand that. "Say what? You're taking your mother-in-law on vacation with you and your husband?"

Michelle chuckled. "Yes."

Having a mother-in-law tag along on vacation with a couple was ridiculous. Amaryllis didn't see the logic in it. "Why?"

"Why not?"

"Uh, maybe because you and James are newlyweds and need to be alone."

Michelle exhaled into the telephone. "James and I are always alone, Amaryllis. It's no big deal."

Amaryllis decided to change the conversation. She accepted the fact that she'll never understand Michelle and some of the things she did. "I talked to your husband this morning, and he's missing you."

Michelle smiled. "James misses me whenever I'm not right beside him, but I love it because the feeling is mutual."

"Maybe I'll know what that feels like someday," Amaryllis said. She was hopeful that her relationship with Charles would grow into what her sister shared with her husband.

"I thought you had a sweetheart. What's up with that guy named Tyrone you told me about?"

Amaryllis exhaled loudly. "Girl, that nymphomaniac got on my last nerve. He's an alcoholic, and I thought that I could deal with that as long as Tyrone wasn't pressuring me for sex. But after he showed up at my home drunk one time too many, I snatched the hairs off his chest and gave that fool his walking papers."

Michelle was sure she had heard wrong. "Snatched the hairs off his chest? Are you serious, girl? I mean, no offense, but when it comes to you, I just have to ask."

"Michelle, he left me no choice. But I have a real sweetie now. His name is Charles Walker. I used to date him back in the day. He says all the right things, and he does all the right things. And I'm still saved, Michelle. Charles is behaving himself."

Michelle loved the new Amaryllis. "Girl, it's so good to hear you talking like that. I'm impressed and so very proud. I wish Daddy could hear you."

"I gotta be honest though. At times it wasn't easy turning Ty away because the brotha was foine with a capital 'F'."

"I don't care how foine with a capital 'F' he was. If he drank like a fish, then he wasn't the one for you."

"I hear you, girl. So far, Charles hasn't pressured me. I just can't understand why every man that approaches me thinks that I'm dropping my thong."

Michelle laughed. "Amaryllis, you certainly have a way with words. Why couldn't you say 'panties'?"

"I don't wear panties."

"Never?" Michelle shrieked.

"Nope, I'm a thong diva. And I suggest you come out of those big bloomers you got on and step into the twenty-first century."

Michelle's mouth dropped wide opened. "Excuse you? I do not wear bloomers. As a matter of fact, I don't wear any undergarments at all."

Amaryllis could easily believe something like that coming out of Bridgette's mouth, but not Michelle's. "Girl, who are trying to fool? I know James ain't turned you out like that."

"You don't know me like you think you do. I'm a married woman now."

"True that, but you're still Nicholas Price's daughter."

"And that means what, Amaryllis?"

"That I'll bet you fifty bucks that you got bloomers on, and I'll raise you fifty that they don't even match your bra."

"Amaryllis, are you crazy? If you're in Chicago, how are you gonna know what I'm wearing, and why are we discussing my underwear anyway? I know this isn't why you called."

"I'll get to the reason why I called in a minute, but first things first. If I can prove that you've got bloomers on and your bra is a different color, you pay me one hundred dollars and take me on a shopping spree the next time I come to Vegas. Is that a deal?"

Michelle chuckled. "Girl, you're crazy."

"Be that as it may, do we have a deal?"

Michelle knew that there was no way possible Amaryllis could find out what she was wearing under her clothes all the way from Chicago.

"Okay, Miss Confident, you've got yourself a deal. But what if you're wrong? What will you do for me?"

"What do you want?"

"I want you to come to my church's women's conference in three weeks. By the way, did you get the flyer I sent you?"

"Yeah, that's the real reason I called. What's a crusade?"

"It's like a seminar where a bunch of women gather together at a church or assembly hall, and a minister comes in and talks to us."

"About what?"

"Anything he or she wants. They mainly teach us how to remain women of God."

"How are you going to be there if you're on vacation?"

"The first two weeks of my vacation will be spent at home and the last two weeks, James and I will be in Aruba."

"Ahh, sooky, sooky, now. Are you gonna come back with a baby?"

"If the Lord permits."

"I would love to come to the conference, Michelle, but my money is funny. Administrative assistants in Chicago don't make twenty-five dollars an hour like they do in Vegas."

"Amaryllis, I'll pay for you to come because you really need to hear Prophetess Anderson. She's the bomb, and she's from your hometown, Chicago."

Amaryllis couldn't believe her ears. "Seriously, Michelle? You'll pay my way?"

"Yes, I will. And if your roommate, Bridgette, wants to come, I'll send for her too."

"Are you serious?"

Michelle had never met Bridgette face to face. But she remembered the telephone call that Bridgette had made to her law office. Amaryllis was working for Michelle but had stepped out for lunch when Bridgette called from Chicago. What Bridgette didn't know was that she was talking to Michelle, not Amaryllis.

Five minutes after Amaryllis left, the telephone rang. Michelle looked at the caller identification and saw that it was a Chicago call. "Price & Associates," Michelle answered.

The first thing Bridgette said was, "So, you still got a job, huh? Your sister ain't kicked you to the curb yet?"

Michelle stated to Bridgette that she had dialed the wrong number.

Bridgette had never spoken to Michelle before. She didn't know that the two sisters had the same voice. She really thought that she was speaking with Amaryllis. "Don't try and act like you don't know who I am, Amaryllis. It's me, Bridgette, your homegirl."

When Bridgette said her own name, Michelle remembered Amaryllis mentioning someone named Bridgette, a coworker, from Chicago. "Oh, Bridgette, this isn't Amaryllis," Michelle said.

Bridgette didn't believe Michelle. "You think I don't know your voice, Amaryllis? Who are you trying to fool?"

Again, Michelle tried to convince Bridgette that she wasn't Amaryllis. Refusing to believe that she was on the telephone with the wrong sister, Bridgette betrayed Amaryllis and told Michelle everything that Amaryllis had confided in her. "Oh, okay, you're Michelle today, huh? What happened, Amaryllis? You wanted to live your sister's life so badly that you hit her over the head, buried her body, and took over her business? All I wanna know is if your sister figured out what you've done yet."

Michelle became curious about what Bridgette was talking about. "What's to figure out?" she asked Bridgette.

Bridgette went in for the kill. She told Michelle that Amaryllis had purposely put her name on Michelle's wedding invitations. Bridgette told

Michelle that Amaryllis had set James up by drugging him and taking nude photos of the two of them and had one photo made into a puzzle. Michelle remembered receiving a piece of the puzzle every week leading up to her wedding. Amaryllis had saved the last piece of the puzzle revealing James's face for last. Michelle received that piece just three days before she was to walk down the aisle to James.

Bridgette hammered the last nail in Amaryllis's coffin. "I bet Michelle doesn't even know that you're the one who sent the puzzle, does she?"

If Bridgette hadn't called the law firm that day, Michelle may never have known what Amaryllis had done. In a way, Michelle felt that she owed Bridgette for exposing her sister and saving her own relationship with James.

"Absolutely. I'll pay Bridgette's way too," Michelle offered.

"Hold on a minute." Amaryllis yelled across the office to Bridgette. "Hey, Bridge, you wanna go to Vegas in three weeks?"

Bridgette was at her desk filing her nails. "Nah, I'll pass."

"It's my sister's treat."

Bridgette looked at Amaryllis and smiled. "Heck, yeah, I'll go."

Amaryllis spoke to Michelle. "Bridgette accepts your invitation, and we both thank you."

"Okay, I'll make the arrangements," Michelle said.

"Be prepared to take me shopping and pay me my money when I get there."

"What are you talking about? You haven't won the bet."

"I'll call you back in ten minutes."

Amaryllis hung up with Michelle and dialed another Las Vegas number.

"Eleventh Precinct, Officer Burns speaking."

"Yes, my name is Michelle Bradley, and I'm trying to reach my husband, Detective James Bradley. I know he's en route; however, I need to speak with him most urgently."

"Hi, Michelle. It's me, Markus."

Amaryllis had no clue who the heck Markus was. "Hi, there."

"My wife and I thank you and James for the lovely gift you gave us. She wanted me to ask where you got it, because she wants to get one for her mother's kitchen."

Mister, why can't you just connect me to James? I don't know what the heck you're talking about or who you are for that matter. "I got it out of a magazine that my sister gave me, and I don't think I saved it, but I'll look for it. If I find it, I'll make sure James gets it to you."

"Thanks, Michelle, I appreciate it. Do you know what other colors it came in?"

Didn't I say that this call was most urgent? "You know, I can't quite remember, Markus. I really need to speak to James, though."

"Sure, Michelle, just a moment."

Amaryllis was connected to James's work-issued cellular phone.

"Detective Bradley speaking."

"Hi, James, it's Amaryllis. I know you're busy, but I got a question for you. Did you witness Michelle getting dressed this morning?"

"Yeah."

"I made a bet with her, so I gotta ask you two questions. Did her bra and panties match?"

James frowned because he wasn't sure if he'd heard Amaryllis correctly. "What?"

"Just answer the question, James."

"Uh, I don't know if I should. What's going on, Amaryllis?"

"I told you that I made a bet with her, but I need your help. Did her bra and panties match?"

"Amaryllis, Mickey doesn't wear any underwear."

If Amaryllis were standing up, she would've hit the floor. "What? Michelle took a walk on the wild side?"

James laughed at her. "Nah, I'm just kidding with you. She's wearing a black bra and pink panties."

"Okay. One more question. Are her panties covering her entire stomach?"

James was too outdone. "What?"

"James, please answer the question."

"Yeah, I guess you can say that."

"Thanks, brother-in-law, I owe you one."

Amaryllis disconnected from him and quickly dialed Michelle's cellular phone.

"Hey, sis," Michelle greeted her.

"You got on a black bra, and your pink bloomers are pulled all the way up to your melons."

Michelle couldn't do anything but laugh, because Amaryllis was absolutely right.

"Girl, how do you know? You got some type of radioactive 3D glasses that you can see me from Chicago with?"

"Nope, but I got a brother-in-law."

"He actually told you what kind of underwear I'm wearing? I thought he was asleep when I left this morning."

"Just be glad that you got a husband that pays that much attention to you. So, Bridgette and I will see you in three weeks, and as soon as we leave the airport we're going straight to the mall. Bring the Navigator because the Jaguar's trunk ain't big enough for all of the stuff I'll be getting."

Chapter 14

Michelle saw Amaryllis coming through the airport terminal before her sister saw her. "Amaryllis."

Amaryllis heard the voice that sounded so much like her own and looked to her left and saw her sister. She dropped her bags, then ran to Michelle and embraced her. "Hey, sis."

"Hey, Boo. How are you? I missed you."

"I missed you too, girl. I'm so glad to be here."

Michelle saw a woman walk up and stand next to Amaryllis. "You must be Bridgette."

Bridgette smiled at a dark-skinned Amaryllis and extended her hand. "Yes. It's nice to meet you, Michelle. You two are identical."

Michelle ignored her hand and pulled Bridgette into her arms. "It's a pleasure to meet you too, Bridgette, and welcome to Las Vegas."

"Thank you. Amaryllis has told me so much about you, and I don't care what she says, I don't think you're snooty at all."

Amaryllis looked at Bridgette, and her mouth dropped wide open. "You ghetto heifer, no, you didn't."

Michelle leaned into Bridgette and lowered her voice. "That's okay, girl, we got the same daddy, and he is snooty, if I do say so myself."

"See? What did I tell you, Bridge? Like father, like daughter," Amaryllis commented.

Bridgette opened her purse and pulled out a Chunky for Michelle. "Amaryllis told me that you're a chocoholic, so I brought you a little something."

Michelle squealed in delight. "Thank you, Bridgette. Girl, I like you already." She looped her arm through Bridgette's and started walking toward the baggage claim.

"Come on, let's get your bags and get out of here. I got a husband waiting on me at home. I've been gone all day."

The two of them walked away, arm in arm, laughing and chatting. They totally forgot about Amaryllis.

Amaryllis called out to them. "Uh . . . hello?"

Michelle turned around. "Oh, I'm sorry, sweetie. I got all caught up in the chocolate."

"This is gonna be a great trip, I can see that already, and we ain't even left the airport," Amaryllis said.

The aroma hit the ladies' noses as soon as they walked in the front door. James heard them come in and walked into the living room from the kitchen wearing an apron that read, I COOK FOR MICKEY. He went straight to Michelle and kissed her lips.

"Hey, gorgeous, I missed you," he greeted his wife.

Michelle indulged in James's soft lips. "I'm not the gorgeous one, baby, you are."

"Not me, you are."

"No, you are."

Amaryllis was used to the greeting her sister and brother-in-law shared, but Bridgette stood looking at them like they were aliens. James and Michelle stared at each other for a long five seconds; then Amaryllis decided to make her and Bridgette's presence known by clearing her throat. "Ahem."

James looked at her and smiled. "Oh, I'm sorry, sis. How are you doing?"

"I'm fine, James. How are you?"

He stepped to Amaryllis and hugged her. "I'm well, thank you."

"This is my friend, Bridgette, from Chicago," Amaryllis introduced.

James extended his hand. "Hi, Bridgette, from Chicago. Welcome to our home."

Michelle picked up their luggage and turned toward the stairs. "Let's get you girls settled upstairs."

James quickly interceded and took the luggage from his wife. "Oh, no, baby. You ain't got no business carrying that. I'll take their things upstairs. Since you've been gone all day, I baked pork chops and made brown rice and crescent rolls because I knew you'd be tired and hungry when you all got in from the airport."

Michelle looked at her man who was too good to be true. "Sweetie, I love you for taking such good care of me."

"It's my pleasure, baby. Dinner is on the table, and I've already prayed over it and thanked God, so you ladies enjoy your meal."

James took the luggage upstairs, and Bridgette stood in the living room to watch him disappear, then looked at Michelle. "Girl, Amaryllis told me that you had a good man, but da . . . uh, I mean, wow." She almost cursed.

Michelle had to laugh at her. "I can truly say that God has smiled on me."

They went into the kitchen and saw their plates already prepared, complete with glasses of grape Kool-Aid. Michelle always kept a pitcher of grape-flavored Kool-Aid in her refrigerator because it was her husband's favorite drink.

Bridgette looked at the feast James had prepared, then looked at Michelle. "Da . . . uh, wow."

Amaryllis and Michelle both laughed at her and sat down to eat. James came into the kitchen with Michelle's slippers and knelt next to her. He removed her pumps, but before he slid her slippers on her feet, he massaged her toes first. Bridgette and Amaryllis looked at him in awe. Afterward, he stood up and talked smoothly to Michelle. "Any back pain today, baby?"

"It's not hurting as bad as it was yesterday. I feel a little bit better," Michelle replied.

"I'm running your bath water with Epson salt. When you're done eating, come on up, and I'll give you a back-rub."

James's special attention toward Michelle was not new to her, but he was blowing Amaryllis and Bridgette's minds. He kissed Michelle's forehead lightly and turned to walk away when she called out to him. "Honey, I forgot to make sure that Bridgette and Amaryllis's bathroom was stocked with soap, toothpaste, and stuff."

"I already took care of that. I made sure that they have everything they need. It's all good. And when you ladies are done eating, leave the dishes. I'll do them after I give Mickey her bath."

When he left the kitchen, Amaryllis spoke to Michelle. "He bathes you, Michelle?"

"Each and every day," she replied. She saw how Bridgette and Amaryllis's mouths were hanging open. "What?" she asked them.

Bridgette was the first to speak. "Girl, your husband washes dishes and bathes you?"

Michelle looked at her. "You don't think he should?"

Bridgette shrugged her shoulders. "It ain't that. I just don't hear that often. Good for you, Michelle."

"I thought your mother-in-law was here visiting," Amaryllis said.

Michelle inserted a forkful of food into her mouth. "Mother Bradley flew back home yesterday. She got a call that her eldest brother was ill. I was looking forward to you meeting her."

After dinner, while Amaryllis and Bridgette were made to feel at home and were in their room for the night, James bathed his wife. Then he wrapped a towel around her and led her into their bedroom where she heard soft jazz music coming from the stereo system next to the king-sized bed.

Michelle saw that her pillow was dented with a box of chocolate-covered raisins, one of her favorites. She looked at her husband. "Every morning when I wake up and look at you still sleeping, I thank God for my man. I honestly

don't think there is another man like you anywhere on this earth."

James untied her body towel and let it fall to
the floor. "Mickey, I'm the one that's blessed."

He picked her up and laid her on the bed, then
opened the box of chocolate covered raisins.
One by one, he placed the candy across her belly
in the shape of a heart. He then bent over her
and ate the candy, piece by piece. For the next
half hour, James enjoyed his wife, and Michelle
enjoyed her husband. The next morning they
were welded together by melted chocolate.

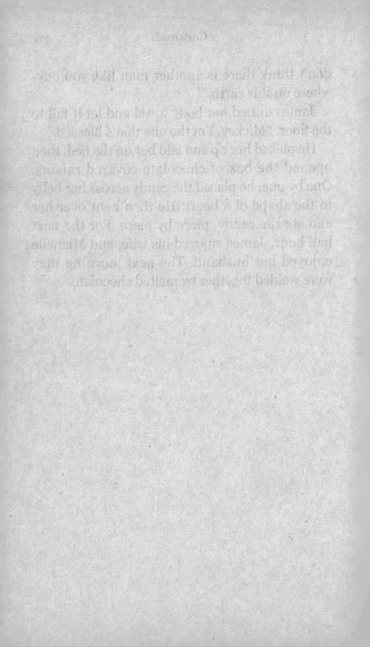

Chapter 15

James opted for a bowl of cereal, and Michelle decided to treat her guests to breakfast at the chicken and waffle house before they went to the shopping mall. Michelle came into the kitchen and saw James savoring his favorite breakfast food while glancing at the sports section of the newspaper. "How's your cereal, honey?"

"I'm coocoo for Cocoa Puffs."

Michelle laughed at her husband and kissed his cheek. "What's on your agenda for today?"

"Well, until someone gets either shot, stabbed, or murdered, I'll sit on the sofa and see what's on ESPN."

"Yuck, who needs sports? Why don't you hang out with me and the girls today?"

"Doing what?"

"What women do best."

James knew what that meant. "Uh-uh, no way. Me, with three women in a shopping mall? I don't think so, Mickey."

Michelle stood behind his chair and wrapped her arms around his neck and purred like a kitten. "Aw, come on, sweetie, pleeeease."

James continued eating his cereal as if he hadn't heard her plea. "Mickey, you know I love you, right? But I refuse to let myself be set up into going shopping with you, your sister, and her friend. It takes you, alone, two hours to go through one store. So, I've learned that when you're in the mood for spending money, to turn you loose so you can do your thang."

"Well, I'm not exactly in the mood. I gotta pay off a bet that I lost, and I just know that it's going to cost me at least three grand. A bet that you helped me lose, might I add."

James stood from the table, grabbed Michelle's waist, and pulled her close to him. "I promise to make it up to you tonight."

Michelle kissed his lips. "I'm gonna hold you to that."

She left James to his cereal and went upstairs to the third floor to wake Amaryllis and Bridgette. She knocked lightly, then opened the door. "Good morning, ladies. It's time to get up."

Bridgette was lying on her stomach and lazily turned over, but Amaryllis didn't stir at all. Michelle walked over to the window and opened the vertical blinds to allow the sunshine to fill the bedroom. "Come on, sleepyheads, it's almost nine o'clock."

At the same time, Amaryllis and Bridgette pulled the sheets over their heads. Michelle knew what it would take to get them moving. She closed the blinds then walked toward the door. "Oh, well, if no one wants to help me spend three grand, that's fine with me."

Immediately covers flew off two bodies as the women hopped out of bed. They collided into one another trying to be the first in the bathroom.

"We'll be ready in fifteen minutes," Bridgette called over her shoulder.

"Please don't leave us, Michelle," Amaryllis pleaded as she pushed Bridgette out of the way and rushed into the bathroom.

The ladies ate breakfast at the chicken and waffle house. The next stop was at Pamper Me Good Salon for a morning of beauty duty. Michelle told Bridgette and Amaryllis that she was treating them to a full-body massage, a facial, a manicure, and pedicure. "I wanna get you ladies relaxed for tonight because Prophetess Anderson is gonna blow your minds."

Amaryllis kissed her sister's cheek. "Sis, I really appreciate this."

Bridgette kissed her other cheek. "Me too, Michelle, I really do."

They sat in the lobby to wait for their names to be called. Bridgette picked up a magazine and saw a picture of a woman whose face and makeup was done to perfection. She held it up to show Amaryllis. "I wonder if they can make me look like this."

Amaryllis looked at the picture. "Uh, Bridge, something like that costs about ten thousand dollars."

"For makeup?"

"For a face-lift, because that's what it's going to take to get you looking like that."

Michelle was sitting next to Bridgette and couldn't believe what her sister had just said to her best friend. "Amaryllis, that wasn't nice."

"What? Bridgette knows good and well that it's gonna take a plastic surgeon, a magic wand, a genie in a bottle, and an exorcist to get that demon called 'Ugly' out of her face to make her look like that picture."

Again, Michelle was stunned. "Amaryllis!"

Bridgette looked at her friend. "I know you ain't talking, Amaryllis. Not the way your breath smells like you've been licking booty pops."

The other women waiting in the lobby heard Bridgette and laughed. Michelle was a regular at the salon, and she didn't come to be embarrassed. "You two are causing a scene. Will you please be quiet?"

Bridgette got up and went to the receptionist's desk and spoke loud enough for everyone in the lobby to hear. "Excuse me, do you do colon cleansing? My friend in the blue jean dress has foul breath all the time, and I think that if she gets her insides cleaned out, it might help her. She's tried everything else."

The waiting room was filled with laughter. Michelle, on the other hand, was not entertained. Even though she was dark skinned, her face was red with humiliation.

Amaryllis approached the receptionist's desk and stood next to Bridgette. "Excuse me. Do you have an M80 I can stick in her nose? Because, the only way to get rid of that type of ugly is to blow up her face."

In a matter of fifteen minutes, the lobby was turned into a circus. One woman was laughing so hard, she had tears in her eyes. Michelle got up and walked to the receptionist's desk and drew a line through all three of their names on the registry list and then walked out of the salon. Amaryllis and Bridgette followed her, but before they got to the door, they heard another lady say, "Can you do one more?"

When they got to Michelle's Navigator, they knew she was steaming. Amaryllis and Bridgette fussed and fought like that all of the time, but no matter how much they argued, they always had each other's back. They got in the truck and said at the same time, "We're sorry, Michelle."

Michelle had to count to ten and calm herself down before she spoke to them. "I can't believe how you embarrassed me in there. For years I've been coming to this place, and now, thanks to you two, I can't show my face there ever again. I spent close to two thousand dollars to bring you here for the weekend and was willing to spend more money to get you ready for tonight. I don't have money to waste. If I wanted to see people signifying on each other, I could've stayed at home and watched Comicview on BET." She started the engine and drove away. Amaryllis and Bridgette sat in silence as they rode to the shopping mall.

At Nieman Marcus, Michelle, Bridgette, and Amaryllis were next in line for the dressing room when a woman who looked to weigh close to two hundred fifty pounds emerged from the fitting room and stood in front of a three-way mirror to model a red stretch dress. Michelle was the first to see her and silently prayed that her sister and her ghetto friend would not see her.

They were talking among themselves when the woman asked Michelle a question.

"Excuse me, how does this dress look on me. Be honest."

Bridgette and Amaryllis stopped talking and looked at the woman. Michelle tried her best to say the right thing. She didn't want to just come right out and tell the woman the gospel truth. Before she spoke, she prayed for the right words. "Well, maybe if you tried another color . . ."

Bridgette stepped next to Michelle. "Michelle, she said 'be honest.'" Bridgette looked at the woman. "Sweet baby, if the spandex company knew what you were doing to their material, they'd sue your big behind."

Amaryllis took her cellular phone out of her purse and pretended to dial a number. "Hello, is this the Spandex Company? I got somebody over here that thinks she's a size three and ain't. Okay, see you in five minutes." Amaryllis looked at the woman. "They're sending somebody over to put you in a straitjacket because you're crazy as heck for even thinking that you could wear something like that."

Michelle placed the dresses she had in her hand on the nearest rack, hung her head in shame, and exited the store. She got in her truck and leaned her head back on the headrest. "Lord Jesus, help me make it through this day."

Ten minutes later, Bridgette and Amaryllis got in the truck. Michelle looked at them both in shame. "You two need to get saved and act like you're saved. Why is it that every time we go somewhere, y'all got to do tha fool and embarrass me? Huh? Can either one of you answer that question?"

Amaryllis looked at her sister. "Michelle, why would you even think of lying to that poor woman. You would actually let her buy that dress and think she's the bomb?"

"I told her to try another color."

Bridgette spoke from the backseat. "Michelle, it didn't matter what color she tried on. She would still look like a sloppy fool, and you know it."

Michelle glanced at Bridgette in the rearview mirror. "Bridgette, since you've been here, I have told you time and time again to watch your mouth. Now, I see why you two are the best of friends—ghetto fabulous and ghetto marvelous."

Amaryllis put her seat belt on. "Yeah, whatever. Come on and take us to the shoe store."

"No, I'm not going anywhere else with you two."

"Come on, sis, we'll be good. We promise." Amaryllis turned around and looked at Bridgette. "Won't we be good, Bridge?"

"Yeah, we'll be good, Michelle. We promise," Bridgette confirmed.

Michelle turned all the way around and looked at them both. "Okay, but if you embarrass me, I promise you both that you're going to a hotel tonight and so help me God, I ain't playin'."

The Jimmy Choo shoe store inside Caesar's Palace was a bit crowded, but Amaryllis managed to get a salesman's attention. He told her that he'd be with her as soon as he was finished with another customer. The three of them were sitting and waiting when Michelle saw a lady across from them trying to stuff what appeared to be a size ten foot in a size eight shoe. Immediately, she lowered her head and told God that if He truly loved her, He wouldn't let Amaryllis and Bridgette see that. Quickly, Michelle started a conversation with them to try and keep them distracted.

"So, how has the weather been in Chi-town?" Michelle asked.

Before either one of them could answer the question, the three of them heard the woman get angry with the shoe salesman. "I don't know what kind of shoes you're selling, because I know that I wear a size eight."

The salesman sat down on a stool in front of her and tried with all of his might to stuff her big foot in the toosmall shoe. "Ma'am, this isn't gonna work. Let me get you a larger size."

"I don't need a larger size. I wear an eight. I wanna speak to the manager."

Michelle looked at Bridgette and Amaryllis and reminded them that if they said one word, they were going to a hotel. Both of them balled up their lips and sat still and watched the woman act a fool.

The manager came and sat in front of her and tried to force the shoes on her feet. "Ma'am, I'm sorry but a size eight is too small for your feet. Let's try a slightly larger size." "No, I ain't trying a bigger size. That's what I get for coming in this cheap store. Y'all ain't got nothing to suit my taste anyway."

Amaryllis was quiet for as long as she could be. "Look, lady, the man was trying to be nice. Why are you trying to force those cruise ships into yachts? Face the fact that you got big feet."

Michelle was too outdone. She placed her face in her hands. "Oh my God."

The woman stood up. "I'm not even talking to you. This is between me and the salesman."

Amaryllis stood and took a step toward the woman. "And it's also between me when I got to sit here and wait until a lightbulb goes on in your head. If you wear a size fifteen, then buy a size fifteen. And get a pedicure every once in a while. You wear your shoes so tight, your toes look like pork crackling."

The woman was ready to fight. "Oh, no, you didn't."

The manager saw that they were attracting too much attention, and he came and stood in between them. "Ladies, please."

Fuming, Michelle got up and exited the shoe store. On her cellular phone she dialed information. "Connect me to a hotel, please, any hotel."

Michelle walked in the front door and went straight into the den where James was lying on the sofa watching a basketball game. She threw her purse on the sofa next to him, then walked and stood in front of the television with her back to him. She placed her hands on the television and bent over. "Kick me, James."

He sat up and looked at her. "What?"

"I need my butt kicked for bringing them here. What was I thinking?"

"Why are you so angry?"

"If they did to you what they did to me today, you'd be angry too. Now come on and kick me, because I deserve it."

James went to Michelle, turned her around, and pulled her into his arms. "It can't be that bad."

Amaryllis and Bridgette walked in the front door and saw James holding Michelle.

Michelle looked in their direction and watched them both go upstairs without saying a word.

"Look at them, James. Lucy and Ethel . They ain't sayin' a word. That's how you know they're guilty."

James sat Michelle down on the sofa, took her shoes off, and gently massaged her feet. "What did they do?"

By the time Michelle finished telling him how her sister and her friend clowned earlier that day, he was on the floor holding his stomach, laughing with tears in his eyes. "That's too funny, Mickey. Now, I wished that I had gone with you."

"James, don't laugh because you'll only encourage them."

"Mickey, they were just having fun."

"Yeah, at my expense. I'm the one who was embarrassed."

"Don't take it personally. Look at it this way, the conference is tonight, and they're leaving in the morning."

Michelle raised her hands toward heaven. "Hallelujah. Thank you, Jesus."

Chapter 16

Later that evening, First Lady Cookie Graham was conducting praise and worship service and flowing prophetically.

Amaryllis and Bridgette heard the women of God speaking in an unknown tongue. They both looked at Michelle, who had her eyes closed, also speaking in tongues.

Amaryllis whispered to her friend, "This is some crazy stuff."

"You ain't lying, but if we can't understand them, we might as well join them."

They closed their eyes, and between the two of them, Michelle heard, "Phe, phi, pho, phum, mama say mama saw ma ma coo saw, zippity do da, chitty chitty bang bang."

Her eyes flew open in horror, and she tapped Amaryllis's shoulder. "What are y'all saying?"

Amaryllis shrugged her shoulders. "We don't know. What are you saying?"

Michelle was so embarrassed she didn't know what to do. "Are you sure that y'all were baptized? I mean, did y'all get in the water? Something ain't right, because you two are not saved, I don't care what you say. And if you really were baptized, then you need to get rebaptized."

Bridgette looked at her. "Why?"

"Because somehow or someway, the two of you missed God. You have been acting a fool all day. I can understand that you're babes in Christ, but my God, you two are ridiculous. You don't just open your mouths and say anything. This is a church. These women are worshiping God in a secret code."

Amaryllis didn't understand. "Why a secret code?"

"So, the enemy can't understand. It's a personal conversation and a gift of the Holy Ghost." They both looked confused, and Michelle didn't have the time to explain it to them. "Look, just shut up and don't say anything."

Just then, Cookie introduced to some and presented to others Prophetess Dr. Michellene Anderson. Everyone began applauding this great woman of God. She stood and walked to the podium with as much grace as God would allow her to carry. Prophetess Anderson was well-known for her quick and very raw anointing power.

"Every woman jump to your feet right now, right now," she instructed.

All of the women stood.

"Look at your neighbor and say, 'Neighbor.'"

The women said in unison, "Neighbor."

"Every female that reaches the age of eighteen is legally considered a woman."

They repeated. "Every female that reaches the age of eighteen is legally considered a woman."

"Now ask your neighbor, 'But are you a lady?'"

The women chanted, "But are you a lady?"

At that moment, the women knew that Prophetess Anderson was on fire for the Lord, and through the Holy Spirit, she was on the verge of disrupting the entire congregation. They encouraged her to do what she did best, which was to get in everybody's business.

"Tell it like it is, Prophetess . . . Don't sugarcoat nothing . . . Come on and give us the word."

From the back of the church someone yelled, "Go ahead and preach!"

The prophetess was as sharp as she wanted to be, dressed in a two-piece silk, sky-blue Marc Jacobs suit. Her jacket fit her every curve and displayed three authentic Swarovski crystal buttons down the center. The long sleeves were cuffed at the wrist, also adorned with crystals at the wrists. The jacket collar had an asymmetrical affect. Her ears sparkled with two and half carat platinum studs at her every move. She was sharp from head to toe, standing in silver glittered shimmers and sky-blue sling-back silk pumps. Sweat beads popped out on her forehead, and she wiped her face with a matching eight-by-ten-inch royal-blue terry cloth hand towel trimmed in silver lace. Her armor bearer brought her Bible and notebook and placed them on the podium in front of her.

Prophetess Anderson looked at what appeared to be about two hundred women standing in her presence. "What a mighty God we serve."

The sanctuary was filled with amens.

"I can't get any help in here. I said 'What a mighty God we serve.'"

"Amen, Prophetess . . . Sho' you right . . . Yes, Lord, we serve a mighty God."

She wiped her face again. "First and foremost, I am privileged to be a child of the King, for without Him, there is no me. I give great honor to the Lord Jesus Christ."

The women were fired up and ready. "Hallelujah, glory to God."

She turned her attention to Cookie. "And to my friend and my praying partner whom I love dearly. The first lady of this fine edifice, Mrs. Cookie Graham."

The women applauded their first lady and blew her kisses.

"Praise God. I'm honored to stand before you today. I've been on a fast all week, receiving what God wants me to minister to you today. Truly the Lord is in this place." She opened her Bible and notebook. "Those of you who have your Bibles, please turn with me to Saint Mark, chapter five, commencing at verse twenty-five and concluding at verse thirty-four." She looked around the church. "If you're standing next to someone without a Bible say, 'Shame on you, but I'll share with you.'"

The women exchanged the comment.

"Ladies, please know that if there was ever a time when we need the Word of God, the time is now. Never, under any circumstances, are you to enter a sanctuary without your Word, amen?"

They answered, "Amen."

"I don't care who's before you preaching or teaching. Don't just take for granted that they're speaking the truth. Read God's Word for yourself and know that you know that you know that the minister is rightly dividing the Word of truth. Second Timothy, chapter three, verses sixteen and seventeen say that 'All scripture is given by inspiration of God, and is profitable for doctrine, for reproof, for correction, for instruction in righteousness, that the man of God may be complete, thoroughly equipped for every good work.' Second Timothy, chapter two, verse fifteen says, 'Be diligent to present yourself approved to God, a worker who does not need to be ashamed, rightly dividing the word of truth.' In other words, you are to study God's Word for yourself."

Prophetess Anderson wiped her face again. "I can remember a few years back when a pastor of a church preached to his congregation that Jesus was coming back on a certain date. He advised his flock to quit their jobs and sell their goods and give all of the money to the church. I sat and watched on the evening news one night and saw the people inside the church repenting for their sins and sending up praises to God.

"Well, lo and behold, Jesus didn't come back that night nor the next night nor the next. The pastor couldn't explain why the saints of God were still here on earth. He said that Jesus had spoken to him and told him that He'd be back on that particular day. In Revelation, chapter three, somewhere around the second or third verse, Jesus says, 'Be watchful and strengthen the things which remain that are ready to die, for I have not found your works perfect before God. Remember therefore how you have received and heard; hold fast and repent. Therefore if you will not watch, I will come upon you as a thief, and you will not know what hour I will come upon you.' And Matthew, chapter twenty-four, verse forty-four says, 'Therefore you also be ready, for the Son of Man is coming at an hour you do not expect.'

"Now the souls of that church were damaged, and they questioned the very existence of God. The Lord had to come in and mend broken and damaged hearts. But had the people read the Word for themselves, they would have known better.

"Ladies, I beg you, do not be deceived by false teachings. Establish a personal relationship with God and know His Word for yourself, and if any of you are being taught anything other than what the Word of God says, I encourage you to seek spiritual leadership where the Word of God is being rightly divided. Can I get an amen?"

"Amen . . . amen . . . amen," the women responded.

"Saint Mark, chapter five, verse twenty-five reads, 'Now a certain woman had a flow of blood for twelve years, and had suffered many things from many physicians. She had spent all that she had and was no better, but rather grew worse. When she heard about Jesus, she came behind Him in the crowd and touched His garment.

For she said, "If only I may touch His clothes, I shall be made well." Immediately the fountain of her blood was dried up, and she felt in her body that she was healed of the affliction. And Jesus, immediately knowing in Himself that power had gone out of Him, turned around in the crowd and said, "Who touched my clothes?'"

"Skipping down to the thirty-second verse, it reads, 'And He looked around to see her who had done this thing. But the woman, fearing and trembling, knowing what had happened to her, came and fell down before Him and told Him the whole truth. And He said to her, "Daughter, your faith has made you well. Go in peace, and be healed of your affliction.' "

When the prophetess had concluded the last verse, she looked out at the women.

"Look at your neighbor and say 'Neighbor.' "

The women obeyed, "Neighbor."

"Whatever your issue is . . ."

"Whatever your issue is . . ." the women repeated.

"Can be made well if you touch Jesus."

"Can be made well if you touch Jesus," the women echoed.

"All right now . . . you better preach," one of the women encouraged her.

"You may be seated, but while you're going down, look at your neighbor on the other side and say, 'I didn't say touch Jesse, Jack, John John, or Junebug. I said touch Jesus.'"

The women stood back up and applauded her. "You're sayin' something . . . go ahead."

"In this particular passage of scripture, Mark talks about a woman who had been hemorrhaging nonstop for twelve years. She had gone to see many doctors who tried to heal her but couldn't. In fact, verse twenty-five says that after she'd seen the doctors, her problem had gotten worse and her funds were depleted while seeking health care.

"I'm reminded of a time when a young lady approached me and confessed that she was addicted to sex. She said, 'Prophetess, I don't understand why I'm like this, but I think about sex all the time and I just gotta have it.'

"I looked at her beautiful face and asked what she meant by she 'just gotta have it.' She said, 'Prophetess I-I just can't help it. Guys call and ask if they can come over and watch a movie, and before I know it, we end up in the bed.'

"So I said, 'Why not go to the theater to see a movie? Why do you have to be at your house?' She answered, ' 'Cause it's more intimate at the house, plus they give me things.'

"Then I asked her what kinds of things men give, and she said that they may pay her rent or car note, and from time to time, they'll give her cash. She said, 'Prophetess, I try to stay away from sex. I wrote to Dear Abby's advice column, I've even gone to see a shrink to get hypnotized to find out if there's something in my past that's making me do this. Finally, I talked to a sex therapist and called a psychic hotline, and they all said the same thing: that I'm hot-blooded, and it must be in my genes.'

"I asked her what happened when men come to her empty-handed and she boldly said, 'Look, I'm high maintenance. I don't come cheap and all of my men know that if I can't get my rent paid or at least my hair and nails done, they don't get none.'

"I explained to this young lady that she's prostituting her body, and she said, 'Oh, no, Prophetess, I don't have sex all the time. Only when they give me stuff.'

"I grabbed the sister by her hand and shook her and told her that it wasn't the sex that she was addicted to, but it was the money and gifts she received from men that caused the addiction."

The audience agreed. "That's right . . . sho' you right . . . teach the truth."

"She had an issue, and the only one who could heal and deliver her from sexual sin was Jesus. Even though she was a young lady who was born and raised in the church, she had no clue who God really was or what He represented in her life."

The women encouraged the prophetess. "Go on and teach . . . preach it . . . Break it down."

"It's not revealed in the book of Mark what the woman's name was, but I like to call her Flo, 'cause she had a nonstop flow of blood. Ladies, can you imagine what it would be like to have your menstrual cycle for twelve years, nonstop?"

The women mumbled. "Uh-uh . . . I'd rather die than go through that."

"Some of us can hardly take the three, five, or seven days a month."

"You're right about that, Prophetess . . . That's sho' 'nuff the truth," the women agreed.

"Then there are those who look forward to it. I'm talking about those of you who are doing what you ain't got no business doing."

The women laughed but couldn't help but to agree with her. "Amen . . . amen . . . Preach on."

"Listen, can I get real and raw with y'all to-night?"

The women responded, "Go ahead and make it plain."

"We're gonna get real and shame the devil in here. Is that all right?"

"It's all right . . . Tell us what we need to hear," the women shouted.

"There were times when I used to actually pray and beg God to send my period. I mean, down on my knees crying and moaning type of begging because I had one of those Momma's that had her own calendar keeping up with my period. I didn't have to count the days because my momma did it for me. If I told her that I was on my period, she'd want to see blood for herself. I'm telling y'all that my momma was from down South. She didn't play. But one time I was late and panicked. I mean I panicked to the point where I made myself sick. I think I was about sixteen, and I wasn't worried about God no more, I was worried about my momma. My prayers had gone from 'Lord, please bring my period and I ain't gonna do it no more,' to 'Lord, please let me die before my momma find out.'

"I knew that if He didn't kill me, my momma was going to. But back in the day, we could get these little white pills over the counter called HUMPHREYS 11. How many of y'all know about HUMPHREYS 11?"

About five women out of two hundred raised their hands.

"That's all right, y'all ain't got to tell the truth."

The women laughed, and about one hundred more raised their hands.

"HUMPHREYS 11 was a pill that kept you from going to the abortion clinic. When I was sixteen I thought I was pregnant. I took about fifteen pills and passed out. I was rushed to the hospital and had to have my stomach pumped. It turned out that I had a blood clot in my uterus that wouldn't let my period flow. That experience scared me to death, along with the beating my momma put on me so bad that I truly repented and asked God to cleanse me. I promised Him that I would never lay with a man again until I was married. Well, as you know, I'm not married, and I'm proud to stand here and testify that God made me whole, and I've been celibate for seventeen years, glory to God."

The women stood and applauded the prophetess. Her voice rose as she wiped her face. "And that's what God wants you to do. He wants you to give Him your issue. Whatever it is, God can make it well."

The women were agreeing with the prophetess. "Hallelujah . . . Praise God . . . Amen . . . Amen."

"Verse twenty-seven says Flo heard that Jesus was in town, and she knew about His healing power, and she pressed her way to Him." The prophetess looked out at the audience. "That's what we gotta do when we need something from God. Flo had been afflicted for years, and no matter what she had to do or who she had to go through, she was gonna get to Jesus by any means necessary.

"But before you give God your issue, you've got to get fed up with yourself. You don't have to live in sin, you don't have to remain backslidden, and you don't have to live beneath your inheritance."

Every woman in the sanctuary was on her feet. "Glory to God . . . Hallelujah."

"I dare you to touch Jesus. He's waiting on you to touch Him. Come on and press your way. He's here, He's here. Reach up and touch Him."

The women had their hands in the air and their heads thrown back, calling out to God.

"That's right. Tell God what you want Him to do for you. Open up your mouths and talk to God, and I promise you that if you tap into Him, He'll immediately heal you. Whatever your issue is, give it to God."

Women were on their knees crying for forgiveness. Others were holding each other. Prophetess Anderson came out of the pulpit and stood in the front of the church. She silently prayed and asked God for direction on what to do at that point.

The Holy Spirit revealed what she was in the midst of. In the sanctuary was an usher who was pregnant by a married deacon, a seventeen-year-old girl who had been pregnant four times, but she was not a mother, a woman on the finance committee that stole at least fifty dollars from the offering basket every Sunday to support her dope habit, and two lesbians who were not saved and were guests of a member of the church. They had gotten married in Canada and were raising two young children together.

As the Holy Spirit revealed, the prophetess moved. She walked and stood in front of Amaryllis, who sat next to Michelle and Bridgette on the front pew. She grabbed Amaryllis's hand, pulled her from the pew on her feet, and looked at her. "Webster's Dictionary defines the word 'dirty' as something being not clean or not pure. When something is dirty, it can become contaminated or even infectious. To be dirty means to be filthy, nasty, and of foul odor."

"Webster's defines the word 'drain' as something that causes depletion or a passageway to discharge or empty things." So that Amaryllis wouldn't be embarrassed at what she was going to say to her next, the prophetess stepped to her, then whispered in her ear. "Your private area is a dirty drain."

Amaryllis's eyes bucked out of her head.

"Many men have discharged their seeds into you. You wonder why every man that approaches you wastes no time saying what's on his agenda. It's because they can smell you. The scent of lustful sex is coming from your body, and it can be detected a mile away. Men are on you like a pack of hyenas on a dead carcass."

Tears streamed down Amaryllis's face. She became so emotional at the words Prophetess Anderson was speaking to her.

Amaryllis felt the prophetess's lips on her lobe. "They can smell your dirty drain, and it attracts them your way. A lion marks his territory by urinating in a certain spot, and the odor carries. Your vagina has been marked with semen. You're walking around with a sewer between your legs, and you stink."

Amaryllis buried her face in her hands and cried openly. The prophetess had spoken the absolute truth. It rained men wherever Amaryllis went. She just couldn't keep them off of her.

Michelle tried to console her sister by hugging her, but the prophetess told Michelle to step away and allow God to come in and do what had to be done. And Michelle knew that was exactly what her sister needed.

Prophetess Anderson continued speaking to Amaryllis. "Vinegar and water is not the answer. The stench is embedded inside your walls, and only the blood of Jesus can cleanse you. You must touch Him and let Him heal you."

The woman of God left Amaryllis standing there crying and moved to Michelle.

"You've lived a sheltered life. God says that in two months' time, He's going to test your faith. Repeat after me, 'Faith ain't fun, and favor ain't fair.' "

Michelle did as she was told, and the prophetess moved on to Bridgette. "Your tongue is your downfall. You don't mind getting folks told. Last week you told a man to kiss your behind, and I'm putting it mildly. Not once, but twice you did that. I see file cabinets and computers. What type of work do you do?"

Bridgette stood in shock because the woman hit the nail right on the head. "I'm a paralegal."

"You applied for a job six months ago, and it was looking promising until your mouth got in the way."

Bridgette fell to her knees, crying and repenting before God. As the prophetess moved on, she looked at Cookie. "First Lady, I hope you'll have me back next year."

All of the women knew that Prophetess Michellene Anderson was a powerful woman of God, and she could see straight through a person.

She stood in front of the dope addict. "Stretch out your arms, daughter."

The prophetess saw what looked like mosquito bites covering the entire inside of the woman's arms. She summoned for a bottle of holy oil and squeezed drops on the woman's arms and massaged it into her skin. "This oil represents the blood of Jesus. With His blood, He has sealed every hole in your arm."

The woman began clapping and thanking God for deliverance. Prophetess Anderson moved on and looked at all the women and saw how they were looking at the drug addict.

"You all are turning your noses up at her like she's the only one here with issues, but hold on, because I'm knocking on your door next."

She got to the pregnant woman and stood in front of her. "What's your name, daughter?"

The woman was already crying and couldn't answer. Prophetess Anderson embraced her and asked her again, and this time, the distraught woman whispered, "Chloe."

"What trimester are you in?"

Chloe's eyebrows raised in fear. "What do you mean?"

"Are you pregnant?"

"Yes, but how did you know?" Her belly hadn't begun to show as of yet.

"The Holy Spirit revealed it to me, and the father of your child is married and has been for eleven years."

Chloe started crying loudly.

"The man's wife is a friend of your mother. Am I right, daughter?"

Chloe was devastated, and the only thing she could do was to cry out for forgiveness.

Prophetess Anderson left the weeping woman and walked to the seventeen-year-old. Immediately the girl started screaming. "I'm sorry, Lord, oh my God, I'm so sorry. Please forgive me, Jesus."

Because the Holy Spirit doesn't bring embarrassment or shame, the prophetess whispered in the teenager's ear. "The last vacuum that entered your body inhaled your entire uterus. You're not even eighteen years old and already your womb has been sold to the devil."

The girl's mother standing next to her held her daughter tightly, and the prophetess looked at her. "You are a single mother who works two jobs, and that has to change. Your daughter needs you to be home at night."

Prophetess Anderson moved on to another woman.

The woman arrogantly looked at the prophetess and boldly spoke to her. "Before you say anything to me, let me tell you that I'm not pregnant, on drugs, I don't curse, I don't have a man, nor am I messing around with anyone else's man, so you can just move on to the next person."

Prophetess Anderson disregarded the young woman's disrespectful attitude and smiled. She lifted the woman's left hand and studied it but saw no ring. "You are a beautiful woman, and I see that you're not married."

The young woman folded her arms across her chest and shifted all of her weight onto one leg. She cocked her head to the side, giving off even more attitude. "No, I'm not."

"But you're sexually active."

The woman's eyes grew wide, and she raised her voice at the prophetess. "See, I knew you were a fake. I told you that I don't have a man."

The prophetess stepped to her and whispered in her ear. "Sweetheart, if I looked in a black box on the top shelf in the rear of your closet, how many types of sexual toys would I see?"

The young woman was embarrassed and speechless.

"Masturbation is an abomination against the body. No one is a professional saint," the prophetess whispered.

Prophetess Anderson moved on. She was getting too close for comfort to the lesbian couple. When she got within five feet of them, they excused themselves and hurried out of the sanctuary.

The Holy Spirit led the prophetess to the rear of the church. She came and stood in front of a woman who was crying. The prophetess studied her face and saw through her makeup and noticed a black-and-blue eye, a semi-swollen jaw, and the busted lip that the ruby red lipstick couldn't hide.

"Get out while you still can. He doesn't love you. If you stay, you'll be dead within five months. There is a better life for you."

The woman didn't say a word.

"Get out while the getting is good. I know he apologizes, but I promise you that the last time wasn't the last time, and it will only get worse. The very next time he puts his hands on you, it will cost you your life."

The woman fell to her knees and cried out to God. Prophetess Anderson called for the first lady to assist her. "Cookie, come and embrace this woman."

The prophetess made her way back into the pulpit and looked at the congregation. Women were lying all over the sanctuary floor. Heads were thrown back and mouths were opened and hands were lifted in the air. Through their praises, Prophetess Anderson spoke to them. "We as women of God must become ladies of God. Any female can say that she's a woman of God, but it takes a special kind of anointing to make you a lady. Ladies of God don't speak in tongues and cuss out of the same mouth. Ladies of God don't chase after a man. God said that it's a man who finds his wife not the other way around. Ladies of God are immaculate all the time. Ladies of God have their toenails painted when they're wearing sandals. And a true lady makes sure that her fingernail and toenail polish match. A lady doesn't wear an outfit that's two sizes too small."

The women were applauding the prophetess. "That's right . . . Speak the truth."

"A lady doesn't accept booty calls. A lady doesn't leave the nightclub at five a.m., then go home to get her Bible and go straight to Sunday School. A lady doesn't raise her arms and allow everyone to see hair with caked-up balls of deodorant. Shave that stuff off. That ain't cute."

"All right, Prophetess . . . Teach it . . . Say that, say that," the women responded to her.

"A lady doesn't wear pants everywhere she goes. Put on a dress from time to time. Take that cap off your head and let your hair down. You're wondering why men won't approach you. It's because they think you're one of them."

The women encouraged the prophetess even more. "You're sho' right about that . . . Preach on . . . Come on and talk about it."

"Take that bounce out of your step and put a sashay in your walk. Ladies don't bounce, we glide. Invest in yourself and buy perfume and scented lotion. You ain't got to wait on a man to make you feel good. Love yourself and treat your own self good."

"Glory to God . . . Hallelujah . . . Yes, Lord," the women chanted.

"Romans, chapter twelve, verse one says, 'I beseech you therefore brethren, by the mercies of God, that you present your bodies a living sacrifice, holy, acceptable to God, which is your reasonable service. And do not be conformed to this world, but be transformed by the renewing of your mind, that you may prove what is that good and acceptable and perfect will of God.'

"You've got to change your minds about how you feel about yourselves. Get it in your mind that you don't have to be a dope addict; you don't have to get your brains beaten out just because your man came home drunk and didn't like the way the furniture was arranged. You don't have to walk around with a sewer between your legs, and you don't have to lay up with every Tyrone, DeVante, and Henry."

When Prophetess Anderson mentioned not laying up with the name "Tyrone," Amaryllis could've shouted. She was proud of herself for not giving in to his sexual advances.

"See, I'ma let y'all in on a secret," the prophetess said. "A woman can easily become a trick if she allows herself to, but a lady will always be a treat."

The sanctuary sounded like a basketball stadium at playoff time.

"Tell yourselves that you are ladies of God. You've graduated from women to ladies today. Reach up and grab your diplomas. God has given you a master's degree in Ladyhood. After today, you may lose some friends because they're not gonna understand the change in you, but that's okay. Some things ladies just can't do, some words ladies just can't say, some places ladies just can't go, and some clothes ladies just can't wear."

The women were delirious. "Yes, Lord . . . Teach it."

"When your friends call and ask what time to meet at the club, you tell them that you're not going because you're a lady."

"Yes, I'm a lady . . . I'm a lady . . . I'm a lady," the women agreed.

"What are you gonna say when Junebug calls you in the middle of the night and asks if he can come over?"

All two hundred women yelled, "No!"

"Why?" the prophetess asked.

They shouted, "Because I'm a lady!"

"Why can't you walk around smelling like a dirty drain?"

Amaryllis shouted the loudest. "Because I'm a lady."

"Why can't you let a man pound on you?"

"Because, I'm a lady," they responded.

"All you ladies in this house come on and give God some praise for your deliverance, for your healing, for your victory, and for your master's degree."

The ladies shouted unto God and began praising Him some more. Prophetess Anderson called for each of the ladies that she personally ministered to, to come and stand at the altar. Once they had assembled themselves next to each other, she spoke.

"God loves you, and He sees you where you are. If you want to be made whole, raise your hands right now and give Him glory."

They obeyed her and started repenting before God. Prophetess Anderson then stepped to Bridgette and blew in her face and immediately she fell into Michelle, who fell into the seventeen-year-old, who fell into the usher, who fell into the lady who had been beaten, who fell into Amaryllis, who fell into the drug addict, who fell into the pregnant lady, who fell into the single lady having sex.

One by one they dropped to the floor in a domino affect. The ladies left standing were praising God for making their issues well and for giving them a new start.

Prophetess Anderson looked at Cookie and repeated her statement. "First Lady, I hope you'll have me back next year."

Chapter 17

When Michelle got home on Sunday evening after taking Amaryllis and Bridgette to the airport, she sat down on the sofa and bowed her head. "Father, you know I love my sister, right? But can you please allow me an entire year before I have to set eyes on her again? Because, Lord, you see, Amaryllis is crazy. And in the three days she and crazy number two were here, they almost drove me crazy. Thank you for however many miles there are between Vegas and Chicago. So, God, can I please have my sanity back? And Lord, whatever Prophetess Anderson meant about you testing my faith in two months, please don't do it, Lord. I'm gonna need at least a year to recover from the crazies' visit."

Michelle sat silently hoping that God would honor her plea. Her cellular phone rang just as she was on her way into the kitchen to search for a chocolate fix. She recognized James's number at the precinct. "Is this my husband?" she said into the telephone.

"You are so beautiful, and I want you," James told her.

Michelle smiled. "Oh, my."

"I love you so much, Mickey."

If Michelle's skin weren't so dark, it would have been easy to see her red cheeks. "I love you too, James. When are you coming home?"

James was on a roll, and he decided to flow with it. "Baby, you mean the world to me. I've been sitting at my desk for the past half hour, thanking God for my wife. And I'm looking at your picture on my desk, and, oh my God, I'm head over heels in love with you, girl. I keep smiling at your picture, and folks around here are laughing and saying that I'm whipped, but you know what, Mickey? I don't care what they say, 'cause I loves my baby." He traced Michelle's face in the photo with his finger. "I'm looking at your hair. I love the way you part it down the middle and let it fall down your back. I'm looking at your pretty brown face. I love your little nose. And the way you're smiling back at me in this picture makes me wanna pounce on you."

Michelle had to sit down on the sofa again. "Oh, my goodness. What's gotten into you?"

"Nothing has gotten into me, but I wanna get inside of you."

Now Michelle got heated and fanned herself. "Whew, watch out there now, Detective."

"You're the one who better watch out, Mickey. Because when I get home, it's on. I just can't stop looking at your picture. I had to call and tell you how much I adore you."

"Well, sweetie, the feeling is mutual."

James paused before he asked, "Are they gone?"

"Yep. I watched the plane take off and get smaller and smaller until it disappeared in the sky."

"We got our house back?"

"Yes, we do. I was just on my way to the kitchen for a chocolate fix."

"I got your fix, Mickey."

Michelle blushed. "Ahh, sooky, sooky, now. Well, bring it on because I got the shakes."

"Mickey, I'm telling you right now, I've been on my best behavior while your guests were here, but I'm coming after you full force when I get home. I'll be leaving the precinct in twenty minutes. I advise you to pray for strength, endurance, and longevity because I'm bringing home the handcuffs."

Michelle hung up from James and glanced at their wedding photo above the fireplace. On the way up the stairs to their bedroom, she said, "Lord, please give me strength, endurance, and longevity because he's bringing home the handcuffs."

Forty-five minutes later, James came in the front door. A string from a red, helium-filled balloon floating against the ceiling greeted him. There was a note attached to it. He pulled the string and read the note.

This is a setup. Do exactly as I say and no one will get hurt. Strip and leave your clothes by the door, then walk into the kitchen.

James didn't have to read it twice. Immediately, he stripped and walked to the kitchen, completely naked. Two steps into the kitchen was another balloon hanging from the ceiling with a note.

In the refrigerator, you'll find a glass of sparkling grape juice. Drink the entire glass then proceed to the third floor. Do not, and I repeat, do not open the door to our bedroom. Go directly to the third floor.

James got excited. He quickly drank the sparkling grape juice then took the stairs two at a time. He stopped on the second floor and pressed his ear against their bedroom door. Soft music greeted his ear, and he got more excited. Grinning, he trotted up to the third floor. At the top of the stairs another balloon and note hung from the ceiling.

I took the liberty of drawing you a bath in the guest bathroom. You are instructed to clear your

*mind, relax, and soak for exactly ten minutes.
At that time you will hear a bell. When the bell
rings, drain the tub, dry your body, and open the
door. An appetizer awaits you next to the tub.
Enjoy.*

Obediently, James walked into the guest bathroom and saw candles burning on the ledge of the
tub. Bubbles were dancing in the heated Jacuzzi.
He carefully stepped over the candles and sank
down in the tub. A bowl of fresh strawberries sat
on a tray next to the tub. He helped himself to a
handful and lay back. James closed his eyes and
smiled. He felt as though he were on a mouse
hunt, better yet, a Mickey hunt. With his eyes
closed, he began to sing. "M-i-c-k-e-y, God gave
you to meeeee."

Exactly ten minutes after James got in the tub
he heard a bell ring from outside the bathroom
door, and he smiled. Just the thought of Michelle
teasing and taunting him this way turned him on
big time. He drained the tub, dried himself, and
blew out the candles. When he opened the door,
there was yet another balloon and note hanging
from the ceiling.

Open the door to the linen closet.

Obediently, James opened the door to his
right and saw a small wicker basket containing
a bottle of Hershey's chocolate syrup, a bottle of

honey, and a can of whipped cream tied together with a note attached. Also in the basket were a long wooden spoon and a spatula with notes attached to them. The note attached to the long wooden spoon read:

Somethin' to stir me with.

James's eyebrows rose. The note attached to the spatula read:

Somethin' to flip me with.

James's eyebrows rose higher as his mouth dropped open. The note attached to the chocolate syrup, honey, and whipped cream read:

Somethin' to rub me down with.

By now, his adrenaline and testosterone were flowing overtime. He grabbed the basket and ran downstairs to their master suite. Outside of the closed door was a fifth balloon with a note attached.

You had your bath, and you had your appetizer. I hope you're hungry because the main course is now served. Open the door!!

All thirty-two teeth in James's mouth sparkled as he eagerly opened the door. The scene before his eyes literally took his breath away. Michelle was lying in the middle of their king-sized bed, nude, with rose petals covering only her breasts and private area. More rose petals lay scattered all around her on the bed. Candles romantically lit the bedroom. James could hear someone blowing the heavens out of a saxophone coming from the speakers of their stereo system. But he concentrated on his wife.

Michelle's hair was parted down the middle and flowing just the way James loved it. She'd taken her time applying makeup to her face, using gold and bronze colors to accentuate her luscious brown skin. James's gaze followed Michelle's perfectly proportioned body down to her petite toes. He thought to himself, I am blessed.

Michelle spoke to him in an extremely seductive voice. "Are you ready to feast?"

"Uh-huh."

"What's in the basket?"

James forgot he was holding it in his hand. "Huh? Oh, um, just some tools to fix you with."

Michelle held her hand out for him to take. "Well, here I am, husband. Fix me."

James almost dropped the basket. Quickly, he tightened his grip around the handle. He had to calm himself before he touched Michelle, because if he touched her at that moment, he'd probably hurt her. He was too excited. It took about twenty seconds for him to realize that she was his wife and wasn't going anywhere.

"What are you waiting on, Detective?"

At the sound of Michelle's sultry voice, he lost it. They didn't know, nor would they have cared, that it would take half an hour in the shower the next day to remove all the goop from the creases in their bodies and Michelle's hair.

Chapter 18

Before Bridgette and Amaryllis walked out of their front door Monday morning, they held hands and prayed. It was the first time the two of them prayed together. The women's crusade left a deep impression on them. On the airplane ride back home to Chicago, it was all they talked about. They were empowered and encouraged.

Amaryllis talked to God first. "Good morning, Lord. First, I wanna thank You for allowing us to experience a weekend that we'll never forget. I personally thank You, Lord, for a new revelation. Please cleanse my body from the inside out. Lord, please don't let another man smell my private area."

Bridgette opened her eyes and looked at Amaryllis. She wanted to laugh, but she knew Amaryllis was sincere in her prayer. She suppressed a giggle as she closed her eyes again and listened.

Amaryllis continued. "Help me, Lord. If I gotta get some ammonia, bleach, vinegar, Ajax, liquid Tide, and Dawn dishwashing liquid and mix them together and soak in the tub for a week, Lord, I'll do it. Whatever I gotta do, Jesus, please, please help me, 'cause I don't want anybody to smell me, Lord."

Bridgette was laughing so hard on the inside she had to force her lips to stay closed.

Amaryllis wasn't done. "Lord, I give my body back to You. All of it. Even my private area. It's Yours, Lord. And You can do what You wanna do with it."

If Bridgette hadn't seen Amaryllis wiping tears from her eyes, she would have given in and hollered out. What in the world could God possibly do with Amaryllis's private area? It took all that was within Bridgette to swallow the laugh, because it was her turn to pray. She held on to Amaryllis's hands and talked to God. "Father, You are awesome and so good, and I thank You for Your blessings. I got a new revelation this weekend too, Lord. And yes, Jesus, I'll admit that my mouth gets me into trouble sometimes. But what am I supposed to say to people when they piss me off?"

Amaryllis's eyes shot open, and she glared at Bridgette.

I know this heifer didn't say that to God.

"All that lady told me, Lord, was that I have a hot tongue. Well, heck, it didn't take a rocket scientist to figure that out. I like to get folks told,

Lord, and You know that. I'm just being me. Bridgette. That's who I am. I cuss folks out. So, God, You tell me what to say to people when I really want to tell them to kiss my #$*&, because I don't know."

Now Amaryllis's mouth dropped wide open. She took two steps backward while still holding Bridgette's hands, because as sure as God was real, He was getting ready to send a lightning bolt down with Bridgette's name on it. Amaryllis wanted to give God ample room to hit the right target.

"Okay, Lord," Bridgette continued, "I'll admit that there have been a few times that I might have gotten a little out of hand—but only a few times. It ain't like I cuss people out every day. Well, actually I do cuss people out every day, Lord, but I think a lot of folks make more out of it than it really is. But sometimes, Lord, I should be justified because You know what I deal with on a daily basis. There are a lot of ignorant folks in this world, and the older I get, the less tolerance I have for silly sh—uh, stuff, Lord."

Amaryllis took another tiny step backward.

"I tell You what, Lord, I promise not to cuss anybody out today, but I ain't making no promises about tomorrow yet. First, we'll see how today goes. And then You and I will take it one day at a time, okay, Lord? Do You feel me? I hope You can feel me, Jesus, because I ask these blessings in Your name. Amen."

Bridgette and Amaryllis stepped off the elevator at 6:20 a.m. Marvin was standing at attention when they got to his post. "Good morning, Amaryllis and Sheneneh."

Amaryllis laughed, but Bridgette didn't think it was funny at all as she looked up toward the ceiling. *You see what I'm talkin' about, Lord? I just promised You that I wasn't gonna cuss today and look what happened. This old fool got jokes. This is a perfect example of what I just talked to You about. So, You best write on my tongue because You know what I really wanna say to this wrinkled mummy.*

Marvin looked at Bridgette, then up at the ceiling, then Bridgette again. "What is you lookin' up there for?"

Bridgette forced a fake smile onto her face. "Good morning, Marvin. How are you today?"

That wasn't the response Marvin was used to. Bridgette threw him for a loop. She was Marvin's caffeine. He needed her to curse. His day wouldn't go right without a heated argument with her. "What you mean, how am I today? Since when you care about me?"

Bridgette set her purse on the counter and placed her hands on top of Marvin's hands.

"Marvin, I've turned over a new leaf. As of today, no cuss words will flow from my lips." *You old bastard.*

Marvin looked at Amaryllis. "Is she for real?"

"I hope so, Marvin, so stop messing with her," she told him.

Marvin took his hands away from Bridgette's. "It ain't gonna last. You cuss in your sleep."

Bridgette placed her purse on her right shoulder. "Marvin, I pray that you have a blessed day. We'll see you tomorrow." *If that corroded heart of yours is still pumping then.* Bridgette was proud of herself for not speaking her thoughts. She smiled and mentally patted herself on the back. It was still early in the day, but so far, Bridgette was keeping her promise to God.

Marvin watched the ladies walk out of the building. Then he went across the street to a café and bought a cup of coffee. It was something he hadn't done since Bridgette moved into the building. He chose to drink it without cream and sugar and frowned at the taste. The coffee was strong, but it couldn't compare to what Bridgette normally did for him.

Chapter 19

The staff at Parker & Parker Law Offices didn't know what to make of the new and improved Bridgette. The first shocker was the fact that she bought doughnuts for everyone. The second shocker came when she greeted those who came into her presence in a friendly manner and with a genuine smile. The ultimate shocker happened when Bridgette sat at her desk, and for the first time in six years, no outburst erupted from her lips.

It was almost noontime, and still no one had heard a peep from Bridgette all morning. Folks didn't know whether to count their blessings that she'd probably taken a sedative before coming to work that morning or to suggest that she see a psychiatrist.

Two file clerks walked by Bridgette's desk, talking between themselves. "Maybe she's got strep throat and can't talk," one guessed.

"I think she's getting ready to blow up. It's always calm right before the tornado hits," the other reasoned.

Bridgette heard their comments but didn't acknowledge them. By two p.m., even Amaryllis was amazed at her friend's new attitude. She dialed Bridgette's extension. "Okay, I know you promised God that you weren't gonna cuss today, but what's up with the silent treatment?"

Bridgette looked across the office at Amaryllis. "First of all, why are you calling me from twenty feet away? Are you that lazy?"

"The word around here is that you are a sitting time bomb waiting to explode, and I didn't wanna be anywhere near you when the match met the dynamite."

"Ha-ha. That's very funny. I'm keeping my mouth shut on purpose because that's the only way I'll make good on my promise. Truth be told, I've been pissed off since eight o'clock this morning."

"Oh, Lord, what happened?"

"My computer was on when I got here, which means somebody was using it. That ticked me off, but I didn't cuss because I made a promise. Then I walked into the break room to get one of the two dozen doughnuts that I bought, not even fifteen minutes after I set them in there, only to find all of them gone. That ticked me off, but I didn't cuss because I made a promise. And that big broad, Barbara, was so busy gossiping about something with April and wasn't looking where she was going while walking my way, and she bumped into me and almost spilled my cup of coffee on my cream linen suit."

Amaryllis knew where Bridgette was going with this. "And that ticked you off, but you didn't cuss, because you made a promise, right?"

"Right, but check this out. Mr. Parker called me into his office earlier and asked if I had given any thought to taking an anger management class. There's a coordinator's position opening up soon, and he'll consider me if I take the class."

"Well, Bridge, if taking the class will get you that promotion, then swallow your pride, take the class, and get paid."

"And let everyone around here think that I'm some kind of nutcase that can't control her temper? I don't think so, Amaryllis."

"Bridge, the man basically told you the job was yours if you want it. Now, you need to ask yourself how bad you want this promotion."

"Not bad enough to be labeled a nutcase."

Amaryllis was fed up with Bridgette's attitude. "Okay, listen. I'm gonna get real with you because I love you, and I'm the only one around here who ain't afraid to tell you about yourself. I don't care about you cussing me out. I'm used to it. So, here's the deal. You are a nutcase. I know it, Mr. Parker knows it, Marvin knows it, and everyone that has ever met you knows it. Even God knows it, okay? Receive in your spirit what I'm telling you. You are just as crazy as Deacon Brown when he thinks he's cute in them teal-blue polyester pants with that white belt and those white patent leather shoes. Now, you know that's crazy. But that doesn't stop him from trying to get his mack on, does it?"

"You know, Amaryllis, you're a couple of ribs short of a full slab yourself. That's why we get along so well."

"This ain't about me, Bridge. I have never said I wasn't a lunatic. I'm not in denial about who I am. I was a crazy sinner, and now, I'm very proud to say that I'm a crazy ghetto saint. What I'm trying to get you to understand is pride will cost you a lifetime of happiness, if you let it. This promotion will be a $15,000 a year increase for you. So what you gotta go to a stupid class for one hour once a week for the next two and a half months? Who cares? And when did you start worrying about what other people think about you anyway? Handle your business, Boo, and do what you gotta do."

Bridgette was sitting at her desk, holding the phone in her hand with tears streaming down her face. Amaryllis was right. She wanted the promotion, and Bridgette decided to do what she had to do to get it. "Thanks, girl. I love you."

"You better. Got me preaching, and I still got two briefs to type before five o'clock."

"I'm worth your time, ain't I?"

"I don't know, are you?"

Bridgette knew that no matter what happened between her and Amaryllis, she could always count on her best friend. "I better be."

"Listen, to show you that I got your back, I'll go with you to the first session of this anger management class," Amaryllis offered.

Bridgette blew her runny nose into a Kleenex tissue. Sniff, sniff. "You will, Amaryllis?"

"Of course, I will. So, go back into Mr. Parker's office and tell him you want that job."

Bridgette wiped her tears. "Okay, let me go and wash my face first."

"Yeah, do that. And you need to invest in Mac makeup because that corner store mascara you wear got you lookin' like a raccoon when you cry."

Half an hour later, Bridgette rushed out of Mr. Parker's office and over to Amaryllis's desk. "Guess what, girl? Guess what?"

Amaryllis was keying ninety words per minute into her computer. "Wait a minute. Let me finish this paragraph."

Through her peripheral vision, she could see Bridgette excitedly stepping from side to side. She stopped typing and watched her friend take three steps backward, then bend forward and touch the floor.

"Bridgette, what the heck are you doing?"

Bridgette turned to her right and took three steps in that direction. "The electric slide, girl. Come on and get with it."

Bridgette took three steps to the left. Amaryllis guessed her meeting with Mr. Parker had gone very well. "So, what did Mr. Parker say?"

Bridgette took a break from dancing and sat on the corner of Amaryllis's desk. "I told him I'd go through the stupid anger management class if he guaranteed me the coordinator's position. He told me the next enrollment for the class begins in three weeks. However, he needs someone to take over that position as soon as possible because Marilyn's last day is on Friday. He wants someone to be in that position on Monday morning."

Amaryllis leaned back in her chair and crossed her legs. "Yeah? And? Get to the part that's got you showing me what you're working with."

"Well, Mr. Parker said that since I volunteered to take the anger management class in three weeks, he'll grant me the promotion today."

Amaryllis's eyes grew wide. "Look at God. Do you see how He worked that thing? All because you made good on your promise, Bridge."

Bridgette was swinging her legs back and forth. "I have to sit with Marilyn for the rest of the week to learn the ropes."

Amaryllis stood up and hugged her friend. "Congratulations, honey. I am so happy for you."

Bridgette stood from the desk and straightened her jacket and pants. "I'm happy for me too, girl. This promotion comes with a corner office with a nice view of Lake Michigan."

"I know, and like I said, look at God."

Bridgette thought about her blessing. "Isn't He awesome, Amaryllis?"

"Even God hasn't created a word to describe just how wonderful He really is, because awesome, amazing, wonderful, and great don't scratch the surface of who and what He is in my life. I guess that's why He says 'I am that I am.'"

Bridgette began to dance again. She took three steps to the right, then three steps to the left. Amaryllis laughed at her. "Go on, girl. Shake it fast. Watch yourself."

Bridgette took three steps backward, and Amaryllis pumped her up some more. "Drop it like it's hot."

She watched as Bridgette squatted down and touched the floor. When she did that, Amaryllis burst out in laughter.

Chapter 20

Within two months, Bridgette was comfortably working in her new position. She passed the anger management class with flying colors. Not one curse word had passed her lips since she gave God her tongue. Marvin still hadn't gotten used to Bridgette's new way of living. Every morning he was like a crackhead waiting on his next fix. He'd gotten to the point where he practically begged Bridgette to curse at him.

"Come on, Bridgette. Give me a little something. I gotta have something to take me through the day."

"I ain't backsliding, Marvin, not even for you."

One Friday afternoon, Amaryllis opened the door to Bridgette's office and walked in. Bridgette was surfing the Internet for prices on cruises to the Caribbean. She looked at Amaryllis as she sat in a chair across from her desk. "Uh, excuse you. You don't just open the door and waltz your way into someone's office. You're supposed to knock first.

Then you wait to be invited in. Now, I know you were raised better than that."

"First of all, you must not know who my momma is. Second, don't make me cut you. Third, I know that ain't my sweater you have on, is it?"

Bridgette quickly changed the subject. "Uh, if we're going on vacation in a couple of weeks, we need to book something now and pay for it in one lump sum."

"How much are we talking?"

"Depends on where we wanna go. Do you know that we gotta have our birth certificates to get into another country?"

"Really?"

"Yep. I gotta go over to City Hall to get a copy of my birth certificate. Where's yours?"

"I lost the only copy I had when I moved from Black's house. I was born in Baton Rouge. I know my grandmother has a copy of my birth certificate. I'll ask her to send me a copy."

"Louisiana?" Bridgette asked.

"Ain't that where Baton Rouge is? I'll call my Nana tonight and ask her send it to me. In the meantime, go ahead and book something for five days in Negril, Jamaica."

Bridgette got excited. "Ooh, Hedonism?"

"No, Bridgette. I ain't trying to get with folks dancing, sweating, and rubbing against each other in their lingerie and thongs, calling it a pajama party."

"Come on, Amaryllis, we're gonna be in Jamaica for your birthday. We might as well get our groove back."

"Do you want God to send you back downstairs, working across the office from me?"

Bridgette didn't answer her.

"That's what I thought. We can't do hedonism."

That didn't hinder Bridgette's mood. "November in Jamaica; I can't wait."

That evening, Amaryllis reached for the remote control on the cocktail table. Her first finger on her right hand made contact against the glass, and she cracked the acrylic on her nail. "Aw, shoot."

She looked at the nail and saw that if she didn't give it immediate attention, she'd snag everything she touched. She walked into Bridgette's bedroom and saw her lying comfortably in her bed, snuggled under the covers, engrossed in a movie on the Lifetime Channel.

"Bridge, I'm gonna run down to Pootang's and get my nail fixed. I just broke it."

Bridgette looked at the clock on her nightstand. "It's twenty minutes to eight. They close at eight on the dot. You'll never make it."

"It's right down the street. I'll make it."

"You know the beauty shop around the corner from the nail salon was robbed at closing time last Tuesday. Why can't you get your nail fixed tomorrow?"

"Because, my name ain't Bridgette. I can't walk around with a broken nail. Especially tomorrow, because I'm wearing my red silk pant suit."

"Well, you don't need to go by yourself. I might as well get a fill-in. Give me a minute to slip into a pair of jeans."

The ladies walked into Pootang's Nail Salon at seven-fifty. MingLee, their favorite nail technician, saw them come in. She'd been doing their nails faithfully for the past year.

"Why you comma heeyah? You jus heeyah three day befoa," MingLee asked Amaryllis.

Amaryllis went and sat down in the chair across from MingLee. "MingLee, I broke a nail. I need you to hook me up because—"

"Yeh, yeh, I know. You alway gotta be cue."

Amaryllis smiled. "All right, MingLee, Sister Girl. I taught you well."

"Yeh, and I tee you well, Mayllis. You comma heeyah when I close shop. You pay me ten dolla moah, 'cause I stay pass eight."

MingLee looked at Bridgette standing. "Why you stan theyah foah? You broke nail too?"

Bridgette sat down at the station next to Amaryllis. "Nah, I want a fill-in."

MingLee gave Bridgette a bottle of acetone and five cotton balls. "You too comma heeyah late. You take own polish off. I take thirdy-fi dolla from you."

Bridgette raised her eyebrows and looked at MingLee. "Thirty-five dollars? I ain't payin' thirty-five dollars for a fill-in. You're crazy, MingLee."

"Breejit, you comma in heeyah when time foah me go home. I heeyah all day. I hungree and period hurt stomak. You pay thirdy-fi dolla, or I set it off in heeyah."

Amaryllis laughed. "Girl, you better take thirty-five dollars out of your purse before you catch a beatdown. Ming-Lee ain't playin' with you. She knows karate."

"So, what? I know crazy," Bridgette returned, rolling her eyes.

MingLee sat down across from Amaryllis and examined her broken nail. "You take own polish off and pay me thirdy-fi dolla, Breejit."

Bridgette didn't respond, but she placed thirty-five dollars on the station, soaked a cotton ball with acetone, and wiped her nails. MingLee saw the amount of money Bridgette placed on the station. "You give tip too, Breejit."

Bridgette wanted to make sure she'd heard MingLee correctly. "Tip?"

"Take long time foah yoah nails. It's time foah me go home. I have family too, Breejit. You pay me ovatime. Ten dolla moah. That be my tip."

Bridgette shifted in her seat. "Oh, I got your tip. Why don't you tip over to the door and lock it before we get robbed."

"You no worry bout dat, Breejit. Someone try rob us, I whoop butt. And I whoop yoah butt too, Breejit, if you no put ten moah dolla on station."

Bridgette placed a ten-dollar bill on the station. "This don't make no sense, MingLee. Not only are you charging me forty-five dollars for something that costs fifteen, but you're making me take off my own polish."

"You comma heeyah late, Breejit. Come late, cost moah."

Bridgette continued to remove the polish from her nails. "That's all right. I ain't never coming in here no more. From now on, I'm going down the street to the Japanese girl."

MingLee glued a nail onto Amaryllis's fingertip. "I no care. Go 'head. They jack up yoah nail, you comma running back heeyah. Koreans do best work, Breejit. You betta aska sommabody."

Chapter 21

Four days later, Amaryllis and Bridgette walked into their building after work and retrieved their mail from the mailbox. Amaryllis recognized her grandmother's handwriting and smiled. "This didn't take long to get here."

They entered the elevator, and Bridgette pressed the button for their floor. The scent coming from Amaryllis's envelope captured her nostrils. She brought it to her nose and inhaled. "Ummm. Good ole, Nana. This smells just like her."

She tore open the envelope. Inside, was a sheet of paper folded in three sections. Amaryllis read what was in the envelope.

CERTIFICATE OF LIVE BIRTH
BATON ROUGE, LA
Last Name: Price
First Name: Michelle
Middle Name: Denise

Amaryllis's heart skipped three beats. She lost her balance and fell into the elevator wall. "Oh my God."

Bridgette looked at the shocked expression on her face. "What?"

"This is Michelle's birth certificate. Why would my mother's mother have this?"

In Las Vegas, James dried the dinner dishes as Michelle washed and rinsed them. Suddenly, Michelle's heart skipped three beats. She dropped the plate she had just washed back into the dishwater.

James looked at her. "Honey, you all right?"

Michelle's heart raced. "Did you feel that?"

"Feel what?"

She pressed her belly forward against the sink for balance. "I don't know. I thought I felt the house shake."

In Chicago, Amaryllis's saucer-size eyes read further.

Mother's Name: Price, Veronica
Father's Name: Price, Nicholas

A small shrill escaped Amaryllis's lips. Her palms got sweaty as she held on to Michelle's birth certificate. Bridgette saw tears streaming down her face. She moved next to Amaryllis and read the paper. "Oh my God. You and Michelle have the same mother?"

In Las Vegas, Michelle broke out into a cold sweat. She was burning hot, yet chilled to the bone. She got dizzy standing at the sink and quickly reached out to hold on to her husband.

James set the glass he was holding in the dish rack and grabbed Michelle gently by her waist and pulled her to him. "Baby, you don't look so good. What's happening to you?"

She could barely get her words out. "We're having an earthquake, James. Can't you feel it?"

In Chicago, Amaryllis's legs were giving out on her. She carefully leaned back against the elevator wall. Bridgette saw a horrified expression on her best friend's face.

"Amaryllis?"

"They lied to us, Bridgette. They lied to us."

Date of Birth: November 16th, 1984
Time of Birth: 10:20 a.m.
Birth Weight: 5lbs., 2oz.
Live Siblings: Price, Amaryllis Theresa-Fraternal Twin

Amaryllis screamed.

"Make it stop, James!"

In James's arms, Michelle was hysterical. He felt chill bumps on her arms as her voice rose. "Make it stop. Please, make it stop."

James had never seen Michelle behave in this manner. "Make what stop, baby? What are you talking about?"

Michelle screamed. "The house is shaking!"

James pulled Michelle's head against his chest and wrapped his arms around her tightly. "Peace be still in this house. In the name of Jesus. Satan, I rebuke you right now. God is the head of this house."

He began to rub Michelle's back and arms. "The blood of Jesus, the blood of Jesus. Peace, peace, peace, peace, peace, peace."

He felt Michelle's body go limp against him. Suddenly, the telephone on the kitchen wall rang. At the sound, Michelle jumped. It was the loudest ring she'd ever heard in her life. James didn't know whether to answer it or continue to shield his wife from whatever was attacking her. Each ring of the telephone screamed louder in her ears. She covered her ears and cried. "It's too loud. Make it stop, James. Please, make it stop."

James let go of his wife and quickly snatched the telephone off the wall. "Bradley residence."

He couldn't make out what the caller was saying. It sounded almost like his wife crying. "Hello? Who is this?"

James pressed his ear into the telephone. He heard more crying and the name "Michelle."

"Amaryllis, is that you?"

Only crying and yelling came through the telephone line. He held the telephone out for Michelle to take. "Mickey, it's Amaryllis. She's crying."

Michelle nervously took the telephone from him. "Sis?"

Because Amaryllis was hysterical, Michelle only made out, "birthday," "Veronica," and "twins."

"What? Amaryllis, you're not making sense, and you're scaring me. Calm down and tell me what happened."

James watched his wife's face turn from dark brown to winter white. He literally saw Michelle's eyes roll to the back of her head. Just as he was reaching out to her, Michelle dropped the cordless telephone and was on her way down with it. James wasn't fast enough. Michelle's face slammed into the kitchen floor.

Chapter 22

Half an hour after Amaryllis had called Michelle, Bridgette answered a soft knock on the door. "Charles, thank God you're here. I can't calm her down."

"Where is she?" he asked frantically.

Bridgette pointed toward the rear of the apartment. "She's lying across her bed."

On his way to Amaryllis's bedroom, Charles kissed Bridgette's cheek. "Thanks for calling me, Bridgette. I appreciate it."

Amaryllis's bedroom door was ajar. Charles poked his head in and saw her lying on the bed in a fetal position, rocking back and forth. He could also hear her moaning and crying. He gently pushed the door open wider and walked in.

Charles spoke softly to Amaryllis. "Hey, beautiful."

Amaryllis didn't acknowledge his presence. He sat on the bed next to her and rubbed her thigh. "Baby, I'm here. Tell me what I can do for you."

Amaryllis's eyes were red and puffy. Her long, beautiful hair was matted to her head. Her rose-colored satin pillowcases were stained with black mascara and eyeliner.

She looked at Charles sitting next to her. "What are you doing here, Charles? I don't want you to see me like this."

"Bridgette called me, and I rushed over."

"Did she tell you?"

"Yeah, baby, she did, and I'm sorry you're hurting."

Amaryllis turned her back to Charles. He saw her shoulders shaking and knew she was crying silently. Charles removed his shoes and lay down behind her and scooted his body next to hers. He pulled her close to him and wrapped his arms tightly around her. With the back of her head pressed against his chest, Amaryllis cried openly. Charles rocked her for twenty minutes until her sobbing turned into sniffles. Finally, she became quiet, and Charles felt her head press onto his bicep; then he knew she was asleep.

Bridgette came into Amaryllis's bedroom and stood by the bed. She saw Amaryllis lying peacefully in Charles's arms, snoring softly. "Thanks for coming, Charles. I'm glad you knew what to do."

"Well, you know she's my baby. Do me a favor, Bridgette. I don't want to move from this position. Can you come and press the power button on my cell phone? I don't want anything to disturb her."

Bridgette honored his request, then pulled the king-size comforter over them.

"I'm going to bed, Charles. Knock on my door if you need anything."

Charles fell asleep holding Amaryllis in a spoon position. In Las Vegas, Michelle had cried herself to sleep in James's arms. The two couples, thousands of miles away, slept in the exact same position until morning.

The next morning, James wrapped Michelle in a huge towel as she stepped from the shower. From so much crying, her eyes were almost swollen shut. He kissed his wife's cheek. "How are you feeling, baby? Are you hungry?"

"No. I don't want anything to eat. I gotta call my sister. She's the one I'm worried about."

James held Michelle by both hands. "I'm all for you calling Amaryllis, but allow me to make you breakfast first. You need your strength to deal with this, Mickey."

"Okay, honey. But don't make a huge breakfast, because I'm really not hungry."

"How about a bowl of oatmeal?"

"That's fine." Michelle thought for a moment. "Why aren't you at the precinct?"

James frowned at her. "Are you serious? Do you honestly think that I would leave you alone at a time like this? You've just insulted me, Michelle. You ought to know me better than that."

James had never called her 'Michelle' before. She knew he was angry. She went to him and hugged him. "Honey, I'm sorry."

"Mickey, let's not ever have this kind of discussion again. I will always, always be your covering. If you doubt that, then I'm not doing something right. There should never be a question in your mind what you mean to me or the lengths I will go to secure your safety and happiness."

"Baby, I don't question your love and commitment. It was a stupid thing for me to ask." She looked up at him with a slight smile. "Forgive me?"

James kissed her lips. "I love my Mickey Mouse."

Fresh out of the shower, Amaryllis walked into the kitchen and sat down at the table. She saw Charles was peeking in the cabinets. "Good morning, handsome."

Charles looked at her and smiled. "Good morning, sleepyhead. Are you hungry?"

"Uh-uh." Amaryllis massaged her temples. "Bridgette's gone already?"

"Yeah, and she said not to worry. She'll make up an excuse to tell your boss why you're missing work today."

"Speaking of work, why aren't you there?"

Charles turned from the cabinets to face her. "Amaryllis, I will not leave you alone at a time like this. I'm here for you for as long as you need me to be. Now, with that out of the way, what do you want for breakfast?"

"Charles, I don't want anything to eat. I'm worried about my sister. I need to call her."

He approached Amaryllis and pulled her up from her chair and held her hands.

"I encourage you to call your sister, but before you do, please eat something. You need your strength."

"I'm not hungry."

"Please, Amaryllis, for me. If I make you a bowl of oatmeal, will you eat it?"

She smiled at Charles. "If you mash a banana in it."

Just as Michelle was reaching for the telephone, it rang. "Hey, sis," she answered.

At the sound of Michelle's voice that sounded so much like her own, Amaryllis's eyes became teary. "How did you know it was me?"

"Caller ID, silly. How are you feeling? Did you get any sleep?"

Amaryllis's head was lying on Charles's lap. He soothed her as he raked her long tresses with his fingers. "Yeah, Charles is with me. He's been beside me all night. How about you? Did you get any sleep?"

Michelle was lying on the living room sofa with her legs stretched out across James's lap. She cooed into the telephone as he massaged her toes. "Yeah, I'm okay. I'm glad Charles is with you. I don't know what I'd do without my husband."

Charles ran the back of his hand across Amaryllis's cheek. She smiled up at him.

"Have you talked to Daddy, Michelle?"

"Nope. I really don't want to. Besides, he and Margaret are on a cruise. They won't be back until next week." Michelle unfolded a piece of paper she was holding. "I got my birth certificate that Daddy gave me. It states that I was born in Las Vegas on April eleventh, 1982 to Diana and Nicholas Price. It also states that I had no siblings. All these years, Daddy's been lying to me. He told me that my mother had a hard labor and died shortly after my birth at the hospital. He said she had hemorrhaged to death. And I remember growing up asking Daddy if I had any aunts, uncles, cousins, or grandparents. He told me that my mother was an only child whose parents had died in a car accident when she was a teenager. He said she didn't have any sisters or brothers.

And as far as any cousins, Daddy told me that he wasn't aware of any."

"Wow. This is crazy, Michelle. Wait a minute. If Veronica is your mother, then who is the lady in the pictures in your house that you thought was your deceased mother?"

Michelle looked across the living room at a photo inside a frame that sat on her mantel. "That's what I wanna know."

"Well, all I know is that Daddy needs to hurry his behind home because we need answers. And now that I think about it, Michelle, I had a copy of my birth certificate that Veronica gave me when I was living with Randall, but it got lost when I moved out. I know it stated that I was born in Baton Rouge on November sixteenth, 1984 to Nicholas and Veronica Price. The word 'twin' was nowhere on the certificate."

"Well, have you talked to Veronica?"

"Nope. And I'm not going to call her, because I don't wanna have to cuss her out. Besides, if Veronica has been lying all this time, why would she tell the truth now?"

Michelle let out a loud sigh. "Well, Daddy is on vacation, and you refuse to talk to Veronica, but we need some answers right now. So, what are we gonna do?"

"Maybe we should leave well enough alone, Michelle."

"Oh, heck, no. I wanna know who's the woman in these pictures that I have all over my house if she's not my mother."

"Well, what do you suggest we do, Michelle? I ain't calling Veronica."

After a long pause, Michelle said, "Let's go to Baton Rouge."

An hour later, Michelle phoned Amaryllis with her and James's flight information. "We land in Baton Rouge tomorrow morning at seven-fifteen."

"Okay, Michelle. I'll call you back with my information."

Amaryllis walked into her bedroom to retrieve her credit card. As she was walking back to the living room, she heard Charles talking on the telephone. "I'm not sure how long I'll be gone, Mike. You're my right-hand man; I trust that you'll keep everything in tact in my absence. You can reach me on my cell phone twenty-four seven."

Amaryllis came and sat next to him. "What are you doing?"

"Taking care of my responsibility."

"Charles, you can't miss work. I don't know how long we'll be down there."

Charles leaned back on the sofa and crossed his left leg over his right knee.

"What's my last name, Amaryllis?"

She frowned at him. "What?"

"What's my last name?"

"Walker," she answered.

"Where do I work?"

Amaryllis smiled because she knew where Charles was going with this interrogation.

"Walker Contracting," she answered.

"That means I'm the boss and I can do whatever I wanna do."

From his wallet, Charles withdrew his Visa gold card. "Put your card away and charge two first-class tickets on mine. I need to run by the company and finalize some things. I also need to go home to pack some clothes, then run a few errands. I'll be back as soon as I can."

Amaryllis called Michelle fifteen minutes later. "Charles and I will land in Baton Rouge at seven-forty tomorrow morning."

"You and Charles?"

"Yeah, girl. He insists on being my shadow. He refuses to leave my side. I ain't mad though, because I need him. He paid for us to fly first class."

Michelle was impressed. "Wow. The brotha is putting it out there like that, Amaryllis? He's dropping $500 dinners, buying expensive furs, and now he's flying you first class.

Plus, he's saved and sanctified. And you ain't even got to lay with him? Da . . . uh, darn. I can't wait to meet this jewel." Amaryllis laughed at Michelle's slip of the tongue. "Oh, yeah. You're my twin. I knew you had it in you."

Chapter 23

James and Michelle retrieved their luggage from baggage claim and walked to the arrivals section in United Airlines to sit and wait for Amaryllis and Charles's flight to come in.

Not far from where they sat, the flight information board listed all of the incoming and outgoing flight times. James searched and found their flight information. "According to the schedule, Mickey, their plane will land on time."

Michelle looked at her watch. "That gives us what, about twenty-five minutes?"

James sat down next to her. "Yep. You want me to get you a cup of coffee or something to eat?"

"No, honey. I'm too nervous to eat anything. Why are you always trying to feed me? Do you want a fat wife?"

"I feed you because you don't eat properly. You've been picky about the food you eat. And why do you always have to smell something before you eat it?"

"Certain things make me queasy, and I can't keep anything down lately."

James held her hand. "I heard you vomiting this morning, Mickey. Are you all right?"

"Yeah, I'm sure it's my nerves." Michelle frowned and placed her hand on her stomach. "Speaking of nerves, I gotta throw up again." She got up and practically ran toward the nearest restroom.

A half hour later, James saw Amaryllis and a man walking toward them. Michelle was asleep with her head rested on his shoulder. Amaryllis saw Michelle and placed her index finger on her lips, motioning for James to keep quiet. She gave Charles her carry-on, then stood in front of Michelle and tapped her shoulder. Michelle sleepily opened her eyes. She saw her sister and jumped up. "Hey, twin."

Amaryllis embraced Michelle and held her tight. "Hey, twin."

James stood up next to Michelle. "What's up, sis?"

Amaryllis kissed his cheek. "Hey, brother-in-law. I want you two to meet my guy, Charles." Amaryllis held Charles's hand. "Charles, this is my sister, Michelle, and her husband, James."

Charles shook James's hand. "God bless you, brother. It's a pleasure."

James tightened the grip. "It's nice to meet you too, man."

Charles looked at Michelle's face and was at a loss for words. Amaryllis saw the way he was staring and nudged him. "Charles?"

Charles blinked twice. "Huh? Oh, uh, I'm sorry. Please forgive me for what I'm about to ask, but I just gotta know. How could you have not known? Except for your skin complexions, you two are identical in every way."

James chuckled. "I guess their complexions threw me off." He recalled a time when his partner, Alexander Moore, had first met Amaryllis when she was visiting in Las Vegas. James and Alexander had stopped by Michelle's law firm to visit. Alexander had met Amaryllis for the first time when she was temping for Michelle's secretary, Chantal. James introduced Amaryllis to Alexander; then the two detectives proceeded to Michelle's office. Once they were inside, Alexander spoke to James, "Wow, Michelle and her sister can pass for twins. They are identical. A black beauty and a yellow beauty."

"We know we're alike in some ways but—" Amaryllis was saying before Charles cut her off.

"In some ways?" Charles looked from Amaryllis to Michelle, then from Michelle to Amaryllis. Their faces, hair, bodies, voices, and even their heights matched. "You are alike in every way."

Michelle looked at her sister. "Do you really think it's possible that we're twins?"

Amaryllis shrugged her shoulders. "That's what we're here to find out."

The two couples exited the airport and got into the waiting limousine that Charles had hired.

Michelle and James checked into suite #2304 of the Marriott, and Amaryllis and Charles shared suite #2305. After Michelle was settled in her room, she went across the hall and knocked on her sister's door. When Amaryllis opened the door, Michelle asked, "What's the plan?"

"I got Nana's address. I say we just go to her house."

Michelle got nervous. "Now? You wanna just show up on her doorstep without calling her first?"

Amaryllis pulled Michelle into the suite and closed the door. "Ain't that why we flew down here?"

"Yeah, but I don't wanna just drop in unannounced. That's not proper etiquette."

"Etiquette? Was it proper etiquette to withhold life-changing information from us?"

Michelle got dizzy and sat down on the king-size bed. "Where's Charles?"

"He went down to the lobby to get a map. Are you all right?"

Michelle fanned herself. "Yeah, it's hot in here, though. I got to be honest with you, Amaryllis. I am so nervous."

Amaryllis sat next to her. "Me too, but we're here now. We've come too far to turn around."

Charles opened the door and came into the suite. "I got directions from the front desk. They should take us directly to your grandmother's front door."

Michelle placed her hand over her mouth, got up, and ran to the bathroom. Charles stood looking at Amaryllis. "Was it something I said?"

An hour later, after showering and changing clothes, Amaryllis called across the hall. "James, are you and Michelle ready?"

"I'm ready, but I can't get Mickey up from the bathroom floor."

"What happened? Did she fall?"

"Nah, she's nervous. She's kneeling over the toilet puking her guts out."

"Open the door for me." Amaryllis hung up from James and walked across the hall. James let her in, and Amaryllis went to the bathroom door and opened it. Michelle was standing at the sink, brushing her teeth. Amaryllis stood next to Michelle and looked at her. "What's wrong with you, Michelle?"

"Girl, I don't know. I can't go through with this. I don't do well under pressure."

"You're an attorney."

"Yeah, but that's a different kind of pressure."

"How about you don't do well under pregnant?"

Michelle dropped her toothbrush into the sink. "Pregnant?"

"Yes, honey. You're pregnant."

Michelle looked toward the bathroom door. "Shh, lower your voice. And how do you know?"

"Because, I can feel it. For the past month and a half, my ankles have been swollen, certain scents make me sick to my stomach, and sometimes I'm moody as heck for no reason. I know I ain't pregnant, because I ain't doing nothing, so it must be you."

Michelle walked to the bathroom door and closed it. "I can't be pregnant because I don't have any symptoms."

Amaryllis looked at her sister. "Duh. You're throwing up. And I got all the other symptoms. When was your last period?"

Michelle lowered the toilet lid and sat down. "I don't know. I don't keep up with that stuff."

"What do you mean you 'don't keep up with that stuff'?"

"Just what I said. I know my period is coming when I start to cramp."

Amaryllis glanced at the ceiling. "Help us, Lord. Michelle, when was the last time you cramped?"

"Maybe around four months ago."

Amaryllis got excited and raised her voice. "You haven't had a period in that long?"

"Would you shut your big mouth before James hears you? I don't know when my last period was, okay? Maybe it was three months ago. I can't recall. I got a big case that I've been preparing for that's been eating up fourteen hours a day, every day, for months. I can't worry about anything else. If my period comes, it comes. If it doesn't, then it doesn't."

"Let me see your girls," Amaryllis demanded.

Michelle frowned at her. "For what?"

"I wanna see something. We're both in a double D cup. If your girls are bigger and fuller than mine, you're pregnant."

Michelle stood and unbuttoned her blouse. Amaryllis raised her own blouse. They stood next to each other facing the mirror and compared sizes.

"Michelle, do you see how you are fuller and rounder than I am?" Amaryllis asked. She pinched Michelle's left breast and showed Michelle her milky wet finger and thumb. "You know what that is, don't you? And if you're able to extract milk, you're probably in your second trimester. You better make an appointment to see your gynecologist when you get back to Vegas."

Michelle ran over to the toilet, vomited, and brushed her teeth again.

Chapter 24

The chauffer pulled up to the curb at 743 Woodland Street, Baton Rouge, Louisiana.

Amaryllis looked at Michelle. "You ready?"

Michelle's stomach was doing somersaults. She'd rather not face the unknown. "I've changed my mind. I don't wanna find out what happened to us. Let's just go back to the hotel."

Amaryllis moved next to her sister and hugged her. "You know we need answers. This is what we came all the way to Louisiana for."

Michelle looked at her husband with pity in her eyes. "Honey, please say a prayer before we go in."

After James's prayer, the two couples found themselves standing on the front porch. Charles had a tight grip on Amaryllis's hand. Because Michelle appeared to need much more moral support than Amaryllis, James held her tightly by the waist.

Amaryllis exhaled, rang the doorbell, and looked at her sister. "This is it, Michelle. There's no turning back now."

"I gotta throw up," Michelle said.

An overweight, gray-haired woman opened the door. She looked at the two couples in their faces, but she concentrated on the girls.

Amaryllis was the first to speak. "Hi, Nana."

Nana's left hand flew to her heart. "Oh my God. Oh, Jesus." She looked from Amaryllis to Michelle, then from Michelle to Amaryllis. "Oh, sweet Jesus. I can't believe you're here. Come in, come in."

Amaryllis stepped into the living room, and Charles followed. Michelle's feet were still firmly planted on the front porch. She didn't have the nerve to place one foot ahead of the other. James nudged her back to get her moving.

Amaryllis walked to her grandmother and embraced her. "It's good to see you, Nana."

Nana returned the hug. "You too, baby."

Amaryllis held her hand out for Michelle to grab. "Nana, this is my sister, Michelle."

Seeing Michelle for the first time caused tears to fall onto Nana's cheeks. She held her arms open for Michelle.

Michelle released Amaryllis's hand and slowly walked to Nana and hugged her. "It's nice to meet you, Nana."

Amaryllis motioned for James and Charles to come closer to where she, Michelle, and their grandmother stood. "Nana, I want you to meet James, Michelle's husband, and my guy, Charles."

James and Charles greeted Nana and kissed her on opposite cheeks.

Nana looked at them all as she sat in a rocker. "Sit down, please. Why didn't you tell me you were coming? I would've prepared a feast."

Amaryllis and Charles, along with Michelle and James, squeezed themselves on a sofa opposite of Nana. The four of them couldn't help but notice the décor of the living room. The dark brown wood paneling on the walls made the room dim and chilly. The drapes were drawn closed, and a crystal ball the size of a bowling ball sat in the middle of the cocktail table. It was surrounded by chickens' feet and rabbits' feet that were scattered across the table. There weren't any family portraits in Nana's living room; however, shelves were filled with books coated with dust. Charles noticed some of the titles of the books.

Feed 'Em And Keep 'Em, Make Her Love You, Five Sure Ways To Guarantee Yourself A Spouse, The Perfect Trick To Become A Perfect Treat, and *The Witches' Guide To Eternal Happiness,* were just a few titles that Charles was able to read through the thick dust.

James saw the door leading to Nana's dining room was made of iron prison bars. The door was ajar with a skeleton key dangling from the keyhole. He got Charles's attention and nodded toward the dining room door. Charles's eyes grew wide and looked at James with an expression that read, "What the heck?"

Amaryllis spoke. "Because this was sort of a spur-of-the-moment thing, Nana. Michelle and I came here for answers."

Nana eyed Amaryllis confused. "Answers?"

"When I asked you to send me my birth certificate, I received Michelle's instead."

Nana's face turned crimson red. "Oh, my goodness. I don't know how I could've made that mistake. I've always been so careful."

"What is there to be careful about?" Michelle asked, not sure if she really wanted to know the answer to her own question.

"About keeping your parents' secret," Nana confessed. "But I guess the secret is out now, since you're here."

Amaryllis scooted to the edge of her seat. "That's right, Nana. And we want you to tell us why we were raised to believe that Michelle was two years older, had a different mother, and a separate birthday."

"Have either of you asked your parents?"

"Amaryllis doesn't talk to her mother and our father is away, unreachable, on vacation. He told me that my mother had died in the hospital shortly after giving birth to me," Michelle informed her.

"Nana, we came here for answers, that, at the moment, only you can give. Don't turn us away," Amaryllis pleaded.

Nana looked at her granddaughters' faces. How could she deny them their right to know their history, their roots? "I don't know where to begin."

"At the beginning," Amaryllis replied.

So that she wouldn't miss one word out of Nana's mouth, Michelle scooted to the edge of the sofa like Amaryllis. "My birth certificate states that I was born in April, 1982. You can go back nine months prior and begin there."

Nana leaned back in her rocker, crossed her ankles, and exhaled. "Your father, Nicholas, came to Baton Rouge to attend a weeklong realtors' convention. One evening, he, along with a colleague, visited a bar. My daughter, Veronica, tended the bar. She fell for Nicholas the moment she saw him. According to Veronica, she and Nicholas became friendly with one another. The more drinks she served him, the friendlier he became. He invited her out for dinner the next evening, and she graciously accepted.

"Over dinner, Nicholas told Veronica that he lived in Chicago and made a lot of money selling houses. Money had always been Veronica's god."

"Ain't that the truth," Amaryllis stated. She remembered the times when her own mother sent her out with men for money and pocketed half of the price. Amaryllis distinctly remembered Veronica's words. 'It's my genes that's got you looking as pretty as you are. Now go on and make that money because closed legs don't get fed.'

"After dinner with Nicholas, Veronica was smitten," Nana continued. "She wanted to make him fall in love with her. But Nicholas would only be in town for two more days, so we had to work fast."

"We?" Michelle asked.

Nana nodded her head. "Veronica asked me to help her, and I did."

"How did you help her, Nana?" Amaryllis asked.

"I put a root on Nicholas."

Michelle's jaw dropped. James and Charles looked at each other and frowned at what Nana had just said.

"A root?" Michelle asked.

"What's a root?" Charles asked Nana. Even though he was there as a silent partner, to only support Amaryllis, he was drawn into the conversation. He blurted out the question without thinking.

Nana shifted in her recliner. "A root is a spell, black magic, voodoo, black art, hocus-pocus, sorcery; it's all the same."

"But that's witchcraft," James volunteered.

Nana looked at him. "It's what I do, honey. Creole women have been practicing witchcraft for generations. My great-grandmother was a witch, my grandmother was a witch, and my mother was a witch. I'm a witch. My daughter, Veronica, is a witch." Nana looked at both Amaryllis and Michelle. "You two are witches too. We're all witches. Any offspring from this bloodline will be warlocks and witches as well."

Michelle vomited on the floor directly in front of her grandmother. She hadn't yet shared with James that she may be pregnant.

Chapter 25

After James cleaned up the mess Michelle had made, he brought her a glass of water and sat beside her again. Michelle's stomach was having a tumultuous affair. She felt the dark walls of the living room closing in on her. She couldn't get enough air into her lungs.

Amaryllis, on the other hand, wasn't as surprised by Nana's revelation. Veronica had taught her long ago how to get a man under her spell. Amaryllis's ex-boyfriends, Randall Loomis and Tyrone Caridine, were so in love with her and did anything she asked of them.

It wasn't only Amaryllis's beauty that had captured their hearts. It was also the specially prepared home cooked meals she fed them. Unbeknownst to Michelle, Nana had been sending Amaryllis secret recipes for years.

Michelle was in shock. Amaryllis's mother, Veronica, was also her mother. The same woman who had used her daughter's body as a way to earn money was also her mother. The woman, whom Michelle had never met, whom she had heard horror stories about, was her mother. The woman who had raised Amaryllis to be promiscuous, devious, a husband stealer, and a professional gold digger, was her mother as well.

Michelle couldn't comprehend or understand or even accept the fact that she too had been born from Veronica's womb. Why had their father lied? What was the big deal? Nicholas had always told Michelle that she and Amaryllis had two different mothers, and that she was two years older than Amaryllis.

Michelle chugged down the entire glass of water, then composed herself on the sofa between James and Amaryllis. "Um, Nana, please help us to understand this. I mean, why were we separated? Why weren't we told the truth? Why all the lies?"

"Because it was what your parents wanted. They thought it was the best thing to do under the circumstances."

"What circumstances, Nana?" Amaryllis asked.

Nana uncrossed her ankles, then crossed them again. "I really wish you'd both ask your parents about this. It's not my place to tell you. If they had wanted you to know, you would have been told long ago."

Michelle massaged her throbbing temples. "It's not your place to tell us, Nana? Was it your place to help your daughter trap our father?"

"We didn't trap Nicholas."

"That's exactly what you did, Nana," Amaryllis stated. "You put something in his food. I know how it's done. You and Veronica taught me well."

Michelle stopped massaging her temples and looked at her sister. "What?"

Amaryllis didn't respond to Michelle's question. She looked down at the floor. She felt ashamed. She was ashamed at how she reluctantly allowed her mother and grandmother to convince her that the only way to get a man to fall in love was to put a root on him.

Amaryllis was only sixteen years old when she cast her first Venus love spell. She had a crush on seventeen-year-old Timothy Mason, a senior and the captain of the football team. Often, Amaryllis would stay after school to watch Timothy practice with his teammates. One evening after practice, she got the nerve to approach him. She waited outside of the locker room for him to make his exit. As soon as she saw him, she walked up to him. "Hi."

Timothy was engrossed in a conversation with a teammate and didn't notice her or even hear her speak to him. He walked right past her.

She walked behind him and tapped him on the shoulder. "Hi, Tim."

He stopped walking and looked at her. "Do I know you?"

Amaryllis smiled and cocked her head to the side in a seductive way, just like her mother had taught her to do. "Do you want to know me?"

Timothy chuckled and looked at his teammate standing to the right of him. The teammate shrugged his shoulders. Timothy looked at her and said, "I don't think so." The two boys walked away and left her standing outside of the locker room by herself.

When Amaryllis arrived home from school, she told Veronica about Timothy and how he had left her standing without a second look. Veronica instructed Amaryllis to take a bath.

"Why?" Amaryllis couldn't understand why she needed to bathe when she had just gotten home from school.

"Do you want the boy to like you or not? Just do what I say and don't ask me any questions!" Veronica scolded.

After her bath, Amaryllis walked into her bedroom and saw the curtains drawn and her mother waiting on her. "Take that towel off."

Amaryllis dropped the towel to the floor and stood nude in front of her mother.

Veronica, dressed in a long black robe with a hood pulled over her hair, grabbed Amaryllis by her hand and led her to stand in front of the full-length mirror.

From the pocket of her robe, Veronica pulled out a clear bottle containing a yellowish liquid. She opened the bottle and poured the liquid in her hand then proceeded to massage the liquid into Amaryllis's skin.

To Amaryllis, it looked like Crisco Oil. "What's this stuff you're putting on me?"

"Ylang Ylang oil. It's perfume."

After applying the perfumed oil over her daughter's entire body, Veronica spread a white sheet on the floor in front of the mirror and told Amaryllis to sit on it and fold her legs into a pretzel.

Once seated, Amaryllis saw Veronica place a red cloth in the shape of a heart, a red candle, and one Venus incense stick, all in the shape of a half circle, in front of her. Veronica lit the red candle and incense stick, then gave Amaryllis seven stick pins.

"Now, pick up the red heart and kiss it seven times," Veronica instructed.

Amaryllis picked up the red cloth and kissed it seven times. "Now what?"

Veronica laid a piece of paper with words on it on top of Amaryllis left thigh, near the candle. "Lay all but one pin on the floor."

Amaryllis did as she was told.

"Read the words on the paper."

Amaryllis proceeded to read. "I call thee, beloved one, to love me more than anyone. Seven times I pierce thy heart, today, the magic of Venus starts. I bind thy heart and soul to me; as I do will, so let it be. Timothy Mason, come to me. Timothy Mason come to me."

Veronica removed the hood from her head. "Now burn the end of the pin in the flame for five seconds and stab the red heart."

Amaryllis followed the instructions, then looked at her mother. "Now what?"

"Pick up another pin, say the chant, and stab the heart six more times."

At midnight, unbeknownst to Amaryllis, Timothy Mason stood outside of her bedroom window glaring up at the full moon.

The next morning at school, Timothy saw Amaryllis walking to her first-period class. He hurried over to her and met her just as she was entering the classroom. When she saw him, she smiled. Timothy was drawn to her scent. He sniffed her neck like he was a bloodhound on the trail of a serial killer. "I wanna know you."

That day after school was when Amaryllis had her first sexual encounter.

Michelle snapped Amaryllis from the thought of her past. "What is Nana talking about, Amaryllis? What did she and Veronica teach you?"

What was Amaryllis to do? She was saved now. God had given her a new life and a new start. Why was her past haunting her? Michelle was right. They should have never come to Baton Rouge searching for answers. All of Amaryllis's skeletons were about to tumble out of the closet. She sat on the sofa next to Charles with tears filling her eyes. "They taught me how to make a man fall in love with me."

Michelle's eyes grew wide. "Oh my God. Amaryllis, what have you done?"

Tears spilled onto Amaryllis's cheeks. "I don't want you to judge me. I am so sorry."

"There's nothing to be sorry about. You did what had to be done," Nana said.

Michelle couldn't believe her ears. "Of course she has something to be sorry about, Nana. Amaryllis deceived men."

"What she did was take control of her own destiny," Nana reasoned.

"By poisoning the minds of men and manipulating them? Nana, you can't possibly think that trickery is good," Michelle countered.

As James sat and listened to Michelle go back and forth with her grandmother, his mind wandered back to a night when Amaryllis was living with Michelle in Las Vegas. James had called Michelle's home after work, and Amaryllis answered. She informed James that Michelle was working late but offered to make him a home cooked meal.

When James arrived at Michelle's house, Amaryllis was dressed in lingerie and had come on strongly to him. He remembered that night like it had just happened yesterday.

When Amaryllis opened the door, James looked at her from head to toe. He had to blink his eyes a few times to make sure he was seeing what he thought he was seeing.

The pink chiffon teddy Amaryllis wore hugged her every curve. It left nothing for his imagination. He stood in the doorway at a loss for words. He was stunned and couldn't move. Amaryllis reached for his hand and tried to pull him inside, but James resisted. He quickly withdrew his hand from hers and remained standing in the doorway.

"You're just in time, James. Dinner is ready. I hope you're hungry," Amaryllis said to him.

James had started to sweat. He'd never been in this situation before, and he didn't know what to do. He asked Amaryllis why she was dressed like that.

"What? This? This is something I just threw on," James remembered her saying, then she turned around to give him a view of her backside.

He asked her where Michelle was, and she reminded him that Michelle was still in court.

James refused to step one foot in Michelle's home. He knew that Amaryllis was trying to set him up. He told her that he didn't think that it was a good idea for him to come inside because of the way she was dressed.

"What do you mean?" Amaryllis asked James.

"The way you're dressed, I don't think Mickey would appreciate it."

Amaryllis told him that the evening was about him and her.

James frowned. "What are you talking about? There is no you and me."

After turning her advances down, he left Michelle's doorway, got in his car, and drove straight to his pastor's house for counsel.

As James thought back on that night, he wondered if Amaryllis planned to put a root on him with the meal she had prepared.

"I'm not proud of what I've done, Michelle," Amaryllis stated. "I've been using witchcraft for years. Veronica helped me cast my first spell in high school. And since then, Nana had been sending me secret recipes."

"Was I one of your victims?" Charles couldn't help himself from asking. He had to know.

Amaryllis covered her face and cried openly. "Oh, Charles, I'm so sorry."

What was he to do? Should he walk out on her and leave her alone with her issues, or should he stay and deal with the bomb that she had dropped on him? Charles remembered a time when he was so in love with her that she could do no wrong. The sun rose and set at her command. Now he knew that she had full control of his heart.

They were in their early twenties when they met. Amaryllis had invited Charles to Veronica's house for dinner. By the time he left that evening, Charles was smitten. The more she cooked for him, the more Charles was in love.

Knowing what Amaryllis had done to him, Charles had every right to leave her to her demons. Instead, he pulled her into his arms. "It's okay. It's in the past." The person Amaryllis was when they were in their twenties was not the woman she was now. She had turned her life around, and because of her willingness to serve God, Charles had also changed his ugly ways.

Amaryllis hugged him and blew her nose. "Nana, please tell us why we were separated."

Nana leaned back in her rocker and crossed her ankles. "Your father insisted that Veronica fly back to Chicago with him. It wasn't three months when she had called to announce that she was pregnant with twins. Veronica was a gambler, and she loved going to the riverboat. The commission your father earned selling houses funded her trips to the blackjack tables and slot machines."

So that's where I got my gambling habit from, Amaryllis thought. She was addicted to the Black Jack table when she was living with Randall. There were times when she had gambled with Randall's tithe money and lost it all. And when Randall had cut her allowance off, Darryl stepped in and funded her habit. But it wasn't for free.

Nana continued with her story. "The finances had gotten so bad that Nicholas and Veronica were about to lose their home. Trusting Veronica to pay the mortgage was a mistake Nicholas had made. When the first foreclosure notice came to the house, Nicholas was livid. Veronica was eight and a half months pregnant by then and turned to other sources to help make ends meet."

"What other sources?" Michelle asked.

"Drugs. She bought marijuana on the street and sold it for profit. One day, in the wee hours of the morning, a dealer and his goons kicked in their front door and put a gun to Nicholas's head and demanded to be paid what Veronica owed them. After pleading for his life and promising to make good on the debt with his next commission check, they left. Two weeks later, Nicholas paid the debt and that same day, on the sixteenth of November, 1984, the two of you were born. Exactly one week later, Nicholas filed for divorced and full custody. The judge ruled that each parent would get custody of one girl. It was Veronica's decision to keep the light-skinned one. Nicholas packed up the dark-skinned twin and moved to Las Vegas."

Nana looked at Michelle. "I never knew why Nicholas told you that you had a different birth date or made you believe that you were two years older than your sister. And I don't know who the woman in the pictures assumed to be your mother is. Those answers you'll have to get from your parents."

Chapter 26

A week later, in Las Vegas, Michelle hung up the telephone from her father. She had asked Nicholas to come over because she needed to talk to him about something important. Since Amaryllis was going on vacation soon, she couldn't take anymore time off from work. She couldn't be in Las Vegas when Michelle confronted their father.

As soon as Nicholas sat at Michelle's kitchen table, she threw both her fake birth certificate that he'd given her and the authentic one at him. The twins knew that their true birthplace was Chicago, Illinois. Michelle also threw a faxed copy of Amaryllis's birth certificate on the table. Amaryllis had gone to the Daley Center to get it as soon as she arrived home.

"Explain," Michelle said to her father.

Nicholas read the authentic certificate first, then looked up at Michelle. "Where did you get this?"

"Explain it," Michelle ordered.

Nicholas leaned back in the chair and ran his fingers through his hair. "I did what I had to do."

"Why did you lie to us all these years?"

"I did what I had to do," he repeated. His voice was calm and relaxed.

Michelle looked at her father. "Is that gonna be your answer for everything? You did what you had to do? Who is the woman in all of those pictures? The woman who you told me was my mother, who is she?"

Nicholas got up from the table, grabbed his keys, and walked past Michelle.

"Daddy, where are you going? Answer me! I know that Veronica is my mother. Who is the woman in the pictures?" Michelle was losing all hope of ever knowing the full truth why she and Amaryllis were separated.

Nicholas stepped back to Michelle and kissed her forehead softly. When he pulled away, Michelle saw tears in his eyes. "Let it go. I did what I had to do." His voice was slightly above a whisper.

When he walked out of Michelle's front door, she knew that since Amaryllis absolutely refused to question Veronica and since she herself didn't succeed when she asked their father about their past, the truth would never be known.

But Nicholas wasn't the only one keeping secrets. Michelle and Amaryllis promised to never tell their father how he had been tricked by the enemy. Both girls knew that by keeping that secret from him, they were no better than he and Veronica were. Michelle knew her father, and she also knew that it would completely destroy him if he found out just how Veronica and their grandmother had deceived him. It was for the best that he didn't know. Just like Nicholas didn't indulge Michelle about her past, Michelle wanted to spare him the heartache and pain of his past as well. She understood that some things were better left unknown.

"So, how did it go with Daddy?" Amaryllis asked Michelle when she had called her.

Michelle exhaled. "It didn't go. He wouldn't admit to or tell me anything."

"Well, did he at least reveal who the woman in your photos is?"

"Nope. He wouldn't go there either. All Daddy said was that he did what he had to do and for me to leave it alone."

"Leave it alone?" Amaryllis shrieked. "He couldn't have been serious, Michelle."

Michelle reflected back to his somber expression. "He was very serious."

"Daddy owes us the truth."

"And so does Veronica, but I don't see you beating down her front door, asking questions."

Amaryllis became silent. She hadn't spoken with Veronica since long before she'd gotten saved. Amaryllis was working on her feelings toward her mother but a lot of damage had been done. Veronica pimped her daughter's body. She abused Amaryllis over and over again. Maybe one day Amaryllis would call Veronica, but not today. Her wounds were still too fresh. She needed more time to heal.

"I'm sorry, sis," Michelle said. "That was a low blow. I know you don't talk to her. But if we can't get anything out of Daddy, maybe you should—"

"Heck, no. That ain't even an option. After all the hell she put me through?"

"I'm just saying Veronica may be our only source."

"Humph, then I guess we'll never know what happened to us."

"And you're okay with that, Amaryllis?"

"Are you okay with it, Michelle?"

"I guess we really don't have a choice, do we?"

"Well, at least we know what our true birth date is," Amaryllis said.

"Yep, and I'm happy to know that I've gained two extra years on my life. Thirty-five seemed too old to become a mother. I can deal with giving birth at thirty-three."

"I hear you, gir—" Amaryllis almost choked. "What did you say, Michelle? Are you pregnant for real?"

Michelle smiled into the telephone. "Yep, it's been confirmed. And you were right. I'm beginning my second trimester."

Amaryllis was happy. "Oh, wow, sis. That's great news. Congratulations. I'm so happy for you."

"Speaking of happy. Happy birthday, sis."

Amaryllis paused. "Oh, my goodness. With so much going on, I completely forgot what day it was. Well, happy birthday to you too, Michelle."

"This is so weird."

"I know. It's gonna take some getting used to. But we'll be okay. We got each other. We got our men. And it won't be long before we have us a little diva."

"Or a little divo," Michelle said.

"I'm rooting for a girl."

"Oh my God. Please don't say the word 'root' when referring to my baby."

Amaryllis understood exactly what Michelle meant. Nana's words about any offspring being born into their family was still fresh in both their minds. "Sorry, sis."

"Let's change the subject," Michelle suggested. "When do you and Bridgette leave for Jamaica?"

"Tonight and not a moment too soon. I am ready to get away."

"Well, have fun but not too much fun. I know what happens in Jamaica."

Amaryllis chuckled. "And whatever happens there will stay there."

"Don't forget how far you've come, Amaryllis. You've been through a lot to get to where you are now. Don't throw that away."

Amaryllis was looking forward to going to Jamaica, but there was no way she was going to allow anything to come between her and God. Besides, she's got a man, a great man that loves her in spite of all of her faults and imperfections. Amaryllis would be a fool to throw that away. "Don't worry, Michelle. I packed my Bible. I won't mess up."

Michelle was impressed. "I am so proud of you, girl."

Amaryllis was no longer at a crossroads. She knew exactly which road to take toward her destiny. She smiled. "I'm proud of me too."

Chapter 27

Sixteen Years Later

After ordering her daughter upstairs to her room, Michelle heard the door slam. "Don't slam any doors in this house, young lady," Michelle yelled. "Do you hear me, Amaris Denise Bradley?"

It was over one hundred degrees in Las Vegas, and Michelle was fit to be tied. Though she was standing in her air-conditioned living room, she felt as though she were standing on her front porch. She just couldn't believe that her sixteen-year-old daughter had ditched school again.

Two hours ago when Michelle's secretary, Chantal, announced that Las Vegas North High School was waiting on line three, Michelle wondered what her daughter had done this time. It had become the norm that either Michelle or her husband, James, would receive a call from the school once a week. Either Amaris had gotten into a fight, cursed a teacher, or had played hooky.

The call today was to inform Michelle that Amaris hadn't reported to her first- or second-period classes, and Michelle knew just where to find her daughter. When she drove up to the house where Amaris's eighteen-year-old forbidden boyfriend, known as Slash, resided, Michelle saw them sitting on the front porch. As soon as Amaris saw her mother's late model black BMW, she tossed the cigarette she'd been smoking into the bushes.

Michelle pulled her car over to the curb and rolled down her passenger-side window. "Get your behind in this car, right now!" she yelled.

She watched as Amaris stood from the porch and made her way to the car.

"How you doin', Mrs. Bradley?" Slash greeted her.

He was taunting Michelle. Both Michelle and James had instructed Amaris to stay away from Slash. He was not permitted to call their home or Amaris's cellular telephone.

Amaris was ordered to not interact with him at all. Last week, when James caught Amaris communicating with Slash on her computer, it had been immediately removed from her bedroom. From then on, if Amaris needed to use a computer to help with her homework, she was to use the desktop in the family room where she could be monitored.

Michelle ignored Slash and focused on her daughter's face and attire. When Michelle dropped Amaris off outside of the school that morning, she was wearing black cotton Capri pants and a pink T-shirt. Only lip gloss was on her lips. Between then and now, Amaris had changed into a thigh-high denim miniskirt and a tank top. Her face had been decorated with black eyeliner, ruby-red lipstick and eye shadow. Michelle also noticed that Amaris was braless.

She started in on her daughter as soon as she opened the passenger door to get in. "What the heck are you wearing? Are you wearing makeup? Where did you get that outfit, and why aren't you wearing a bra, Amaris?" Michelle regretted that Amaris had already been wearing a C cup since she was just thirteen years old. "You know that your boobs are too big to go braless," Michelle fussed.

After tossing her backpack into the backseat, Amaris got in the car and slammed the door shut. She then turned her entire upper torso toward her mother. "Can I please buckle my seat belt before you flood my eardrum with all of that yin yang?"

If Michelle didn't think she'd go to jail, she would have wrapped Amaris's seat belt around her neck and strangled her with it. "Who in the heck do you think you're talking to?"

The defiant teen glanced in the backseat, then connected her eyes with her mother's. She didn't say a word, but Michelle knew that her smart-aleck daughter's gesture was asking, "Do you see anyone else in this car?"

Though she hadn't spoken the words out loud, Michelle wanted to smack her in the mouth regardless. She put the gear in drive and pulled away from the curb, but she wasn't letting Amaris off the hook about her clothes. "Where are the pants and T-shirt that you wore to school this morning?"

Amaris smacked her lips before she spoke. "In my backpack."

"You know what, little girl? I suggest you lose that attitude because it's not doing you any good right now. And didn't your father and I forbid you to see that boy?"

Amaris smacked her lips again. "Forbid?"

The smacking of the lips infuriated Michelle. She desperately wanted to pull the car over and go one on one with her rebellious daughter. "You heard what I said. I didn't stutter. Yes, you were forbidden to see Slash. You know that you aren't suppose to speak with him or see him. And I watched you enter the school doors this morning. What did you do? Wait until I drove away before you walked out?"

"Something like that," Amaris answered while picking at her newly coated acrylic fingernails.

Michelle inhaled the smell of nicotine. "Have you been smoking?"

"Maybe."

Right then and there, Michelle decided that it would be best if she didn't continue the conversation with her daughter in the car. The temptation of going upside the disrespectful girl's head was too great. Amaris's nonchalant attitude was pushing Michelle over the edge. The wise thing to do would be to wait until they got home. Michelle thought that being behind closed doors where there were no witnesses would be the best way to deal with her hot-to-trot daughter.

As she drove home in silence, she spoke to the Lord. *Father, I was a virgin until marriage. I've served You all of my life and stayed true to You. I've never given Daddy any trouble whatsoever. I was an honor student and graduated at the top of my class. I'm a successful lawyer, and I pay my tithes and offerings faithfully, Lord. What did I do to deserve a replica of my sister?*

Michelle and James were ecstatic when Amaris was born. Amaryllis and Charles, who eventually married, had flown from Chicago to Las Vegas for the birth of Amaryllis's niece. They were sitting in the waiting area when James came and told

Amaryllis that her niece had been born and she could go see her. When Amaryllis walked into Michelle's delivery room, the first thing she said was, "Oh my God. She's a mini me, Michelle."

The seven-pound three-ounce baby girl was light skinned with a head full of black curly hair. She had inherited her aunt's color, pinched nose, and full lips. Both Michelle and James were dark skinned, and Michelle didn't understand where her baby had gotten her high yellow skin from until her sister had walked into the delivery room. It wasn't until Amaryllis said those words that she realized that she had just given birth to another Amaryllis.

When their father, Nicholas, walked into the delivery room and saw his granddaughter for the first time, he said, "That's Amaryllis all over again."

For months prior to the delivery, Michelle and James had disagreed on what name to give their baby girl. Even on the day of her birth they still hadn't come to an agreement. Grateful that Amaryllis had come from Chicago for the birth of her niece, Michelle and James had allowed her to name their daughter.

Amaryllis sat in a chair next to Michelle's bed and held her niece and thought about a fitting name.

"All I ask is that you don't name her anything freakish like Margarita, Alize', or anything pertaining to liquor," James said.

"And don't give her any of your ghetto friends' names like Sharylonda, TyQuandra, Bodrene, or Saturn," Nicholas added.

"Oh, God. Please don't name her anything like that," James begged.

"I agree with Daddy and James. Don't give her any name that'll be too hard for the world to pronounce or spell," Michelle added.

"Like mine?" Amaryllis asked them all.

James laughed. "Yes, like yours. Haven't you ever noticed that I always call you, 'Sis'? That's because I can't pronounce your name correctly."

Amaryllis looked down into her niece's sweet, little face. "You're a mini me. I shall call you, Amaris."

Amaryllis looked at James's face, then Michelle's face, and then her father's face.

They didn't say a word, but they all looked at each other, then back at her.

"Her name is Amaris Denise Bradley," Amaryllis stated loudly.

"I like it," Nicholas said.

Michelle smiled. "It's cute. Thanks for giving her my middle name."

Amaryllis looked at her brother-in-law. "Well, Papa?"

James caressed his beard. "Amaris Denise Bradley, huh?" He contemplated for a long ten seconds. "I guess I can live with that."

Michelle and James had no clue that when Amaryllis had said that their baby girl was a mini version of herself that Amaryllis was speaking prophetically. In the years to come, Amaris would take them on a journey. A journey that her aunt Amaryllis had taken. A journey of promiscuity, deception, lies, secrets, and plenty of heartache. The name "Amaris" was indeed short for "Amaryllis."

Michelle stood in her living room and thought back sixteen years prior to when their grandmother in Baton Rouge had informed her that any offspring born to their family would be witches and warlocks. Michelle often wondered if it had been a mistake allowing Amaryllis to name her daughter after her.

If Amaris was indeed cursed, Michelle vowed to break it by any means necessary. Either she'd break the generational curse, or she'd break Amaris's behind.

Loud rap music had begun to play from the upstairs bedroom, and Michelle was on her way up the stairs to silence the noise when her cellular phone rang. She took her phone out of her purse and saw James's cellular number on the caller identification. So, instead, she plopped down on the sofa, then answered her husband's call. "Hi, honey."

Michelle wasn't chipper like she normally was whenever she answered his call and, James knew it.

"Uh-oh" was all he said.

"Uh-oh is right. We got problems."

"I called the law office, and Chantal told me that you had gone to Amaris's school. So, what did our lovely junior in high school do this time? No, wait! Don't tell me. Let me guess. She got into another fight?"

Michelle ran her hands through her hair. "Nope."

"Did she disrespect one of her teachers again?"

The music coming from upstairs made it difficult for Michelle to hear James clearly. "Hold on a minute, honey." Michelle yelled toward the stairs. "Amaris, turn that doggone music off, right now!" She brought the telephone back to her ear. "I'm getting ready to go to jail, James. I'm going to kill her."

"What did she do, Mickey?"

"She ditched school again. I found her sitting on Slash's front porch."

"What?"

"And I don't even wanna tell you what she was wearing. She may as well have been naked. And, James, she wasn't wearing a bra."

Years before, James had lost his mind when Michelle informed him that their eight-year-old daughter was ready for a training bra.

"She's only in the third-grade, Mickey."

"I know that, James. But have you taken a good look at your daughter lately? We gotta face it. Her breasts are developing fast, and we can't let her continue to walk around without some type of support."

James had begged Michelle to wait awhile longer before she took their daughter bra shopping. Buying a bra told him that his daughter was becoming a woman, and that was a fact he didn't want to accept. But when Amaris had walked into the kitchen the next morning wearing a thin T-shirt, James saw that her breasts were standing at attention.

"Are you cold?" he asked her.

Amaris looked at her father with a weird expression on her face. "No. Why did you ask me that?"

He looked at her breasts again. It was indeed time for a bra. He told Michelle to make sure to buy padded bras.

James, a homicide detective, was in Milwaukee, Wisconsin, on business. "I'm coming home, Mickey."

"James, you can't come home. I can handle our daughter just fine."

"I'm sorry I can't be there to help you with this."

Michelle ran her hands through her hair again and exhaled. "I just gotta do what I gotta do, honey."

Those words worried James. He had to constantly play referee between his daughter and his wife. If it weren't for him, Michelle would have indeed been locked up a long time ago. "What does that mean, Mickey?"

"That means that by the time you get back home, I'll be incarcerated and your daughter will be six feet under."

Michelle ended her call with James and marched up the steps to her daughter's room. Amaris was lying on her bed with her hands extended behind her head. Michelle walked over and sat next to her.

"What's going on with you, Amaris?"

Amaris looked at her mother but didn't offer a response.

Michelle looked at her daughter's face. In spite of the makeup, Amaris was very beautiful with soft features. It worried Michelle that she was seeking validity from boys when she didn't have to. Both she and James often told her that she was a beautiful girl.

"Why can't you see that Slash is no good for you? He didn't graduate from high school, he doesn't have a job, and he has no future. Why would you wanna throw your life away for a bum? He's not worth it, sweetheart."

Amaris turned to stare at the wall.

"Don't you want a respectable boyfriend?" Michelle continued. "Don't you want a boy that sets goals and strives to achieve those goals?"

Still no response from Amaris, so Michelle tried another approach. "Tell me what you like about Slash. Help me to understand your attraction to him."

Amaris sat up and swung her legs around to place her feet on the floor. "Slash is fun. He's just cool to hang around with. You and Daddy won't even give him a chance to prove himself because the first time you saw me talking to him at school, you didn't like his appearance."

What Amaris had said was true. The first time Michelle saw Slash, she had driven up to the front of the high school to pick up Amaris. Michelle saw her daughter hanging on to every word that the boy was saying to her. He wore his hair in French braids. He had earrings in both ears. His jeans were sagging so that everyone could see his briefs. Tattoos covered his entire neck area, and a cigarette dangled from his lips. When Michelle honked her horn, Amaris grabbed him by the hand and proceeded toward the car.

Amaris opened the passenger door and asked Michelle a question. "Ma, can you give my friend a ride home?"

Michelle examined the boy up close. His braids were long overdue to be redone, his eyes were glazed, and fresh wounds on his arms were visible. To Michelle, the wounds looked like cuts.

"Does your friend have a name?" Michelle asked Amaris but kept her focus on the boy.

"His name is Slash."

Michelle looked at Slash from his overgrown hair to his feet. "Is that your birth name, young man?"

"Nah, it ain't the name my moms gave me, know what I'm sayin'? It's a name I picked up from around the way, know what I'm sayin'?"

When Slash opened his mouth to speak, Michelle saw nothing but gold. "Uh, no, I really don't know what you're saying. Are you a student here?"

"Nah, I gave that up a long time ago, know what I'm sayin'? I couldn't get with the whole school thing, you know what I'm sayin'?"

Michelle looked at Amaris. "Get in the car."

Slash attempted to open the passenger rear door, but Michelle stopped him. "Uh, not you."

She looked at Amaris again. "I was talking to you."

"Well, can we give Slash a ri—" Amaris started.

"No, we can not!" Michelle answered sternly.

Amaris stared at her mother in disbelief. "Why? He doesn't live far."

Michelle became upset that her daughter wouldn't obey and do what she'd been told. "Because I said so, that's why. Now get your behind in this car. I'm not gonna say it again, Amaris."

Amaris exhaled loudly and turned to Slash. "I'll catch up with you later, Slash."

"It's all good, cutie. You know where I'll be, you know what I'm sayin'?"

Finally, Amaris got in the car and looked at Michelle.

"Thanks for embarrassing me, Mother. That was rude. I don't know if I can face Slash again."

"Well, that won't even be a problem because you will not see him again."

"Oh, so now you're gonna pick my friends for me?"

"Look into my eyes, Amaris," Michelle ordered. She waited until her daughter met her eyeball for eyeball before she spoke. "He's not a student here, therefore, he shouldn't be hanging around. He's a lowlife, a bum, a degenerate, and you are not permitted to talk to him ever again. Is that understood?"

"So, uh, let me get this straight. Just because Slash dropped out of school and has tattoos and wears baggy pants, he's a lowlife? Oh, that's classy, Mother. You're judging Slash before you even get to know him."

"What makes him a lowlife is going by the name of Slash with cuts on his arms to complement the name. And he's a school dropout that looks like he hasn't had a bath in months. You are not to see him again, and that's all I have to say about it."

"You never gave him a chance," Amaris whined.

"Because he won't give himself a chance. He's throwing his life away, and I refuse to let you go down his path."

"Whatever, Ma."

And "whatever" was the attitude Amaris still seemed to have today.

Michelle stood up from the bed. "Wash that makeup off your face, take that skirt off, and put on some decent clothes."

"But I like this skirt."

Michelle's eyes grew wide. The disrespect had to stop. "I don't give a rat's behind what you like. I didn't buy that skirt for you. It's too short. Who gave it to you?"

"A friend."

Michelle placed her hands on her hips. "What friend, Amaris?"

Amaris exhaled and looked at her mother. "Just a friend. Dang."

Michelle closed her eyes and prayed. With every breath she took, her nostrils swelled. "Take . . . it . . . off!"

"Okaaaaay. Dang," Amaris stated but didn't remove the skirt. She stood still looking at Michelle. "Can I have some privacy?"

Michelle took two steps closer to her daughter and folded her arms across her chest. "Not in my house. Take the skirt off—Now!" she ordered.

Amaris unbuttoned the skirt and slowly slipped it down her thighs. That's when Michelle let out a loud scream.

Chapter 28

Forty-five minutes later, Michelle sat next to Amaris as her gynecologist examined her daughter. When the exam was completed, Amaris was asked to get dressed and wait in the lobby while the doctor spoke privately to Michelle.

"She hasn't been touched," Michelle's doctor confirmed.

Michelle released a sigh of relief. "Thank God. There's still time then."

"Time for what?" the doctor asked.

"I want you to write her a prescription for birth control pills." The doctor saw Michelle's hands shaking. "Are you sure you want to do that? How can you be sure she'll take the pills daily?"

"Because I'm gonna shove them down her throat myself. That's how I'll know."

"But there's still the matter of sexually transmitted diseases," the doctor said. "You know that birth control pills alone won't prevent her from contracting a disease. And she's still a virgin, Michelle. Amaris is a good girl. I'm sure you can advise her against intercourse."

Tears dripped from Michelle's eyes. "You don't understand, Doctor. My daughter is living my sister's life."

The doctor didn't understand what Michelle meant. "And that means what?"

Michelle wiped the tears from her face. "She's cursed."

Michelle and Amaris rode home from the doctor's office in silence. When they arrived home, Amaris marched straight upstairs to her room. Michelle sat on the sofa and cried openly. When Amaris revealed that she wasn't wearing any panties, Michelle panicked and drove her straight to the clinic.

She was still a virgin, but Michelle knew that it was only a matter of time before that changed. She got up from the sofa and went into the bathroom for tissue to blow her nose. Michelle looked at her reflection in the mirror. "Where have I gone wrong?" she asked herself.

Michelle left the clinic with a prescription for birth control pills, but she hadn't gotten it filled. Putting Amaris on the pill would clearly give her the green light to have sex, and Michelle didn't want to do that. Besides, James would blow a gasket if he found out that his daughter was taking birth control pills and Michelle hadn't consulted with him.

She walked into the kitchen to make herself a cup of tea. After she filled the teapot with water and set it on the open flame on top of the stove, she opened a cabinet and grabbed a mug and placed it on the counter. From a container in another cabinet, she pulled out a chamomile tea bag and placed it inside the cup. Michelle then sat at the kitchen table to wait for the kettle to sing. Her telephone rang, and she slowly stood to answer the cordless telephone on the wall.

"Hello?" she answered.

"Michelle?"

At the sound of her pastor's wife's voice, Michelle started to cry openly again. "Cookie, I don't know what to do. James is not here, and I just don't know what to do with this girl."

"Calm down. I'm on my way," Cookie said.

Later in the afternoon, Michelle told Cookie the events of the day.

"Well, you and James certainly have your hands full, Michelle. But nothing is too hard for God," Cookie encouraged her. "You have to keep Amaris lifted in prayer. She's at that age when young girls act out."

"I understand that. But we're not talking about Amaris not cleaning her room or not doing the dinner dishes. Cookie, she didn't have on any underwear. And don't forget she had been smoking. To me, that surpasses acting out." Michelle paused before she spoke again. "I got Amaris a birth control pill prescription."

Cookie quickly shook her head from side to side. "Putting that girl on the pill is absolutely the wrong thing to do. You may as well say, 'Amaris, you have my permission to have sex just as long as you don't get pregnant.'"

Michelle threw her hands in the air. "Well, then, tell me what I'm supposed to do, First Lady. Being darn near naked with that boy tells me that my daughter won't be a virgin for much longer. And the more James and I fuss about her seeing Slash, the more defiant she gets. I mean, besides birth control, what other choices do I have?"

"Michelle, you have to pray," Cookie said.

Michelle looked across the kitchen table into Cookie's eyes. "I've been doing that. And it seems like the more I pray, the worse she gets. I make her go to church, I watch to make sure she does her homework every night, James and I take her cellular phone and computer away when she breaks a rule. How many times have the three of us sat in front of you and Pastor Graham for counseling because of something she had done? Countless times, Cookie. James won't let me lay a belt to her butt. And truth be told, that's really all that Amaris needs. She's a spoiled brat that has had everything handed to her on a silver platter. I should have pulled her reins years ago. But her latest stunt terrorizes me. My gut tells me that my daughter will have sexual intercourse soon."

More tears spilled onto Michelle's face. Cookie got up from her chair and went to embrace her. "I have a suggestion that you may not like, but I think it'll help with Amaris."

Michelle wiped her tears. "I'll try anything."

"You said that Amaris is living the life of your sister, Amaryllis."

"Yes, she is. Everything that Amaryllis has done, Amaris is doing."

"Maybe Amaryllis is the one person who can get through to her. Who better than Amaryllis could talk with Amaris and actually relate to the way she's behaving?"

"I don't know about that, Cookie. Amaryllis may be saved and living the straight and narrow now, but when she was a teenager and young adult, she was a pistol. I don't think that turning Amaris over to her aunt would benefit her."

Just then, Amaris walked into the kitchen with her purse on her shoulder and house keys in her hand. She saw Cookie and spoke. "Hello, First Lady."

"Hi, sweetheart," Cookie smiled.

Michelle and Cookie watched her go to the refrigerator, open it, and take out a can of Pepsi.

"Why do you have your purse and keys? I know you don't think you're leaving this house," Michelle said.

"Why not? It's Friday. There's no school tomorrow."

"Amaris, after what you did today, I don't understand how you could even fathom the idea of stepping outside of this house."

Amaris exhaled loudly. "So, what? You're gonna hold me captive forever? I'm just going across the street to Rhonda's house."

Michelle stood and snatched the purse off her shoulder and keys from her hand. "You ain't leaving this house."

Amaris looked at Cookie, then back at Michelle. She then slammed the can of Pepsi on the counter and stormed out of the kitchen.

Michelle sat down at the table, ran her trembling fingers through her hair, and looked at Cookie. "And all you want me to do is pray?"

Cookie nodded her head toward the cordless telephone on the kitchen wall. "And call your sister." She got up from the table and grabbed the telephone, then brought it back to Michelle.

Michelle refused to take it.

"Listen to me, daughter," Cookie said, "if anyone can reach that girl, it's Amaryllis."

Michelle slowly took the telephone from Cookie's hand and dialed her sister's number.

In Chicago, Amaryllis answered Michelle's call. "Hey, twin."

"Hey," Michelle responded.

Amaryllis could tell from her voice that she was despondent. "Is everything okay?"

More tears fell onto Michelle's face. "No. Um, I need you to talk to Amaris. She's out of control. Today she ditched school again, and I found her at a boy's house with no underwear on."

Amaryllis knew that her niece acted out on occasion. Often Michelle would call her and share the horror stories of things that she had done. Amaryllis had offered to come to Las Vegas and have a heart-to-heart talk with her niece, but Michelle had been against it.

"What? Did she—?" Amaryllis began.

"No, she's still a virgin, but she won't be for much longer. How soon can you get here?"

Amaryllis wasted no time. "If there's a flight to Vegas tonight, I'll be on it." She disconnected the call from Michelle and immediately dialed Southwest Airlines. She knew exactly what Amaris was doing because she had done it. But she absolutely refused to let the devil steal her niece. Amaryllis had wanted to speak to the girl about her behavior the first time Michelle confided that she was misbehaving. The good news was that Amaris was still a virgin. Amaryllis was prepared to go to war on her niece's behalf to keep her pure. She would join forces with her sister and break the curse once and for all.

Chapter 29

Later that night after Amaryllis had paid the taxicab driver, she proceeded to walk up the front steps of Michelle's townhome with her carry-on bag on her shoulder. She figured she didn't need to bring many changes of clothes, because what she had flown to Las Vegas to do wouldn't take long.

She had a lot to think about on the four-hour flight from Chicago. When she had spoken to Michelle earlier that day, she heard desperation mixed with tears in her sister's voice. Her niece was out of control. Amaris's life needed to be protected, and her soul needed to be saved. She was a rebellious brat who had become immune to lectures and time-outs. They no longer worked. Amaryllis herself had walked down the path that her look-a-like niece was treading upon. Amaryllis had a plan, a tough plan that would surely prevent Amaris from self-destructing.

When she reached the top of the steps, she heard yelling coming from inside. "Amaris, the topic of you going to any party at this late hour is not up for discussion," Michelle stated.

"You never let me do anything," Amaris screamed. "I hate you, I hate Daddy, and I hate this crappy house."

Amaryllis knocked on the front door. As soon as Michelle opened it, Amaryllis set her carry-on bag on the floor next to the door. She looked at Michelle. Gray strands of hair were visible around her temples. Deep creases ran across her forehead. Amaryllis studied the dark circles beneath her eyes. She would bet money that her sister hadn't slept in the last seventy-two hours. At forty-nine years old, Michelle looked every bit of sixty-five.

"Where are your car keys?" Amaryllis asked her sister.

Michelle looked at her confused. "What do you need my car keys for?" She glanced at the time on her wristwatch. "I thought your flight was landing in another two hours. Why didn't you call me? Amaris and I would've come to the airport to pick you up."

"I caught an earlier flight." Amaryllis repeated her question. "Where are your car keys?"

Michelle pointed to the cocktail table. "Over there. Why?"

Amaryllis walked into the living room and grabbed Michelle's keys from the cocktail table, then turned to her niece. "Let's go."

Amaris didn't move. Instead, she looked at her mother.

"Where are you taking her, Amaryllis?" Michelle asked.

"To a part of Vegas where the lights don't shine."

Michelle didn't try to stop Amaryllis as she grabbed Amaris firmly by her elbow and walked out of the front door. Michelle didn't know where her sister was taking Amaris, but this was the reason why she was called. The one thing Michelle did know for sure was that Amaryllis loved her niece. She had spoiled the girl rotten over the years. The sky was the limit, and money was no object where Amaris was concerned. One year ago when Michelle had refused to purchase the newest design of the Fendi purse Amaris had begged her for, it was delivered to the front door two weeks later.

"I can always count on my auntie," Amaris had bragged as she modeled the purse on her shoulder. "I know she loves me."

After her sister and niece left the house, Michelle walked upstairs to her bedroom and stripped from her clothes. She slipped into a nightgown, sat on the bed, then looked at the telephone on the nightstand and decided to call Cookie.

"Hi, Michelle," Cookie greeted her, having seen Michelle's home number on the caller ID.

Michelle inhaled deeply, then exhaled. "Well, Amaryllis is in town. She knocked on the door, asked for my car keys, then took Amaris away."

"Just like that?" Cookie asked.

Michelle chuckled. "Yep. Just like that."

"Okay, well, I want you to do something for me."

"What might that be, First Lady?"

"Go to sleep."

Michelle chuckled again. "What?"

"Get some sleep, Michelle. Your sister's got this."

Cookie was right about that as Amaryllis drove Michelle's BMW twelve blocks south and parked it in a grocery store parking lot. After locking it, she and Amaris walked to the corner and waited for the next bus.

"Aunt Amaryllis, where are we going?" Amaris had been silent until that point.

"To a place where people go to get away from their parents when they hate them."

A bus drove up, and the two women got on. Amaryllis pulled money from the front pocket of her jeans and paid their fare. Before she and

Amaris got in the car back at Michelle's house, Amaryllis had taken money, photos, and her driver's license from her purse. She shoved them in her pocket, then put her purse in Michelle's trunk.

"Go to the back and sit down," Amaryllis instructed her niece.

Amaris wasn't afraid, but she was nervous. Her aunt was behaving mysteriously. This wasn't like all the other times when the two of them had spent time together. They'd shopped together, told jokes, and laughed together. This time, Amaris felt like she had been kidnapped by a stranger.

When they were seated at the back of the bus, Amaryllis pulled some photos from her pocket and handed one to Amaris. "I want you to see this."

Amaris took the photo from her aunt and looked at it. "Where did you get this picture of me?" She studied the photo and frowned. "I never wore my hair like that."

"That's me at your age," Amaryllis informed her.

The girl's eyes bucked out of her head. She brought the photo closer to her eyes. "This is you, Auntie?"

"Uh-huh. I was your age. Sixteen years old." Amaryllis remembered being a junior in high school and having sexual intercourse for the first time after casting a spell on a boy she had a crush on.

Amaris couldn't take her eyes off the photo. "But this is me, Auntie. I mean, this could really be me."

Amaryllis gave her another photo.

Amaris gasped when she saw it. "What happened to you?"

"That picture was taken when I was admitted to a hospital. I went to a man's house to have sex with him. But he had other plans for me. Three of his friends were there, and they also wanted to have sex with me."

Amaris looked at her aunt with a horrified expression on her face. Then she looked at the picture again. "They beat you up?"

Amaryllis looked at the picture Amaris was holding. She remembered that day like it was yesterday. The busted lip, swollen black eye, and broken pelvic bone. "Humph, they did more than that. They took turns raping me. When one climbed off me, another climbed on. They held me down until they were done. I got beaten because I fought back. And the guy that I went to see was somebody I really liked. Sometimes I would ditch work to be with him."

"Really?" Amaris asked. That was the same thing she had done that day. She ditched school to be with a guy she really liked.

"He made me laugh, and we could talk about anything. At one point, he had me convinced that he was the only person in the world that understood me. But it was all a lie. He set me up to trust him, and then he betrayed me."

Amaris listened closely to her aunt, but she didn't comment. She kept staring at the photo.

"I wish somebody had warned me about him," Amaryllis said. "I wish someone had loved me enough to tell me to stay away from him." She looked into her niece's eyes. "But you wanna know what I wish for the most? I wish I had a mother who loved me like your mother loves you. If just one person had been praying for me, I wouldn't have lost my virginity when I was sixteen."

Amaryllis looked out the window and saw that they had arrived at their destination.

"We're getting off at the next stop," she told Amaris.

The stench of the neighborhood flooded Amaris's nostrils the moment she and Amaryllis stepped off the bus. Broken glass, empty beer bottles, and scattered sheets of newspaper lay at their feet. Graffiti decorated the front and sides of abandoned buildings. Amaryllis grabbed her niece's hand and started walking.

Amaris lived a sheltered life. She never knew this world existed. "Aunt Amaryllis, I'm scared. Where are we?"

"In hell," came the reply.

Amaris saw a lady staggering in their direction. She wore a dirty rag on her head and a filthy trench coat that she held closed with her grimy hands. She was thin, frail, and hunched over. Dingy gym shoes without laces were on her feet. She walked right up to Amaris. "Can you spare a dollar?" She released the coat and held out her hand. Amaris saw that she was completely nude beneath the coat.

The stench of stale urine jumped off the woman into Amaris's face. Like a two-year-old does whenever a stranger approached and spoke to them, Amaris stepped behind her aunt and hid. Amaryllis moved out of the way. "What are you hiding for? The lady asked you a question."

Amaris looked at the lady like she was a monster. She was afraid to speak.

"Well?" Amaryllis asked.

Amaris started to shake. "No. I-I don't have a dollar."

The lady closed her trench coat and moved on.

Amaryllis grabbed the teen's hand and started to walk again. "You're not scared are you, niece? You don't have to be afraid. Everybody here hates their parents just like you."

By now, Amaris was holding on to her aunt's hand for dear life.

Amaryllis pointed across the street. "Look over there."

For the first time ever, Amaris saw a drug deal taking place. She witnessed a man remove a small, clear plastic bag from the crack of his butt and give it to another man.

"I wanna go home, Aunt Amaryllis. I don't wanna be here," the young girl pleaded.

"I brought you here to show you what could happen when you don't obey your parents and when you ditch school."

A young boy not much older than Amaris lay on the sidewalk in a fetal position shaking.

"What's wrong with him?" Amaris asked.

"He's a dope addict. Instead of going to school and making something of himself, this is the way he chooses to live. He probably hates his parents too."

"Where's my money, ho?"

Amaris and her aunt heard those words and looked over their shoulders, where they saw a man punch a woman in her face before asking her the question again. "*%#@*, you smoked up my ^$#@* money?"

Amaris let out a small shriek and started to cry when the man punched the woman in her face again.

"I don't wanna be here no more, Aunt Amaryllis. I wanna go home. Please. Let's go home."

"You are home. This is it for you. Get used to it. You may as well blend in and get to know everybody here, because these are your peeps. See, this is what happens when girls ditch school and sneak off to smoke cigarettes and joints with their no-good boyfriends. This is where girls end up when they aren't focused. Girls who wear short skirts with no panties end up here."

Amaryllis released Amaris's hand and looked at her wristwatch. "Well, it's time for me to go."

She started to walk in the direction in which she and Amaris had come from.

Amaris hurried after her and grabbed her hand again. "No, Auntie. Don't leave me here."

Amaryllis stopped walking. She removed her hand from Amaris's. "You can't go with me. This is your home now. You belong here."

Amaris became hysterical at the thought of her aunt actually leaving her. She wrapped her arms around her aunt's waist and cried openly. "I don't wanna be here. Auntie, please. I promise I'll be good. I'm sorry, Auntie. I'm so sorry."

Tears began to flood Amaryllis's eyes. Listening to her niece beg reminded her of the time when she went to Michelle's church and threw herself at her sister's feet and begged for forgiveness.

Amaris tightened her grip around Amaryllis's waist. "I'll be good, Auntie. I promise, I'll be good. I just wanna go home. I wanna go home."

It was almost three a.m. when Amaris burst through the front door. She took the stairs two at a time up to her mother's bedroom. Without knocking, she opened the door, rushed inside, ran to her mother's bed, and jumped on top of her. "I'm so sorry, Mommy. I'm so sorry, Mommy."

Michelle didn't know what to think. She had been in a deep sleep and was startled when Amaris had dived on her. "What happened?"

Amaryllis had appeared in the bedroom doorway.

Amaris hugged Michelle and buried her face in her neck. "I love you, Mommy. I love you and Daddy too. I'll be good. I promise I'll be good."

Michelle still didn't know what took place that had caused her daughter to surrender. She saw Amaryllis standing in the doorway with a sure smile on her face.

"The curse is broken," Amaryllis said softly. "The curse is broken."

Book Club Discussion Questions

1.   Amaryllis Price was once considered a bad
      seed, but she completely turned her life
      around. How difficult was it for her to do that?
      What was the sin that caused her setbacks?

2.   Do you think it's even possible for someone
      like Amaryllis to stay on the straight and
      narrow?

3.   Was it wrong for Amaryllis to torture Tyrone
      the way she did? Why or why not?

4.   Charles Walker reemerges from Amaryllis's
      past. Is it realistic for the two of them to
      have a celibate relationship when they were
      once hot and heavy?

5.   Bridgette knew that her tongue was out of
      control. What was the turning point when
      she realized that she had to make a change?

6.   Is it believable that both Amaryllis and Mi-
      chelle didn't know that they were fraternal
      twins?

7. Was it wrong for Nana to expose their parents' secret?

8. Is it true that a human being can cast a spell on another person? Is practicing witchcraft a myth?

9. Bridgette and Marvin, the security guard, were at each other's throats daily. Why do you think Bridgette raced to the hospital to see about him?

10. Considering all of the heartache and pain that Amaryllis had caused a lot of people, is it difficult to accept her character as a bad girl gone good?

of course, your prayers. We plan and then we sit
back and let God guide us.
book club. We hope to make comfortable in,
our opinions, and reviews that build up, rather
than tear down our authors.

UC HIS GLORY BOOK CLUB!

www.uchisglorybookclub.net

UC His Glory Book Club is the spirit-inspired
brainchild of Joylynn Jossel, Author and Acqui-
sitions Editor of Urban Christian, and Kendra
Norman-Bellamy, Author for Urban Christian.
This is an online book club that hosts authors of
Urban Christian. We welcome as members all
men and women who have a passion for reading
Christian-based fiction.

UC His Glory Book Club pledges our commitment to provide support, positive feedback,
encouragement, and a forum whereby members
can openly discuss and review the literary works
of Urban Christian authors.

There is no membership fee associated with
UC His Glory Book Club; however, we do ask
that you support the authors through purchasing, encouraging, providing book reviews, and

of course, your prayers. We also ask that you respect our beliefs and follow the guidelines of the book club. We hope to receive your valuable input, opinions, and reviews that build up, rather than tear down our authors.

What We Believe:

—We believe that Jesus is the Christ, Son of the Living God.

—We believe the Bible is the true, living Word of God.

—We believe all Urban Christian authors should use their God-given writing abilities to honor God and share the message of the written word God has given to each of them uniquely.

—We believe in supporting Urban Christian authors in their literary endeavors by reading, purchasing and sharing their titles with our on-line community.

—We believe that in everything we do in our literary arena should be done in a manner that will lead to God being glorified and honored.

We look forward to the online fellowship with you.

Please visit us often at:
www.uchisglorybookclub.net.

Many Blessing to You!
Shelia E. Lipsey,
President, UC His Glory Book Club

Coming Soon

April 2014

Damsels In Distress

A novel by

Nikita Lynnette Nichols

Chapter 1

Am I My Sister's Keeper?

It was the third Saturday evening in April. The spring rain fell hard. Heavy thunderstorms accompanied by dangerous lightning blasted throughout the windy city. Chicago had been given that nickname, decades ago, for its angry winds. The sewers overflowed on South Ada Street. The same street that twenty-seven-year old Ginger Brown modeled a royal blue two-piece satin suit inside her house. Her best friends, Portia Dunn and Celeste Harper encouraged her to sashay and turn then turn and sashay.

Ginger had recently purchased the suit at Macy's. The following Sunday would be Women's Day at church and as the emcee for the afternoon program Ginger had planned on looking good.

Portia and Celeste were seated on opposite ivory lounge chaise chairs in Ginger's immaculate living room. White Berber carpet, white stone cocktail and end tables matched the white plantation shutters that covered the floor to ceiling bay windows.

Ginger had broken a strict rule. She had been warned that no one, not even herself, who owned the house, was ever allowed to step a foot inside the sterile living room. Ginger, her live-in boyfriend, and guests must enter the house, through the back door, at all times. But her significant other, Ronald, who enforced the rule, was not home. Therefore Ginger felt bold enough to entertain her friends in what she considered to be the most beautiful room in her home.

The thirty-two-inch space between the women seated served as a catwalk for Ginger to strut.

"All right, Ginger, girl. Show us what you're working with," Celeste encouraged.

Ginger unbuttoned the suit jacket, slipped it off of her arms, then swung it over her left shoulder to reveal the silver-gray satin camisole she wore underneath. She turned away from Portia and Celeste then strutted back to her starting point just at the archway that separated the living room from the dining room.

As Ginger walked away, Portia's smile quickly vanished when she noticed black and blue bruises on Ginger's right shoulder, next to the spaghetti strap of her camisole. She sat straight up on the chaise chair. "Ginger, what the heck is that on your shoulder?" Portia's outburst startled both Ginger and Celeste.

Ginger had no clue that the boxing match, from the previous night, with Ronald, was evident. She was usually extremely careful not to allow any bruises to show. Had she known the marks were visible, Ginger never would've taken off her jacket. "Oh, girl, it's nothing." She quickly put the jacket back on. "Ronald got a little high last night. Y'all know how he gets."

Ginger's poor excuse for being a punching bag was for her own benefit. Truth be told, she was quite embarrassed. How could she have been so careless and allow anyone to see the bruises?

When Ronald came home, the evening before, with his eyes glazed, Ginger knew he had brought trouble home with him. She was in the kitchen, standing at the stove, frying pork chops.

Ronald approached Ginger reeking of marijuana. He lifted the lid of a pot that sat on the stove. "What is this?" he asked. His speech was slurred and his voice was just above a whisper.

Nothing infuriated Ginger more than when Ronald asked her a question that he already knew the answer to. Anyone in their right mind could see that the pot was half filled with white rice. Evidently smoking weed had taken Ronald's common sense away.

Ginger exhaled a loud sigh of frustration. She hated when he asked stupid questions. "It's rice, Ron. I'm gonna make gravy to go with it."

Ronald placed the lid back on the pot then turned to walk away. Ginger thought the conversation was over but was mistaken when Ronald spun back around. He slammed his open palm against Ginger's face and with all the strength he had, Ronald pushed Ginger backward. He sent her flying down but on the way to the floor, Ginger's right shoulder connected with the edge of the marble-top kitchen table. She screamed out in pain.

"Who are you huffin' and puffin' at? Huh?" Ronald stood over Ginger glaring down at her. He drew his leg back in preparation to kick Ginger in her abdomen but stopped short. "I told you about catching an attitude every time I ask you a question."

Ginger lay on the kitchen floor moaning and wincing in pain. Her right shoulder was on fire.

"I don't want rice and gravy," he spat. "Throw that garbage out and make me some corn." With that being said, Ronald exited the kitchen.

Celeste stood, went to Ginger, and forcefully pulled the jacket off her shoulders to get an up close and personal look at the marks. Portia came and stood next to Celeste. The bruises were blue, black, and purple. They stopped just above Ginger's right elbow.

It wasn't the first, second, or third time Celeste and Portia witnessed bruises on Ginger. They had been begging Ginger to end her abusive relationship with Ronald ever since she moved him into her home three years ago.

Last month Ginger showed up at church with a swollen busted lip that she tried to hide with lipstick. Portia and Celeste were so angry that they wanted to go to Ginger's house and confront Ronald but just like all the times before, Ginger had begged them not to interfere. Now the three best friends stood in Ginger's living room facing the issue again for what seemed like the one hundredth time.

"Is that fool still pounding on you, Ginger?" Celeste asked.

Ginger's heart raced as tears began to run down her chocolate colored face. "Celeste, please understand," she pleaded.

Portia frowned. "Understand what, Ginger? That fool is out of control and you need to get away from him."

"I'm calling the police." Celeste returned to her chair for her purse. Her cell phone was inside.

Ginger was quickly on Celeste's heels. As soon as Celeste pulled her phone from her purse, Ginger snatched it out of her hand. "No, Celeste."

Celeste placed her right hand on her hip and shifted all of her weight onto one leg. "No? What the heck do you mean 'no'? Ronald needs to be locked up and you need to be institutionalized for allowing him to beat on you."

By the expression on Ginger's face, Portia knew Celeste's words had hurt her. Celeste had basically accused Ginger of being crazy.

Portia came and stood next to Ginger. "Celeste, I know you're upset but—"

"Upset?" Celeste had cut Portia's words off. "Furious is what I am, Portia. And why are *you* so doggone calm about this? We've been dealing with this crap for three years. Did you get a good look at her back?"

Ginger placed her face in her hands and cried. Not only was she embarrassed but if a call was made to the police and Ronald found out about it, Ginger knew she'd be in even more trouble with him.

Portia wrapped her arms around Ginger. "It's okay, Sweetie. We're gonna get through this. We'll work it out."

Celeste couldn't comprehend Portia's attitude about the situation Ginger was in. "How do you suppose we work this out, Portia? Huh?"

Portia guided Ginger to one of the chaise chairs and sat her down. "I don't know, Celeste. Let's talk about it."

In Celeste's mind, talking with Ginger wasn't necessary. The only talking that needed to be done was on a 911 call. She hastily left the living room and walked toward Ginger's bedroom. "You and Ginger talk. I know what I'm gonna do."

In Ginger's bedroom, Celeste opened the closet door. She found a small suitcase and threw it on the bed. She snatched blouses, dresses, and pants off of racks and threw them on top of the suitcase. Ginger and Portia came into the bedroom and saw Celeste on a rampage. Just as

Celeste was headed for the dresser, Ginger ran and stood in between it and Celeste.

"What are you doing, Celeste?" Ginger asked her.

"I'm helping you get through this. That's what I'm doing. Get out of my way."

More tears ran down Ginger's face. "Ron apologized. He promised to never hit me again."

"That's what he said the last time and the time before that, Ginger," Portia interjected from the doorway. "When are you gonna learn that Ronald is sick?"

Ginger looked at her best friends through teary eyes. "Y'all just don't understand. He told me . . ." She couldn't finish her sentence as she choked back tears.

Celeste placed her hands on her hips again. "He told you what?"

Ginger knew that if she revealed what Ronald had told her years ago, all heck would break loose. She hesitated. She wondered how she could pacify this situation and calm Portia and Celeste down.

"He told you what?" Celeste's outburst startled Ginger.

Ginger opened her mouth and spoke softly. She looked into Portia's eyes because she didn't want to see the expression on Celeste's face. "Ron once told me that he'd kill me if I ever left him."

Both Celeste and Portia's eyes grew wide. *"What?"* They screamed at the same time.

Celeste became enraged. She was even more eager to pack Ginger's clothes and get her out of that house. "Move out of my way, Ginger."

Ginger pleaded with Celeste to calm down. "Celeste, please understand."

"Why do you keep saying that, Ginger? What is it that you want us to understand? You ain't married to that fool. Ron won't even give you his last name. He's too darn lazy to get a job. All he does is smoke weed all day. He's living in *your* house while *you* go to work every day. *You* pay the mortgage, utilities, and *you* buy the groceries. Ron has you so twisted that he makes you ask his permission to go to church. Plus he's ugly. I don't see how you can stand to look at him let alone sleep with him. You deserve better, Ginger. So, since you don't have enough brains to pack your bags, I'm gonna do it for you." Celeste pushed Ginger aside and opened the top dresser drawer then grabbed a handful of bras and panties and threw them on the bed.

Ginger grabbed her underwear from the bed and brought them back to the dresser. "Stop it, Celeste."

Celeste ignored Ginger and proceeded to another drawer. She grabbed another handful of clothes and took them to the bed. On her second trip, she looked at Portia standing in the bedroom doorway. "What the heck are you just standing there for? You should be helping me."

Portia didn't move. She was torn. She knew Celeste was doing the right thing by packing Ginger's clothes and of course she should be helping Celeste. But Ginger just said that Ronald would kill her if she left him.

Portia watched as Celeste transferred clothes from the dresser to the suitcase then she watched Ginger transfer clothes from the suitcase back to the dresser. Portia knew Celeste was out of control but then again, enough was enough.

Ginger was crying and begging Celeste to stop trying to pack her clothes.

Celeste forcefully took the clothes from her hand and looked at her. "Look, Ginger. I'm sick of this crap. Now, either we pack your clothes and you come home with me or we pack Ron's clothes and sit them out on the curb. One of you is getting the heck out of here tonight. Now, since this is your house, I'll let *you* decide. Because if he touches you again, I'm gonna pay somebody to touch *him*. So, who's leaving, you or Ron?"

Ginger didn't answer Celeste. She stood in the middle of her bedroom crying. Celeste waited five seconds then threw the clothes on top of the suitcase and proceeded to the dresser to grab more. Ginger reached out to try and stop Celeste but lost her balance and fell. She managed to grab a hold of Celeste's left leg. Celeste stumbled but was able to deliver the suitcase's deposit. Ginger begged and cried for Celeste to stop packing her clothes. "Celeste, please. Please, Celeste."

Celeste drug Ginger from the dresser to the bed as she continued to pack her clothes. "Portia, get her off of me."

Portia had a decision to make. She could only pray that Ginger would eventually forgive her and Celeste for doing what had to be done. She went to Ginger and pulled her arms from around Celeste's legs. "Ginger, we gotta do this."

Ginger stopped fighting. She knew that her friends were relentless and they were not going to let her stay in her home as long as Ronald resided there also. But Ginger also knew that she needed to come up with a plan to get Portia and Celeste to leave before Ronald got home. "Okay.

Okay, I'll go to the police station." She told them what they wanted to hear.

Portia released Ginger's arms. "You will?"

"Now you're talking like you got some common sense," Celeste said. She grabbed a suitcase by the handle and instructed Ginger and Portia to take one each. "Ginger, you're coming home with me after we leave the police station."

"Okay." Ginger didn't argue. She wanted them to leave. She had a plan.

Celeste, Ginger, and Portia rode in silence to the police station. It was when Celeste drove into a parking spot and put the gear in 'park' that Ginger said from the back seat, "I'm not doing it."

Both Portia and Celeste turned around and looked at her.

Celeste was furious. "What the heck you mean you're not doing it?"

Ginger turned her head away from her friends and looked out of the window. "I've changed my mind."

Portia looked at Celeste and exhaled loudly. "Now what?"

Without a word Celeste removed her key from the ignition. "I'll be right back." She opened the door and got out of the car. Celeste shut the door and pressed a button on her remote. The feature that Celeste had on her car was the same feature that the police use as car bait. Once a button is pressed on the remote, the car can't be opened from the inside. Because the windows were raised, Celeste couldn't hear the foul names Ginger called her as she ran, through the rain, inside the police station.

Five minutes later Celeste returned to her car with an African American female. Celeste felt that a black lady cop would be better suited than a man to convince Ginger to press criminal charges on Ronald and leave him for good.

The rain had lightened up to a drizzle. Celeste pressed the button on her remote again and opened the passenger door. "Ginger is the one sitting in the back seat," she told the female officer.

The lady cop knelt and looked in the back seat. She asked Portia to get out of the car. With Portia out of the way, the lady cop sat in the front passenger seat and faced Ginger. "Are you Ginger Brown?"

Ginger sat in the back seat with her mouth shut.

"I'm Sergeant Phyore Montgomery. I'm here to help you. Have you been abused?"

Not a word from Ginger. *What kind of name is 'Phyore'?* she wondered.

Celeste stuck her head inside the car. "Open your darn mouth, Ginger."

Sergeant Montgomery patted Celeste's arm. "Mrs. Harper, please calm down. Give her time."

Celeste rolled her eyes at Ginger and walked away.

Sergeant Montgomery saw tears streaming down Ginger's face. "Miss Brown, I've been on the force for twenty-three years. I've dealt with all kinds of abuse. Nine times out of ten, domestic abuse turns into murder because the victim is too afraid to report it. Your friends brought you here because they love you and want to help you."

Ginger looked through the rear passenger glass window and saw Portia and Celeste standing on the sidewalk glaring at her. "They kidnapped me. Isn't that a crime? Can I file charges against them for bringing me here against my will?"

Ginger had just lied to Sergeant Montgomery. Back at her house she had agreed to come to the police station just to get Portia and Celeste to leave before Ronald arrived home. Ginger had gotten into Celeste's car voluntarily. Telling Sergeant Montgomery that she had been kidnapped by her best friends was Ginger's anger speaking. Celeste and Portia were constantly meddling in her personal business. It would serve them right if Sergeant Montgomery slapped handcuffs on both of them.

Sergeant Montgomery had already gotten the full story from Celeste why she and Portia had brought Ginger to the police station. "They brought you here to save your life." She didn't entertain the thought of allowing Ginger to press charges against her best friends. "Have you been abused?" She asked Ginger again.

Ginger turned her head in the opposite direction. Tears ran down her face. She refused to answer the question.

"Miss Brown, I can't help you if you don't talk to me," Sergeant Montgomery said. "Your friend, Celeste, said that your boyfriend threatened to kill you if you told that he physically abused you. Is that true? If it is, I will personally see to it that you're placed in protective custody. I can have him picked up tonight."

Nothing from Ginger.

Portia became frustrated. "Ginger, tell her about the time when you were five months pregnant and Ron kicked you in the stomach. That caused you to miscarry."

Sergeant Montgomery gasped. Her eyes grew wide and her mouth fell open. "Is that true?" She asked Ginger.

A tear dripped from Ginger's chin. "I really don't wanna be here," she said.

Sergeant Montgomery pled with her. "The only way to stop this is to press charges. If you don't press charges, it won't stop. He's not worth your life. No man is. I know you're afraid but you have to admit to me that he put his hands on you."

Ginger focused on someone walking across the street. Sergeant Montgomery sat in silence for a few seconds. "You are a beautiful black woman. Learn to love yourself. It hurts me deeply to get called to a house and find one of my black sisters unresponsive from domestic abuse. And I'm gonna tell you something, Miss Brown. Eventually he *will* kill you. It happens like that all the time. So, get out while you can."

Sergeant Montgomery waited another twenty seconds for Ginger to confess. She then got out of the car and walked over to where Portia and

Celeste were standing. She looked at them both. "I can't do anything without a complaint from her."

That didn't please Portia. "This is bullcrap. Look at her shoulder."

"I understand but I can't make an arrest unless she files a formal complaint."

"So, what are we supposed to do?" Celeste asked.

Sergeant Montgomery shrugged her shoulders. "There's nothing anyone can do. Miss Brown has to help herself first."

"But what if we say that we actually saw her boyfriend hit her?" Asked Portia.

Sergeant Montgomery sighed. She understood Portia and Celeste's frustration. But she couldn't take a false statement. Neither of them had actually seen Ronald put his hands on Ginger. They had only seen the marks he left behind.

"If Miss Brown is not willing to file a complaint, according to the law, to heck with what anyone else says."

Celeste stormed around to the driver's side of the car, got in, and slammed the door. Portia sat in the passenger seat. Sergeant Montgomery watched Celeste's tires burn rubber as she pulled away from the curb.

"This is absolutely ridiculous," Celeste said angrily as she sped away.

She drove back to Ginger's house so that Portia could get her car. Celeste pulled into the driveway and parked next to Ronald's car. "The fool is home. Hurry up and get out, Portia."

Ginger yelled from the back seat. *"Let me out, Celeste!"* She knew Celeste was gonna try to take her home with her.

"No!" Celeste yelled back at Ginger.

Portia looked at her friend. "Celeste, Ginger is a grown woman. We can't make her do anything she doesn't want to do. Look what just happened at the police station."

"I don't care. If you hurry up and get out, I can drive off."

Ginger yelled again. "Celeste, I wanna get out of this car."

Celeste switched the gear to 'park', took her foot off the brake pedal, then turned her upper torso around to face Ginger. "You know that if you go in there with your bags, Ron's gonna go off."

"Well then keep the darn bags, Celeste. I'll get them from you tomorrow."

"If you live that long." Celeste commented.

Ginger couldn't believe what her friend had just said to her. "You know what, Celeste. Just because you live in a fairy tale world with the perfect husband and the perfect job don't make you any better than anyone."

"What the heck are you talking about, Ginger? I'm trying to keep this fool from killing you. You better wake up and realize who really loves you. I'm tired of begging you to save your own life. If you wanna let Ron knock your brains out, then that's on you 'cause I'm through with it." Celeste opened her door, got out, and then pressed the seat forward.

Ginger climbed out of the backseat. Portia exited the passenger seat and walked around to the driver's side where Ginger and Celeste stood.

Ginger looked at both of them. "I love y'all. I will see you at church in the morning."

Portia hugged Ginger. "I love you too, Honey."

Ginger let go of Portia and looked at Celeste. "I'm sorry for yelling at you. I know you love me."

Celeste made no effort to hug Ginger. She was angry. "Yeah, whatever. I gotta go." She got in the car and slammed the door shut. She backed out of the driveway.

"You know Celeste is a hothead," Portia said to Ginger when they were left alone in Ginger's driveway. "But she only wants what's best for you. We both do."

"Portia, I love Ronald. And I know that he loves me too."

Ginger made the statement as though she was simply telling Portia what time of day it was.

It saddened Portia that Ginger may have actually convinced herself of that lie. "Ginger, is he loving you when he's bouncing you off the walls?"

Ginger lowered her head and didn't respond. Portia proceeded to her car and drove off.

Ginger walked to the garage door and stood before the security panel mounted just beneath the security light. She keyed in the four digit code and the garage door lifted. Once inside the garage Ginger walked to the interior door that led to the breezeway. She pressed the 'close' button on a different panel and went inside.

Ginger walked through the kitchen. On the way to her bedroom she saw Ronald lying on the sofa, in the living room, watching a basketball game. The same white, sterile living room that Ginger was forbidden to enter. Ronald was wearing a pair of gray jogging pants and a white ribbed tank T-shirt known as a wife beater. Ginger wondered if Ronald was dressed to beat her.

Ronald had heard Ginger come in. He knew she was standing at the archway to the living room. He looked up at her. "What did I tell you about leaving this house with dirty dishes in the sink?"

Ginger became nervous. "I'm sorry baby, I forgot."

Ronald looked at the suit she was wearing. "Why do you have on a suit and where have you been?"

Ginger nervously looked down at her attire. I went to see a lady from the church. She's a seamstress. I needed to get my skirt hemmed for church tomorrow." Ginger's lies to Ronald had become more and more effortless.

Ronald repositioned himself on the sofa. "You went to church last Sunday. You ain't going to-morrow."

Ginger started to panic. Her name was on the church programs. She'd been looking forward to emceeing the Annual Women's Day program for the past three months. In preparation for the service, Ginger had been walking around the house pretending to hold a microphone in her hand, practicing her speech. What would hap-pen if she didn't show up at church? Folks were depending on her to be there. Ginger had to be at church, she just had to.

She walked to Ronald, knelt down to kiss his lips softly before heading to the kitchen to wash the three glasses and saucers that she, Portia, and Celeste had drank tea and eaten cookies from.

"Next time, I'm not gonna ask any questions about dirty dishes being left in the sink, Ginger. If you're gonna act like a two year old, then I'll treat you like one.

"It won't happen again," Ginger said over her shoulder.

"Make me a sandwich," Ronald ordered.

Five minutes later, Ginger brought Ronald a bacon, lettuce and tomato sandwich on a small wooden lap dinner tray. Next to the sandwich was a glass of grape Kool-Aid.

"Where is my napkin?" Ronald asked. "And you know I like ice in my Kool-Aid."

Ginger quickly returned to the kitchen for a napkin and to put ice cubes in the glass of Kool-Aid. "Can I go to church tomorrow?" She asked when she returned from the kitchen with the napkin and Kool-Aid.

Ronald looked at her. "You went last Sunday."

"But tomorrow is the annual Women's Day celebration. I've been asked to be the Mistress of Ceremony. Had I known that you wouldn't have let me go to church two Sunday's in a row, Ron, I would've missed last week just so that I could be there tomorrow. "

Ginger stood in the middle of *her* living room, looking at an unemployed man who was *not* her husband, lie on *her* sofa and watch the television *she* paid for, praying that he would *allow* her to go to church. It dawned on Ginger that Celeste was right. Ronald was very ugly. His face was oily, his French braids were long overdue to be re-braided and he needed to shave. The hair on Ronald's chin was nappy and it looked like taco meat.

Ronald drank from the glass and swallowed. He took a bite of his sandwich. "I shouldn't let you go anywhere 'cause I'm tired of telling you about leaving dirty dishes in the sink."

"Portia and Celeste stopped by this evening. We had tea and cookies. I modeled my suit for them and that's when Portia suggested that I get my skirt hemmed. She said it was way too long. So we had to leave in a hurry to get to the seamstress's house before it got too late. I had totally forgotten about the cups and saucers."

"You're gonna have to start entertaining those broads outside of this house. They don't like me and the feeling is mutual."

The hatred Ginger's friends felt toward Ronald was not unknown to him. The very first time Ginger told Portia and Celeste that Ronald had slapped her face they drove to Ginger's house and confronted him. They threatened to kill Ronald if he touched her again. Ronald told Ginger that if her friends insisted on interjecting themselves in their personal relationship then they would be banned from the house altogether. From that moment on Ginger had rarely invited the girls to her home and if she did it was always at a time when she knew that Ronald would be out of the house.

Ginger didn't respond to Ronald's latest demand. If he didn't want Celeste and Portia to visit then she would see to it that they didn't. With her suit still on, Ginger sat next to Ronald and pretended to be into the basketball game he was watching. When he had finished his meal and drank the last of his Kool-Aid, Ginger took the plate and glass into the kitchen and washed them. She turned the kitchen light off then came and stood nervously by the sofa. "Honey, I know you're into the game but I was wondering if you've decided to let me go to church."

Ronald ignored Ginger for a long thirty seconds while he continued to watch the game before he looked up at her and asked, "What's in it for me?"

Ginger didn't say a word. She knew what to do next. Right there in the living room, she stripped naked then knelt before Ronald. He grabbed Ginger by the back of her head and guided her face toward his lap.

Celeste walked in the front door and slammed it shut behind her. Her husband, Anthony, was talking on the telephone with their pastor. He watched as Celeste threw her purse and keys on the sofa next to him and stormed toward the rear of the house.

"It was good talking with you too, Pastor. Celeste and I will see you at church in the morning." Anthony disconnected the call and went to find his wife. He found her in the master bathroom sitting at her vanity removing make-up from her eyes with a cotton ball. In the mirror, Celeste saw Anthony leaning against the door frame watching her. She didn't acknowledge him but by how far Celeste's lips were poked out, Anthony sensed that she was upset.

Celeste tossed the cotton ball toward the trashcan but missed. Anthony picked it up from the floor and threw it in the trashcan then came and sat next to her. Celeste inched over to allow him more room.

Anthony faced his wife. He exhaled. "Let me guess. Ginger and Ron, right?"

"Yep, you guessed it." Celeste opened the cabinet next to her left leg and grabbed a bottle of Sea-Breeze astringent. She soaked a cotton ball with the blue liquid and began rubbing it all over her face.

Anthony extended his legs and crossed his ankles. He leaned backward and placed his elbows on Celeste's vanity. "What did that punk do this time?"

Celeste threw the cotton ball into the trash can. "He hit her again, Tony. You should see her shoulder. Bruises are all the way down her arm."

"She showed them to you?" Anthony asked.

"No. Evidently, Ginger didn't know the marks were there. Portia and I saw the bruises while she was modeling the suit she's wearing to church tomorrow, that is if Ron even allows her to go to church."

Anthony could only imagine how Celeste be-
haved when she saw Ginger's bruises. "You didn't
freak out did you, Celeste?"

Celeste was applying moisturizer to her face
when she stopped and looked at her husband.
"Heck yeah, I freaked as I should have. What
would you do if your best friend was getting his
butt whipped all the time?"

"Look, baby. You and Portia have to come to
the conclusion that Ginger is an adult. You can't
live her life or make decisions for her, nor can
the two of you fight her battles. Yeah, Ron is a
punk. But until Ginger decides that she's had
enough of his crap, there's nothing you, Portia,
or anyone else can do." That wasn't the first time
that Anthony had to remind Celeste to stay out of
Ginger's business.

"*My* concern is you," Anthony stated. "You're
my wife and I don't want you to have a stroke or
develop ulcers over Ginger and Ron's issues. The
only thing you can do for Ginger is pray for her
and be there when she needs you."

Tears ran down Celeste's face. "Portia and I
took her to the police station but she wouldn't
even get out of the car. I went inside and got a
female cop, a sister, and brought her to Ginger

but she sat in the back seat and wouldn't open her mouth. Portia and I looked like two fools."

Anthony grabbed Celeste's hand and kissed her open palm. "You and Portia have been going through this with Ginger for years. Nothing will change until she faces reality and realize that it's up to her, and *only* her, to get away from Ronald. So let's change the subject. How did your doctor's appointment go this morning?"

Celeste wiped the tears from her eyes. "And that's another thing that's getting on my nerves, Tony. I'm sick of being disappointed every month. We try and try and try but I always get my period. Today Dr. Bindu took my temperature and gave me an ovulation predictor. He said that our best chances of becoming pregnant is between now and next Friday."

Anthony stood behind Celeste and massaged her shoulders. What he didn't know was that his loving wife, the wife he cherished, and the wife he desperately wanted to have a baby with, had just lied to him. Those were not Dr. Bindu's words. He had sent Celeste home with bad news. The ovulation predictor was a purchase that she'd made at Wal-Mart after her appointment. But she had wasted her money. Doctor Bindu told Celeste that her chances of conceiving a baby were slim to none.

"So, what are we waiting on?" Anthony asked.

Celeste dismissed Anthony's question and asked one of her own. "What am I gonna do about Ginger?" She was not in a rush to make a baby because a baby would never be made.

Anthony let out a loud sigh. "Celeste, I want you to let Ginger take care of Ginger. And I want you to come to bed so I can take care of you."

In her bedroom, Portia pressed the 'play' button on her answering machine. She listened to her messages as she undressed.

"Hey, beautiful. What's up with you? It's me, David. I've been calling you all day. Hit me on my cell when you get in." (Beep)

David insisted that Portia only called him on his cellular phone. She wasn't worthy of his home number. His wife could answer.

"Hi, Portia. This is Greg. I've been trying to hook up with you for two weeks. What's up? Are you missing in action or what?" (Beep)

Every two weeks, like clockwork, when Gregory's wife got a headache, he wound up in Portia's bed.

"Portia, this is Richard. Why are you avoiding me? You think a brotha ain't got nothing else better to do than track you down?" (Beep)

Three days ago, Portia received a dozen red roses at the car dealership where she worked as an Administrative Assistant. The inside card read, 'My dearest Tamara, I love you always, Richard.'

Portia did a little detective work and found out that Tamara was Mrs. Richard Clark.

The fool had mistakenly written his wife's name on the card.

"Hey, Beautiful. I'm in town for a few days. Let's get together. Give me a call at my mother's house. 555-3743. I would love to see you." (Beep)

The last message was from Gary Stokes. He is stupid fine and had always been Portia's weakness. She returned his call.

Forty-five minutes later, Portia stood at her stove and unwrapped a king-sized milk chocolate *Hershey's* candy bar. She placed it into a small saucepan then added two pats of butter. She heated the saucepan on low then stirred the chocolate and butter until the mixture melted and blended well. On the sink next to the stove was a bowl of fresh, ripe, juicy sweet strawberries. Portia removed the melted chocolate from the heat then dipped the strawberries, one by one, in the chocolate and laid them on a plate. She placed the plate in the freezer then showered while the chocolate hardened.

Fifteen minutes later, Portia removed the plate of strawberries from the freezer and sat it on the sink next to an open bottle of *Pink Moscato*. She filled a syringe with the wine and carefully inserted the needle into each strawberry and emptied it. She smiled when she heard a soft knock on the front door. It was time to play.

She carried the plate of chocolate covered strawberries into the living room with her. Portia greeted Gary wearing a white sheer teddy and a smile. "So glad you could come over."

Gary stood in the doorway looking as fine as he wanted to look. Retired from the National Football League where he was a wide receiver for the *Chicago Bears* for nine seasons, Gary's broad shoulders, buffed arms and thick neck were easy on Portia's eyes. Six feet three inches and two hundred sixty pounds of solid muscle walked passed Portia. He left a whiff of *Usher* cologne in the wind.

Portia shut the door and leaned against it. She admired Gary's smooth bald head. His goatee mended greatly with his mustache. His caramel colored skin was as smooth as silk. "Umph, umph, umph. It's a shame your wife lets you travel alone."

Gary's mischievous smile melted Portia. "Why is that?"

"Because you don't know how to behave yourself."

"That's not true. I'm always on my best behavior when I'm away on business. It's only when I come back to Chicago that I get into trouble."

Portia walked to Gary and wrapped her left arm around his broad neck while holding the plate of chocolate covered strawberries in her right hand. "Is that what I am, 'trouble'?"

He pulled Portia's body closer to his. "With a capital 'T'. But you're the kind of trouble I don't mind getting into, if you know what I mean." Gary seductively bumped his torso against Portia's.

Portia picked up a chocolate strawberry from the plate and inserted it into Gary's mouth. He bit into it and when he tasted the wine, he smiled. "Umm, yummy."

Portia returned the smile. "You like?"

"I love." Gary answered sinfully.

She sat the plate of strawberries on the cocktail table and stood on her tippy toes to kiss Gary's forehead, his left cheek, and his right cheek. Portia took her time and ran her tongue along his mustache from left to right. Gary picked Portia up and she wrapped her thighs around his waist. The married man carried Portia to her bedroom and it wasn't any shame in their game.

Notes

Notes

ORDER FORM
URBAN BOOKS, LLC
97 N18th Street
Wyandanch, NY 11798

Name (please print):_____

Address:_____

City/State:_____

Zip:_____

QTY	TITLES	PRICE
	3:57 A.M Timing Is Everything	$14.95
	A Man's Worth	$14.95
	A Woman's Worth	$14.95
	Abundant Rain	$14.95
	After The Feeling	$14.95
	Amaryllis	$14.95
	An Inconvenient Friend	$14.95

Shipping and handling-add $3.50 for 1st book, then $1.75 for each additional book.
Please send a check payable to:
Urban Books, LLC
Please allow 4-6 weeks for delivery

ORDER FORM
URBAN BOOKS, LLC
97 N18th Street
Wyandanch, NY 11798

Name (please print):_____

Address:_____

City/State:_____

Zip:_____

QTY	TITLES	PRICE
	Battle of Jericho	$14.95
	Be Careful What You Pray For	$14.95
	Beautiful Ugly	$14.95
	Been There Prayed That:	$14.95
	Before Redemption	$14.95
	By the Grace of God	$14.95

Shipping and handling-add $3.50 for 1st book, then $1.75 for each additional book.
Please send a check payable to:
Urban Books, LLC
Please allow 4-6 weeks for delivery

ORDER FORM
URBAN BOOKS, LLC
97 N18th Street
Wyandanch, NY 11798

Name (please print):_____

Address:_____

City/State:_____

Zip:_____

QTY	TITLES	PRICE
	Confessions Of A Preacher's Wife	$14.95
	Dance Into Destiny	$14.95
	Deliver Me From My Enemies	$14.95
	Desperate Decisions	$14.95
	Divorcing the Devil	$14.95

Shipping and handling-add $3.50 for 1st book, then $1.75 for each additional book.
Please send a check payable to:
Urban Books, LLC
Please allow 4-6 weeks for delivery